CATCH A FALLING STAR

The CASA Chronicles – Volume 1

Keith Julius

*RAE:
THANKS FOR
THE SUPPORT.
ENJOY!*

Published by Keith Julius

Temperance, MI   48182

Copyright © Keith Julius 2016

Cover Photos © Keith Julius 2016

All Rights Reserved

First edition – May 2016

www.KeithJulius.com

ISBN: 978-0-9969607-2-4

Printed by CreateSpace

This is a work of fiction. Any similarities

between actual persons, places, or things is

purely coincidental.

This book is dedicated to all the wonderful CASA volunteers everywhere. Without your dedication and commitment to the children you serve the world would truly be a sadder place.

While writing this book I received advice and support from some people who deserve recognition for their assistance.

To the Bedford Library Evening Book Club – in particular Joanne Guyton-Simmons, Kris Houstin, Michelle Buberniak, and Patricia Hofmann – thank you for your comments concerning my early drafts.

To Debbie Lipson, formerly an attorney with CASA, I owe a tremendous amount of gratitude. Debbie gave me valuable advice while pointing me in the proper direction concerning some questions I had. Her suggestions increased the presence of Beverly Stone in the story and helped me to emphasize the good work performed by CASA volunteers around the country.

Barbara Baumgartner, whom I met through CASA, also offered advice and guidance concerning the flow of events, while Maiya Niangadou – who became so involved with the story she chastised me for certain events I chronicled – helped to shape some of the closing chapters of the book.

Belinda Brooks offered something that was very important to me – a personal perspective. Having lived with a daughter who became a heroin addict, she was able to read my work with an eye to authenticity that I could get nowhere else. Her words of encouragement and support helped greatly.

Thank you everyone who assisted me. And thank you to all those who take the time to read my book. This is for all of you.

Chapter One:

ALEISHA TURNER FELT TIRED, WORN OUT from walking. Her muscles ached. Not just her legs, though the miles she had put on today were beginning to have their affect on her, but her arms and lower back as well, with a soreness that was much too prevalent lately and stubbornly refused to go away. She realized it wasn't the walking alone that made her uncomfortable. The fatigue and general listlessness she experienced was a condition that had lingered for months now – for longer than she could remember – the discomfort seeming to increase with each passing day.

But she had come to accept the fact. Like so many things in her miserable life it was merely something else she had to put up with.

Turning the corner onto Maple Street, heading west now toward the setting sun that tentatively attempted to peek through the accumulation of evening clouds, Aleisha continued her leisurely stroll along what had become in the past few months her usual route. The motion was an automatic maneuver anymore. She barely noticed the buildings she passed. Mickey's Pawn Shop. The First National Bank. Subway. Ernie's 24-Hr Grill. She had seen them all so many times before that Aleisha didn't need to look at them to know they were there. They didn't interest her anyway.

She would have liked to go home, to just crawl into bed

and forget about everything else, but she knew there was no escape in slumber. Sleep was a temporary respite only. It couldn't compare to the escape she was so eagerly anticipating.

As the sun sank lower in the sky, blocked now by the buildings of downtown Toledo, an unexpected chill approached, the summer day losing the warmth it had exhibited earlier in the afternoon. Aleisha felt colder now in her shorts and halter top, the breeze raising a row of goosebumps along her bare arms, but she couldn't do anything about it. So she walked, ignoring her discomfort, eyeing the passing vehicles, her thoughts focused on the score she needed, motivated by the release that awaited her at the end of the long day.

The blue Ford slowed as it drew closer. She had noticed the car a few minutes earlier, when it had driven by and then taken the turn onto Cherry Street. This time it pulled to the curb ahead of her, the maneuver betraying all the signs of a last minute decision.

As she approached the window went down on the passenger's side, a beckoning invitation to the young woman. Aleisha's movements were casual, as though she had all the time in the world and wasn't about to hurry for anyone else. It was better not to appear too eager. To make them think they had to earn her attention.

She rested her arms on the side of the door as she leaned in, presenting what she hoped was her most radiant smile. She noticed with smugness that the driver's concentration seemed to be focused on the halter top, and the attributes barely concealed within, rather than on her expression. Which was fine with her. It meant she had him hooked already.

She sized-up the individual in a few seconds, her professional experience processing the information in a calculating manner. About her own age, in his mid-twenties, he was slightly overweight and casually dressed. He didn't look particularly prosperous, his clothes having a worn and somewhat soiled look to them, but at least he had shaved recently and looked relatively clean.

Not that it mattered to her. She wasn't planning on spending that much time with him.

He looked to be good for fifty anyway, she decided before making her pitch.

"Hello, Honey," she began, using the lilt in her tone the men seemed to expect.

"You need a ride?" His voice was quiet, barely reaching to her side of the car, as though he didn't want to disturb anyone nearby.

Or didn't want to be heard making his offer.

"I might. Where ya headed?"

He shrugged. "No where in particular. Just cruising. Looking for some fun."

The words she wanted to hear.

"Works for me."

With casual ease she opened the door and got in the car. She closed the door behind her but didn't bother to latch the safety belt, tugged instinctively at her halter top in adjustment, then turned in her seat to face him.

"So ya like ta party?" she asked.

"Who doesn't?"

"You not Police are ya?"

"Do I look like Police?"

"A girl can't be too careful, ya know."

"No. I'm not a cop."

"That's good. Don't need no cops giving me a hard time tonight. So what ya got in mind?"

He hesitated, as though searching for the words. Finally he attempted an answer, his voice again the whispered tone he had first greeted her with. "How much for...?" He stumbled once more before managing a meek reply. "You know."

Aleisha laughed at his obvious discomfort. He seemed more than a little nervous. She couldn't help wondering how often he had done this. "Damn, Honey. If ya can't even say it how ya gonna do it? How much ya willin' to spend?"

His answer came with no hesitation, like he had thought long and hard on the question ahead of time and the reply was firmly planted in his mind. "Sixty dollars."

She considered for only a moment before answering. She would have liked more, but it was above what she had originally figured him for. At least it was enough to get her through the next day or so. Beyond that she wasn't too concerned. Something else would come up by then. It always did.

"That will work," she informed him, presenting another one of her smiles. "And I promise ya won't be disappointed with what you're getting."

Now that the business transaction had been agreed upon there was no sense wasting further time. The sooner she got this over with and ditched the asshole the sooner she could get on with the rest of her evening.

"Let's not sit here no longer attractin' attention." She pointed ahead. "Just start drivin'."

The car pulled away from the curb, entering the light flow of traffic.

"Ya from around here, Honey?"

"Just visiting."

Possibilities floated through her head. "Where ya stayin?"

"We can't go there." He offered nothing further and she didn't press for an explanation. There was always some sort of reason. She'd heard them all before. "Don't you have anyplace?" he asked at last.

"I know a house we can go ta. It's safe. Pete's a good guy. Won't give us no trouble. But it will cost ya another ten."

He answered immediately. "Okay. Where to?"

"Just keep drivin'. I'll tell ya when we get there."

8

As the car moved along the driver cast occasional glances her direction, his eyes taking in the entire package. She offered her most enticing come-get-me look and shifted to face him more directly, thrusting her breasts forward with the maneuver. They always liked her breasts. Aleisha considered them her best feature, and most of the Johns seemed to agree. She had lost weight lately but at least had managed to maintain what she needed on top.

"What's your name, Honey?"

He hesitated, no doubt considering his reply. "Ray," he answered at last.

She was certain Ray wasn't his name.

"I'm Aleisha," she supplied. "So, ya ever done it with a black girl before?"

"No."

"No? Never had no brown sugar before?"

He shook his head.

"Then you in for a real treat." She leaned toward him, running her hand over his right thigh until it came to rest between his legs. She allowed her hand to linger there a moment before withdrawing, then turned to look out the windshield. "Yeah. We're gonna have us a good time tonight."

The young man smiled, no doubt pleased with the prospect.

Aleisha's mind was already on what she was planning to do with her earnings.

After several turns that threaded through lesser traveled streets, and eventually down a trash-strewn alley, Aleisha instructed the driver to pull over.

Pete's place wasn't much to look at, a rundown house with a droopy porch and saggy windows. Several of the windows were boarded over, the plywood lettered with names and obscenities in the bold colors of city graffiti everywhere. Not that the house stood out. It blended in well with the other residences on the block, a conglomeration of dwellings that must have been new at one time but gave the impression of having been perpetually old and worn. The small plot of grass in front of the place was ragged, interspersed with patches of dirt. A broken bicycle, one tire missing, lay abandoned in the weeds. Dog droppings littered the lawn.

"Don't worry," she assured him as the car drifted to a parking place in front. "It's safe."

He followed her up the wooden steps, his eyes focused more on the attributes of the young woman in front of him than on his surroundings. Aleisha knocked a quick beat on the door then immediately opened the panel, walking in uninvited, comfortable with the routine she had done countless times before. "Come on in," she prompted.

Once both of them were inside she closed the door behind him.

The hallway was dark and cluttered, with barely enough room for a path through the obstacles. From a room ahead on the left a television could be heard, its volume overpowering.

"Ya got the ten for the room?"

Wordlessly he fished the bill from his pocket and handed it to her.

"Wait here, Honey."

She entered the adjoining room. Pete was a big man, not tall but with an overabundance of girth to him, dressed in baggy pants and a white t-shirt that somehow managed to contain all the bulges beneath. He sat on the couch puffing on a cigarette, his form vaguely indistinct due to the accumulation of smoke already filling the cramped space. No lights were on in the room, the only illumination the glare from the television. The ever-shifting scene projecting from the screen painted Pete a rainbow of colors with its glow.

"Hey, Pete. 'Kay if I use the back room?"

He made no acknowledgment other than a slight nod.

"You're a doll." She bent over provocatively, presenting Pete a closer view of her breasts. It was a favor she always granted him. Sometimes it seemed the brief glimpse was worth more to him than the ten for the room. She slipped the bill on the table in front of him, deliberately taking her time with the procedure so he wouldn't feel cheated.

Returning to the hallway she led the man who called himself Ray to the back of the house. The room they entered was cold, with a coldness that seemed to emanate from every surface, as though the heat hadn't been turned on all year. A mattress lay on the floor, rumpled blankets covering it, the only other piece of furniture a worn dresser beside the window. A closet door stood slightly ajar, overflowing with debris.

"The money goes on the dresser," Aleisha directed.

As he retrieved his wallet from the rear pocket of his jeans Aleisha closed the blinds on the windows. The chore completed, she glanced at the bills, making out the three crumpled twenties, then closed the door, satisfied with the transaction.

Turning, she smiled in reassurance. "Don't worry. No one's gonna bother us."

He stood by the bed, as if uncertain what was expected of him.

"What say we get comf'able?"

It only took a moment for the halter top to come to rest on the floor at her feet.

Ten minutes later the blue Ford drove away. Ray was alone in the car now, Aleisha having stayed behind to confer with Pete concerning other transactions.

Chapter Two:

THE TWO CHILDREN SAT TOGETHER IN front of the television, the glare from the set highlighting their young faces. Willard Turner was the oldest at age eight. His six year old sister, Nataya, sat beside him. She slumped against her brother, as though seeking warmth from his closeness. Her arms held a tiny doll in a garish purple outfit. Though she seemed unaware of the plaything's presence her arms continually caressed it, as though it was a security blanket she held and not a plastic figurine.

Both children were captivated with the activity on the small screen in front of them, immersed in the undersea adventures of the yellow sponge creature and his ridiculous companions. Neither uttered a sound, other than the occasional laughs that punctuated the funny moments of the show. They were simultaneous expressions that issued from both of them, as though there was a synchronized bond between the two siblings. Once the moment passed they would lapse again into silence.

When the show paused for a commercial Nataya looked at her brother. "I'm hungry." She spoke quietly, in whispered tones, the way she always expressed herself. "When do we eat?"

Willard shrugged in answer. "Prob'ly not 'till Mom gets home."

"Can we have a snack?"

He sighed, intending at first to drop the matter, then

realized he was hungry as well.

"I'll go see," he finally decided.

Leaving the tiny bedroom at the end of the hall that the two children shared, Willard stepped onto the cold wooden floor of the hallway. Time had worn the flooring smooth in the center, buffing away any semblance of grain, though the edges betrayed the telltale marks left from the dogs of previous owners. The floor had apparently been stained several times in the past, as evidenced by the varying shades of wood, though it had been so long ago and the passage of countless footsteps had so worn the planking that it would be difficult to say which color was the most recent of those present.

Passing Michael's room Willard could hear the infant stirring in his crib. As the baby moved a rattle sounded, the snake-like cadence accompanied by the faint stirring of blankets and bed clothes, the tentative motions of the child in the early stages of awakening.

Willard hardly noticed. He didn't even bother to look in.

Heading downstairs he entered the living room at the front of the house. His step-father sat on the couch. Mark Bradley's attention was focused on the hockey game in front of him, the roar from the television speakers reverberating off the walls of the room as he added his own shouted comments to the pandemonium. The table his feet rested upon held – along with an assortment of papers – a half-empty bag of potato chips, two cans of Budweiser, and a selection of candy bar wrappers. Some of the contents had managed to fall onto the floor, forming a small pyramid on the far side of the table.

Willard stood there a moment, saying nothing, waiting to be noticed.

After thirty seconds he finally spoke up. "We're hungry, Mark."

No reply.

"Mark?"

"I heard you."

"Can we have somethin' to eat?"

"When your mother gets home."

"When will that be?"

"How the hell should I know? She'll be home when she gets home."

Willard realized there was no sense in arguing about it. He started to leave when something else occurred to him.

"Michael's awake."

"So?"

"He's gonna be hungry."

"Then fix him a bottle. Christ, do I have to do everything around here?"

Shuffling to the kitchen, Willard grabbed one of the bottles off the counter and filled it halfway with milk from the refrigerator. It never occurred to him to question whether the bottle was clean or dirty. He spilt a little of the milk, having misjudged how quickly it would gush from the gallon container, and wiped absentmindedly at the counter with a soiled dishrag. He actually managed to remove some of the mess with the maneuver.

Leaving the cap off the baby bottle he placed it in the microwave and set the timer for thirty seconds. While the seconds counted down he moved over to the cupboard, stealing a quick look behind him to be certain he wasn't being watched. There wasn't much to choose from. Eventually he decided on a selection. Removing the box of saltine crackers he reached in and withdrew a handful.

When the timer went off the box of crackers was already returned to the cupboard. The young boy tightened the nipple on the container of milk, shook the bottle a few times, then headed back through the living room – the crackers safely hidden behind his back – to go upstairs.

As he mounted the first step he heard the scraping of the

key in the front lock. The door opened and his mother entered.

Aleisha Turner walked in slowly, as though in a daze. She failed to notice her son on the stairway as she closed the door behind her. The motions were meticulous and precise, as if they were the most important actions in the world to her.

Her halter top drooped on the right side, evidence that it had been hastily thrown on. The legs of her shorts were uneven, the lining of one of the pockets peeking out from beneath the material in a haphazard manner. Her hair was in disarray, her lipstick smeared.

She started up the stairs, actually stepping over Willard in the process, who moved to allow his mother to pass. She had only taken four steps by the time Mark made it to the front of the house.

"Where you goin' 'Leisha?"

She halted. Her shoulders slumped slightly, as though she was exasperated with a situation she had been hoping to avoid. She didn't bother to turn around as she answered. "I'm tired. Headin' ta bed." Her words were slurred. Mumbled. Like she had a difficult time forming them.

"Like hell you are."

His words funneled up the stairway, as though projected through a bullhorn. Instantly the baby began to cry, startled by the loud tone, and tiny footsteps raced through the hall as Nataya scampered to the top of the stairs, halting abruptly at sight of her mother.

Mark noticed none of it as he reached up to grab Aleisha's arm, spinning her around as he took a step on the stairs. His fingers dug into her arm, though she failed to exhibit any reaction to the grip. His hands felt warm against her skin, which had a cold, clammy feel to it.

"Your kids are hungry. Why don't you pretend you're a mother that gives a damn and fix them somethin' to eat?"

She tried to pull away but Mark still had hold of her.

It was then he noticed the telltale signs on her arm – the fresh prick of the needle, the dribble of dried blood left as a reminder of the event. The vein running down her forearm stood out with a blue boldness, like some sort of slithering creature crawling beneath her skin.

"Son-of-a-bitch."

He glared at her.

"I thought you were through with this nonsense?"

She cast her head down, refusing to make eye contact, and only then noticed her son crouched on the stair step. She turned from him as well.

"Where'd you get the money for this, 'Leisha?"

She spun to face him. "I earned it." Defiance was in her eyes as she met his gaze.

He pulled her toward him as his right arm swung at her face. Her position afforded a poor target, so it was little more than a glancing blow, but it managed to knock her off balance anyway. Mark released his grip as Aleisha fell away from him. Tumbling down the stairs she landed in a heap against the front door, making no movement as she lay sprawled on the floor.

Mark stared for a moment, his features an utter lack of concern. Stepping over her he headed back to his hockey game. "Fucking whore."

Nataya, still standing at the top of the stairs, began to cry, soft undulations that shook her tiny body. She stared at her mother, bewildered with what was going on.

Willard recovered more quickly. As soon as Mark left the room Willard was at his mother's side, grabbing her shoulders and shaking gently.

"Mom? Are you all right?"

No answer.

"Mom?"

He shook her again, getting no response.

His next words were shouted so Mark, already seated in front of the television, could hear.

"She ain't breathin'. Do somethin'! She ain't breathin'."

Chapter Three:

O: ALL CASA VOLUNTEERS

From: CASA Office Toledo Ohio

Subject: Can you help these children?

Family of three – 1 boy age 8 yrs – 1 girl age 6 yrs – 1 boy age 8 months

Mother overdosed on heroin and is currently recovering at Toledo Hospital.

Father of two older children unknown. Children are currently residing in Foster Care.

Father of younger boy cited for alleged Domestic Violence. Child currently placed with Paternal Aunt.

If you can find it in your heart to be the CASA for these three loving children please let us know. They are in need of someone who cares.

Thank you.

Rebecca Poole
Lucas County Juvenile Center
CASA – Court Appointed Special Advocates

Chapter Four:

THE THREE-STORY RED-BRICK structure on Washington Street still intimidated Beverly Stone. It was five years old now, having opened the year before she started volunteering for the CASA office, and though it wasn't necessarily imposing of itself it sometimes frightened Beverly to consider the purpose of the building – the reason for its very existence – and what it had to say about our Society.

The plain sign in front announced it as Lucas County Juvenile Center. Many people walking past on the busy Toledo sidewalks no doubt failed to even acknowledge the building's existence. Or, when they did, didn't stop to think of what went on inside.

But Beverly knew how important it was. She had been part of the process for the last four years, serving as a volunteer advocate, and understood there was a lot more to the place than a fancy exterior.

Within its brick walls decisions were made that determined the future of entire families. Whenever a child abuse or child neglect case surfaced it was sent here for review and consideration. Rulings were decided upon that had far reaching ramifications for the participants involved, often changing a young person's life forever. Families were reunited here. Or, depending on the circumstances of the case, they could just as easily be torn apart.

Here too came the juvenile delinquents. These weren't necessarily bad kids, but rather children who had lost their way and wound up on the wrong side of life, often due to situations and circumstances far beyond their control. They were housed in the basement of the building, away from the public eye, in a state-of-the art detention center that kept them isolated from outside influences.

Beverly had toured the facility a few years ago. Clean and well-maintained, it had more the appearance of a live-in school than a dormitory for runaways and young offenders. There were classrooms, and a cafeteria, and art projects decorating the walls, all helping to maintain an illusion of normalcy.

But as you looked further you noticed other things, disturbing differences that, at least in Beverly's mind, brought home the reality of the situation. Like the ever-present video cameras, monitoring all activities.   Or the uniformed guards strategically posted at key points.   Most sobering were the community bathrooms, which allowed for little if any privacy to the inmates.

It disturbed her to think of what these children were going through, what they had done to prompt their incarceration, as well as what life had in store for them once they left.

Setting aside her forebodings Beverly entered The Juvenile Center, pausing at the security checkpoint, and placed her purse on the counter and moved silently through the metal detector. For some reason she always found herself catching her breath with the passage, as though she had something to hide and was fearful of being discovered, and somehow holding her breath would prevent the detection of the deed. She followed the same procedure at airport security, an incident Russell had never failed to make fun of when they used to travel together.

She breathed more comfortably once she received the approving nod from the uniformed officer manning the door.

The first floor of the building was occupied with administrative offices, classrooms, and a lecture room for public presentations and such. In her mind Beverly considered this floor the public presence of the Juvenile Center.

The second floor housed the courtrooms. There were five rooms presided over by magistrates and two larger rooms for the judges. This was where the nuts-and-bolts business took place. Where cases were reviewed. And presented. And argued. And, ultimately, where rulings were handed down that would affect many of these children for the rest of their lives.

Beverly reflected on this information, as she always did under these circumstances, while the elevator took her up to the third floor.

Her floor.

Lucas County Children's Services, the watchdog for the youngsters of Toledo Ohio, occupied most of the floor. But tucked away in a tiny corner, unnoticed by many who walked the nearby halls, was the CASA office.

Russell's death five years earlier had left a gaping hole in Beverly's life. She had retired from teaching the previous year and her husband was at the time six months away from leaving his job at the Jeep plant. Their future stretched before them with unlimited possibilities. The house was paid for. The kids were grown. They could spend the rest of their lives doing whatever they wanted to do.

The possibilities had dwindled to nothing the night of the accident.

She tried not to think about it anymore. Of course it was always with her, a part of her life that could never be forgotten. But for months following the crash she had brooded over it, moping around the house in a daze, finding it difficult to move on. With time – and thanks in no small part to the constant attention and support of her children – she had realized there had to be more to her life.

Beverly had finally accepted that she had a void to fill, an emptiness to overcome, and after some searching online came across the CASA program, or Court Appointed Special Advocates. It sparked an immediate interest.

When cases of child abuse and child neglect were presented by Children's Services the battles they waged took them to this building. These courtrooms. Every parent had the right to legal representation, with each of the parties going to court with an attorney at their side.

The children were another matter. They were frequently defenseless in the legal tug-of-war that took place between the various parties. Defenseless and often, due to their age and circumstances, speechless.

That's where the CASA volunteer came in. Appointed by the courts, the trained volunteers took on the task of representing the interests of the children in all cases involving child neglect or child abuse. In a truly legal sense they became the Guardian of the child, with a duty to safeguard their interests and see to their safety and well-being. It was a responsibility they accepted with grave seriousness.

A case could last two years or longer, and during that time the volunteer – people just like Beverly Stone – would investigate and research the allegations. They would talk to the parents and other family members. With the backing of the court firmly behind them they were permitted to confer with doctors and medical personnel, police departments and school officials, and anyone they felt instrumental in guaranteeing the welfare of the children they protected. Reports would be written, court hearings attended, and anything that needed to be done for the child's benefit to see the case through to a successful conclusion was taken in stride as part of the assignment.

It was a labor of love that exposed them to the heart-wrenching realities of life.

First and foremost they were there for the children. At least once a month the CASA volunteer would visit each child for every case they were assigned to. This was to be certain the children were in a safe environment and dealing successfully with their current situation. The CASA would be a friend to the child, a mentor and guide, taking time to listen and learn and understand. They could then advocate for what was in the best interest of the youngster in their charge.

And when it came to the hearings they would speak out, if necessary, for the child's rights. Regardless of what the parents said or felt, or how they wanted to resolve the issues, the CASA always had their say. Their convictions carried a lot of weight with the courts.

And rightly so. The children were depending on them.

Upon entering the CASA office the first person Beverly met was Susan Grant. Sue sat at the front desk and routinely intercepted everyone who walked in the door with a cheery greeting. Today was no exception.

"Good morning, Bev. You're looking good today."

"Thank you Sue. How are you doing, Dear?"

"Busy. I suppose that's a good thing. I'd much rather be doing something than just sitting at my desk twiddling my thumbs all day.

"Unfortunately," she continued, with a heavy sigh, "it also means the cases keep coming in and it's all we can do to keep up with things. One of the sad realities of my job."

Her frustration appeared obvious with her tone.

"So what can I do for you today, Beverly?"

"I'm ready to take on another case."

"I'm glad to hear it. Becky's in her office if you need to see her."

Beverly knew the way, and moments later was in Rebecca Poole's office. Rebecca was responsible for obtaining the preliminary information for the various cases that came through the office. She assimilated reports from Children's Services and contacted, generally through email, each of the volunteers on the roster. She also dealt with the CASAs directly; assigning and overseeing their case loads, reminding them of court dates, and passing along any pertinent information received through the office.

"I'm here about the email you sent out," Beverly began. "The two boys and a girl?"

"Goodness! I just sent that out this morning. I'm glad to see someone responding so quickly."

Moments later Rebecca had the information on her desk, contained in a slim folder of printed material.

"The mother's name is Aleisha Turner. 25 year old black girl. She's been picked up a few times for suspected drug use but nothing was ever proven. No convictions against her. But, in light of what happened, it's pretty obvious she's been using for a while. This time she nearly went too far and wound up in the hospital from an overdose. She seems to be recovering fine, but is still being held for observation. We suspect she may have been prostituting herself to support her habit but nothing in her record substantiates it."

She handed over a few sheets of paper, particulars concerning Aleisha Turner, including birth date, Social Security number, and both former and present residences. The woman's history was spelled out in a few stark pages, as though a person's life could be encapsulated that easily. Beverly gave the pages a brief glance before setting them down.

"And the father?"

"We don't know with the two older siblings. We're not even certain they have the same father, though the mother says it's a possibility. She lost touch with all the potential candidates. Some of them she couldn't even give a name to. So they're out of the picture completely."

"How about the baby? A little boy, isn't it?"

"That's right. The mother's been living with the same man now – Mark Bradley – for a couple years. They were married six months ago, after the birth of the child, though Aleisha opted to keep her own last name. Mark is white, and the child appears to be bi-racial, so he could be the father. The child is listed on his birth certificate as Michael Bradley, so it may even be true. But considering the mother's behavior it's not a sure thing."

"So where are the children now?"

Rebecca consulted her paperwork again. "The youngest one, eight month old Michael, is with a Paternal Aunt. Mary Bradley."

Beverly searched through the papers until locating the proper name, along with an address and contact information.

"And the other two?"

"In a foster home. Mr. and Mrs. Robert Kale are the foster parents. They're good people. They've been taking in kids for years now. I've worked with them before and never had any problems with them."

"That's reassuring."

Performing a final glance through the file, Beverly caught a quick glimpse of what was there. Included were Police Reports, case studies, and background histories, all pertinent information that would help her as the case progressed.

"Looks like this will get me started."

"Just call if you need anything. The Adjudication hearing is in five weeks. Good luck."

As Beverly headed for the exit a formidable looking man entered the office. He wore a dark navy blue suit that fit him as though he was born to it. His eyes flashed with a fiery intensity. His name was Malcolm McDougal, and he was the Director of the CASA office. Though undoubtedly a busy person, he always found time to praise and support the volunteers that assisted in the hundreds of cases that wound up on the agency's doorstep each year.

"Hello Beverly."

"Mr. McDougal."

"I see where the Benedict case reached a satisfactory conclusion."

"That it did," she replied, amazed as always that someone as busy as Malcolm would remember an individual case from one of the volunteers. "I had my doubts for a while," she continued, "but it was a pleasure to see the family reunited after all they'd been through."

"I'm sure they owe a lot of their success to you."

"I don't know about that."

"Don't underestimate yourself, Beverly. The work you do is important. These kids depend on the CASA office and, as you're well aware, we couldn't do it without people like you devoting your time and energy to the cause."

"It's my pleasure."

"I'm glad you feel that way. So what brings you here today?"

"Starting another case."

"Good for you. That's exactly what we want to hear. Don't forget, if you ever have any questions or concerns don't hesitate to stop by or give the office a call. That's what we're here for."

His pep talk complete, Malcolm turned and disappeared into the inner sanctum of the offices while Beverly made her way downstairs.

Chapter Five:

IT WAS STILL EARLY AFTERNOON. AS LONG as she was in the city already Beverly could see no reason not to jump into things. She could have gone home and studied the paperwork, to familiarize herself with the case, but Beverly preferred to walk into things with an open mind. She didn't want to make a hasty judgment of the people involved from a few random bits of written information in a case report.

By approaching the matter with fresh eyes she wouldn't prejudice herself with erroneous facts. A cursory look at the sheets provided by the CASA office had given her enough background information to get started. The details could be filled in later.

A large portion of the work involved in any case could only be handled by talking with the participants on a one-to-one basis. It was important to be aware of a person's reactions to questions; not just the words they employed, but their inflections and motions and the body language that accompanied what they had to say. The clues picked up from careful observation could often be as important as the words that were discussed.

Beverly made it a habit to often stop in unannounced during her cases. Though required to make visits, she didn't need to make appointments ahead of time. As a court advocate she was entitled to stop in at any time to visit with the children she was representing, regardless of where they were.

The downside of this approach meant that sometimes she would arrive at an empty house, the people she needed to talk to being away for the moment. But that didn't bother her. If she missed them the first time she would just stop again later.

It was late afternoon by the time she reached her first destination.

Robert and Margaret Kale lived in a neighborhood that, while not affluent, was well-maintained and orderly. It looked like a solid middle-class area, with working families managing to keep their heads above water but not high enough for the fancier frills of life. Many of the houses had swing-sets in back. Not fancy wooden contraptions, like the kinds prevalent in the more prosperous neighborhoods in the suburbs. These were the old kind, with tubular A-frames and metal slides; the tried-and-true type Beverly had grown up with. Beverly could see above-ground swimming pools in some of the backyards, but they were the exceptions and not the rule.

The car parked in the Kale driveway fit the house; not brand new but serviceable. A child's car seat, from the immaculate looks of it recently obtained, perched on the rear seat.

Pulling to the curb, Beverly shut off the engine and placed her keys in the outer pocket of her purse. From the same pocket she withdrew the plastic ID tag issued by the court, identifying her as a CASA Volunteer. The name on the tag read Beverly Johnson. Johnson had been her mother's maiden name. It was policy at the CASA office for the Volunteers to not use their real names when dealing with their clients, some of whom weren't the most reputable of characters. The name Beverly Johnson was registered with the court as legally binding for the work that needed to be performed, so as soon as she stepped out of the car she left Beverly Stone behind.

Spying no bell in front Beverly rapped lightly on the door's window. The knock was answered by a teenage boy who looked to be of high school age, a pimply-faced youth with gangly legs and arms that he had yet to grow into.

"May I help you?" His voice cracked slightly as he enunciated the words.

"I'd like to speak to Robert or Margaret Kale. Is one of them available?"

"My father's at work. But Mom's here. What's this about?"

"I'm here regarding Willard and Nataya Turner. The two children your parents are taking care of."

"Oh. Come on in. I'm sure Mom will want to speak with you."

The teenager led Beverly into a simply furnished living area that looked like it hadn't received a face lift in a long time. The furniture, though obviously not new, looked well cared-for and maintained, as though the owners understood the importance of getting their money's worth out of things. There was a certain amount of utilitarianism to it – nothing showy or flashy, just what was required to be live-able.

A few paintings adorned the walls, with assorted knick-knacks on the shelves, but there was nothing overwhelming. Just enough decoration to add an accent without providing accompanying clutter.

The teenager offered the visitor a seat and then retreated from the room to search out his mother.

Beverly had barely sat down when a youngster entered, a young boy with curly black hair and a precocious smile. Small in stature, he entered with a carefree easiness, as though he was in charge of things. In someone older the movement could have been described as a swagger, but there was no pretentiousness to the youngster.

He paused at sight of the unfamiliar woman sitting on the sofa.

"Who are you?" The question was announced with the

simple innocence of youth.

"My name's Beverly. Are you Willard?"

He nodded in reply.

"Well, it's nice to meet you Willard."

"What are you doing here?"

His bluntness was somehow refreshing to Beverly. The child wasn't shy about voicing his thoughts. He spoke his mind. Or, perhaps, he was just accustomed to looking out for himself, and his frankness was an attitude he had developed as a coping mechanism.

"I'm here to talk with you and your sister, Willard. And see how things are going. Do you like it here?"

He shrugged an answer. "It's all right, I guess. At least they have Cable TV."

"And you and Nataya would be lost without it, wouldn't you Willard?"

The new voice took Beverly by surprise. The woman had entered quietly from the room behind Beverly, her arrival unnoticed until she spoke up.

Barely missing a beat Beverly continued with her end of the conversation, her attention still focused on Willard. "So what do you like best about Cable TV?"

He answered with no hesitation, a smile on his face as he spoke. "Disney Channel. Especially the cartoons."

"I like cartoons myself. Though I imagine the cartoons I grew up with are different than the ones you watch. Do you know who Daffy Duck is?"

"Nope. SpongeBob's my favorite."

"I'm sure he's funny, too."

A pause came into the conversation, allowing the woman who had recently entered the opportunity to bend down beside the boy. "Can you go get your sister for me?"

He nodded and left the room.

Beverly stood, offering her hand. "You must be Margaret

Kale?"

"Call me Peggy," she offered. "And you are...?"

"Beverly Johnson. From the CASA office."

"Of course. I've dealt with CASA before. If I had known you were coming I would have had the children prepared to meet you."

"That's okay. I wanted to observe them when they were being themselves. How are they adjusting to things?"

"As well as can be expected. You wouldn't know it to look at them now, but they were a sight when they got here. Their hair looked like it hadn't been washed in ages. And their clothes!" She shook her head, reflecting on the matter. "I can only imagine the filth they must have grown up in. I don't know how people can live like that. That mother of theirs'...."

Beverly, hoping to avoid the subject for the children's sake, interrupted. "The mother has problems of her own."

"I'm aware of that. And I'd be the last one to speak ill of somebody else. But to treat your kids like this.... There's just no excuse for it."

Willard entered at that moment, leading a young girl into the room with him.

Nataya was much darker complexioned than her brother. The shading gave her a sheen that accented her delicate features. Her eyes, though expressing little in the way of emotion, nevertheless shone in comparison to her skin, lending her an almost bewitching style of cuteness. Beverly couldn't help thinking this was a girl that would be breaking a lot of hearts when she got older.

Beverly walked over, stooping on bent knees to more directly face the little girl. "So you must be Nataya."

No reply came.

"Do you like it here, Nataya?"

Once again she failed to voice a reply, though she managed a meek shrug of her shoulders.

"She likes it here okay," her brother supplied. "She just don't say much."

"There's nothing wrong with not saying much. Sometimes I think I'd stay out of trouble more if I didn't say so much." Beverly chuckled, making light of the moment, but neither child responded.

Willard turned to face Margaret Kale. "Can we go back to our room now?"

"Of course you can. I'll let you know when dinner's ready."

After they were safely out of earshot Beverly resumed with her questions. "Is she always this quiet?"

"Pretty much. Her brother does most of the talking for her. But you know kids. They're resilient. Even though they've been through a lot I'm sure they'll bounce back."

Beverly knew from experience that wasn't always the case, but she failed to share these forebodings with the other woman.

"How about their baby brother?" Beverly asked at last.

"Michael?"

"Yes. Do the children have much contact with one another?"

"They haven't yet. It's still pretty early, you understand. They've only been here a few days and we're all still getting adjusted to things. I wanted to give them time to establish some routines before we add too much to their lives. And with the mother in the hospital she's been pretty much out of touch with things as well. Once she gets feeling better I'm sure the kids will want to visit with her."

"What about the step-father? Mark Bradley. Has he been in contact with you?"

Peggy hesitated a moment. "You have to remember, he's only the baby's father. He's no relation to Willard and Nataya."

"He married their mother," Beverly pointed out. "That

32

sounds like a relation to me."

"That's not the way these people think." Her enunciation of the words left little doubt as to what she thought about *these people*. "They jump in and out of relationships as easily as they change clothes. A marriage license isn't anything more to them than a slip of paper, that's all. When things get tough they don't bother to hang around."

"So you don't think Mark will show an interest in the older children?"

"Well, he hasn't so far. That should tell you something."

"Have the children asked about their mother?"

"They know she's sick." She accented the last word with her hands, forming imaginary quotation marks around the word. "Other than that they haven't questioned it. I suspect they're pretty accustomed to their mother not being there for them. They don't seem to even find it out of the ordinary. I get the impression she wasn't around much. That they were pretty much left to fend for themselves."

"I just think it's a shame the children have to be separated from the baby. It's bad enough they're away from their parents. And then to not see their brother as well...."

"Hey, don't complain to me about that. I took two of them in, didn't I?"

"Nobody's faulting you, Peggy."

"Well, they better not be. I'd love to have all three kids. Really I would. But I'm not set up to take care of an infant. I still have one of my own that's in school, you know."

"Yes. I met your son when he let me in."

"David's been good about it. My husband and me taking kids in and all. It detracts from his time with us, you know, but I think it's helped him to see what a tough world it is out there. It's a good learning experience for him."

"I'm certain it is."

"Believe me, two extra kids is enough of a handful

already. It gets pretty hectic around here at times."

"I'm sure they keep you busy. And it's wonderful that you're providing a place for them."

"Give it time. I've had lots of children over the years as a foster mother. Things will work out. You'll see."

Chapter Six:

ALEISHA TURNER SAT IN THE DARKENED room, staring at the blank wall opposite her bed.

She ached all over, her muscles cramping with even the smallest expenditure of effort, so she found it easier to just sit and do nothing, her arms hanging listless at her sides. Her mouth felt dry, her throat scratchy. She had a hard time concentrating on anything, and found the images before her eyes to be a weird kaleidoscopic mishmash, making it difficult to perform even the simplest of tasks. The light from the hallway beyond was a glaring accent to the shadows in her room, an accent that stung her eyes and forced her to turn away from the harshness of the light.

Even the sounds outside her room – quiet sounds of muffled footfalls and whispered voices – seemed to be enhanced, as though she had developed new perceptions and a new awareness of the world around her. But the perceptions were harsh and unrelenting, cutting into her head like the cold edge of a knife, while the awareness became a cluttered orchestration of noise that made her head ache, even when she cupped her hands over her ears in a futile attempt at blockading the assaulting sound.

So she sat in silence and made no movements as she struggled against her whirling senses.

With time she was able to bring herself under control once

more, feeling her body return to a sense of near normalcy.

She breathed a sigh of relief, hoping that the next relapse would be less extended.

For a moment Aleisha reflected on what had brought her here.

They told her she was no longer in danger; that she had weathered the worst of it since coming out of her overdosed induced condition. Her breathing had failed her, they said, a normal enough occurrence when under heroin's influence, with the body failing to control the involuntary motions needed for a person's survival. Had the Rescue Squad arrived much later she would now be in The Morgue. Instead she found herself in a long-term rehabilitation facility.

Things were looking up, they informed her. Her move from the hospital was an important step on the way toward recovery.

But as much as she considered the concept – the idea that things were improving in her life and she had weathered through the worst of – the more difficult it was for her to believe that was the case.

Muddled thoughts swirled through her head, confusing her even further, a recollection of events that seemed real enough to touch but, for all she knew, could have been merely heroin-induced imaginings; waking up in the hospital with an IV feed attached and a battery of instruments monitoring her vital signs; a bevy of doctors and nurses scampering about, examining her and poking her and asking questions she didn't know the answers to then and couldn't remember now; the constant need to empty her stomach, her sickness convulsing for what seemed days on end.

The past week was a blur, a portion of her life lost to her forever. Which was perhaps just as well. It was a nightmarish dream time that eluded her with its vagueness.

How much time she passed in the aimless meanderings of her mind would be difficult to say. But at last a uniformed nurse approached the room, calling out her name.

"Aleisha?"

She turned, slowly, to acknowledge the summons.

"Your doctor is here to see you now."

Her doctor. Like she had any say in the matter. Like she hadn't been just thrown into a room and assigned the first Psychiatrist that happened to have an opening on his schedule.

Making no response, willing herself to react, she stood and followed the nurse to a tiny cubicle of a room. Most of the space was occupied by a steel desk. Behind this perched the doctor, an overweight specimen of a man with a thin pointy beard that reminded Aleisha for all the world of a Halloween Devil's mask. He wore a long white lab coat over a suit that looked wrinkled and worn, as if he had slept in it. His hands smelled of disinfectant, but beneath the lingering soapy odor Aleisha detected cigarettes.

She disliked him on the instant.

He made no attempt to acknowledge her presence until, after allowing her to linger for perhaps two minutes standing in the doorway, his gravelly voice barked out.

"Have a seat, Miss Turner."

He indicated a chair on her side of the desk while his eyes remained riveted on the folder in front of him. For another full minute she sat there ignored, the doctor lost in his perusals, until at last he set the papers down to look her squarely in the eye. She immediately felt on the defensive, like she had already been judged and been found wanting.

"Heroin overdose." The exclamation matched his demeanor, a no-nonsense tone that brooked no argument. "Sounds to me like you're pretty lucky to be here."

She felt some response was necessary but had no idea what was appropriate. "If you say so."

"Don't you think you're lucky to be here?" He gave her five seconds to answer before proceeding. "Would you rather be dead?"

She turned away, reluctant to face him. "No," she mumbled.

"What's that?"

"I said no."

"So you wouldn't rather be dead. In other words, then, you *are* lucky to be here."

"Sure."

"I thought as much. How long have you been doing heroin, Miss Turner?"

"Couple years."

"How long have you been mainlining?"

"A few months. I guess. I don't know." She shook her head in an attempt to clear the confusing thoughts. His rapid-fire way of speaking left her rattled and unsure of herself. "I don't remember."

"Of course you don't remember. The only thing you remember is how to get your next fix. Once that poison gets into your system nothing else matters, does it?"

"If you say so."

"You know it's true. How do you pay for your drugs, Miss Turner?"

The change of topic threw her, and Aleisha nearly blurted out an answer. Instead she replied with silence.

"I suppose you've been selling yourself on the streets?"

No answer was necessary. She doubted he expected one.

"These are dangerous habits to pursue, Miss Turner. Heroin. Prostitution. These are habits that ruin a person. Or kill them."

He shifted position then, and when his voice resumed it was like a new person had taken his place. A kindlier, more gentle person. "You can't keep doing this to yourself, Aleisha.

No good can come of this behavior. For you. Or your family.

"I want to help you. I *can* help you. But I can't do it alone. It's up to you. You have to trust me. You have to be honest with me. And you have to tell yourself you can beat whatever demons you're fighting that keep forcing you to choose heroin over life."

He leaned back in his chair and the old tone of voice returned. "Or the next time something like this happens the ambulance may not get there in time."

She fought back the tears, saying nothing, waiting for him to continue.

"How are you feeling since your move from the hospital?" he asked at last.

The abrupt change in the conversation surprised her. For a few seconds she said nothing before finally managing a weak answer.

"Better."

The reply was non-committal at best, Aleisha feeling the urge to say something but confused with what was expected of her.

"Is there anything you need?" The words bespoke a friendliness that wasn't apparent in his tone. It was as though the man behind the desk was unaccustomed to being amiable and the position was uncomfortable to him. He proceeded nonetheless, as though he felt compelled to continue along this new line of questioning. "Are there any personal items you can use?"

Aleisha shrugged.

"If you need anything don't hesitate to ask, either myself or any of the attending personnel on the floor. We want your time here to be the start of something good, Miss Turner. The people here have an earnest desire to assist you and see you through your recovery. So if there's anything you want...."

"I want ta go home."

"I'm certain you do. But...."

"Why do I have ta stay here? Locked up and watched like there's somethin' the matter with me." She felt herself growing stronger now, with the need to rebel against her situation. "I don't belong here."

"That's where you're wrong." His voice, reacting to her manner, assumed a colder tone. "You brought yourself here, Aleisha. With your lifestyle and bad habits and total disregard for your own health and safety."

"It's my life. Why don't I get any say in things?"

"Because you need help. You can't continue the way you have been. It's no good for you. And it's no good for your family."

She said nothing, staring at him with defiance but failing to find the words to continue.

"You haven't asked anything about your children, Aleisha. Why is that?"

"My children are fine. They tough. They gonna get along just fine." Then, as an afterthought, she added a concluding comment. "Once I get outta this fuckin' hellhole ya got me in."

"I know you feel constrained right now. That your life is being controlled by others. But don't think of this place as a prison. You have to look at this as an opportunity. An opportunity to recover. An opportunity to learn about yourself, and grow in awareness. Good things will come from all this if you only allow it."

She made no reply, her face turned downward as she stared at her hands resting on the stiff white fabric of the gown she wore.

He stood, effectively ending the interview.

"I'm Dr. Antonio Bargalony. Your case is in my hands now, so if there's anything you need I'm the one to talk to. Understand?"

Aleisha nodded in reply.

"You can return to your room, then. I'll stop by

tomorrow to see you again."

Chapter Seven:

THAT NIGHT BEVERLY FOLLOWED HER normal evening routine, though with a minor variation. She fixed her cup of tea at 9:00 as usual – the herbal green that she found so relaxing – alongside the crackers with peanut butter and cheese she invariably chose for a snack. Retiring to her bedroom she set the items on her nightstand while donning her comfiest pajamas, the ridiculous looking Minnie Mouse outfit her daughter Jennifer had given her last Christmas.

The small television in the corner she turned on, with the volume down low. She failed to recognize the faces that came into view once the aging set warmed up, though it didn't matter anyway. She never watched television at night. It was a habit she failed to develop.

Russell had been addicted to the small screen, switching it on as soon as he entered the room. Regardless of what was on he had to be watching something or, if not watching, at least listening to it. The device served as a constant background chatter he seemed to be lost without.

She approached her computer, which occupied a desk in the corner, to check her email. She had an account set up for her CASA work and referred to it on a daily basis, to be certain there wasn't any new information coming her way. She noted a message from Patrick Zimmerly, the case worker who was initially called in on the complaint regarding Aleisha Turner. Patrick was assigned to the case now, which meant he would be Beverly's contact at Children's Services. She had sent him a note earlier in the day, requesting some information regarding Mark Bradley and his sister, and Patrick had replied with what she needed. She had never met the case worker before, but from her experience all the employees at Children's Services were hard working, dedicated people concerned about the young charges under their supervision. She had no reason to believe that Patrick was any different.

Having gleaned all the information she could from her computer Beverly approached her bed. Snuggling under the blankets, feeling the comforting warmth that enveloped her, she declined to pick up the novel she was reading, which is what she normally would have done. Instead she varied her routine, spreading out the information from the CASA folder, arranging it into orderly piles on the bed's quilt.

Before her eyes was a history of two people – Aleisha Turner and Mark Bradley – told through a series of DUI's, neighborhood complaints, and traffic citations. A background of their families was included, or at least what information had been obtained in the short time the allegations had been under review. A report from Children's Services, detailing what they discovered the day they arrived on the scene following Aleisha's overdose, was also on hand.

It was all there in black and white. Not Beverly's normal late night reading fare, but information she had to familiarize herself with.

She took a sip of her tea, savoring the warmth of the liquid, then set her cup down on the night stand and reached for the first pile of papers.

As time wore on Beverly blocked out the sound of the television, concentrating on her reading, until she was in her own isolated world. She jotted down notes in a loose leaf binder, facts she thought were important or information that was unclear to her, until she found herself becoming more familiar with the events.

At last she had seen enough, absorbing all she could for the evening. Setting the papers aside she became aware once again of the sound from the television in the corner.

There was a couple on the screen – she recognized them as husband and wife from a popular sitcom – and they were arguing about something. The laugh track accompanying the show seemed much louder than the dialogue, as though the show's makers felt the need to inform the audience where the funny parts were. The laughter made Beverly feel there were other people nearby, watching the show along with her.

And for a moment, a brief instant in time, it was as if her husband was right there in the bed beside her again. As if she could reach out and feel his closeness, and experience once again the warmth they used to share.

She cherished the moment, hoping it would never end, but as it did on every night the moment passed, leaving her once more alone and lonely.

Beverly got out of bed, turned off the television, and crawled back under the covers.

Chapter Eight:

BEVERLY DIALED THE NUMBER FOR Mary Bradley, the paternal aunt who had temporary custody of the youngest of the three children in the case she had taken. She didn't want to drop in unannounced to visit eight month old Michael. Somehow it seemed wrong to do that to someone who had recently taken over the responsibility of caring for her brother's infant child. No doubt the woman had her hands full adjusting to the new schedule a baby subjects a household to without dealing with surprise visitors on top of things.

With this in mind Beverly opted to phone ahead first, so Mary wouldn't be caught unaware. She waited, and after five rings the call went through to voice mail. Beverly left a brief message explaining who she was and that she would call again, then set her mind to other activities.

It was time to visit the mother.

Beverly was fully aware of the sad reality facing many of the families she dealt with. Single parents – most notably single mothers – were often dragged into the system due to an inability to handle the day to day stresses confronting them. It wasn't that they were stupid, or uncaring, or any of the countless excuses people found to belittle others. It's just that they were on their own and unprepared for the enormity of the task they faced. With little or no support, the fathers often absent or unwilling to be of assistance, the overwhelming task of providing for their children often fell to young women barely more than children themselves.

As such the mother was often the key to the children's future. A successful family reunification depended largely on how willing the mother was to adapt to the situation; to follow through on her case plan and change her lifestyle to one more conducive to raising a family, rather than reverting back to the destructive behavior that had come close to ruining them in the first place.

Upon arriving at Toledo Hospital, where Aleisha Turner had been admitted following her overdose nearly a week and-a-half ago, Beverly discovered the young woman was no longer a patient there. Instead she had been moved to Riverfront Rehab, a care facility that specialized in long term rehabilitation of people suffering through the trauma of addiction, whether it be from alcohol or one of the dozens of drugs so prevalent on the streets of the city. Riverfront also worked with patients expressing suicidal tendencies, providing a safe haven while they worked through whatever issues were plaguing them, all under the guiding hands, and watchful eyes, of trained therapists.

Beverly was encouraged with the move. She had heard only good things from other CASA volunteers concerning Riverfront. Being transferred from the hospital implied the young woman was over the worse of her immediate medical problems and was working to put her life back together again. It could only be a positive step in the case.

Beverly had initially resisted the suggestion, put forth by her children several years ago, that her old cellphone wasn't adequate. According to them she was becoming out-of-date, relying on antiquated technology. By her reckoning a basic phone was fine. As long as she had something that kept her in touch, and allowed her to make calls in the event of an emergency, what else did she need? It was a means of staying connected that would have been unheard of twenty years ago. How antiquated could it be?

Two years ago Jennifer and Joey had gone in together and bought her a Smart phone and the accompanying service plan. It seemed like overkill to her; much more than she could possibly make use of.

That opinion changed as she got further into her CASA cases. She now took the time, at the start of an assignment, to enter the name, address, and contact information of everyone involved with the case into the device. This gave her a notebook of information at her fingertips. It was easy to get hold of the people she needed to, as well as allowing her to screen incoming calls.

Another feature she took advantage of, and had come to rely on more and more, was the GPS capabilities. She was often unfamiliar with the neighborhoods she had to visit. One touch of her phone, to activate Google Maps, and the friendly voice told her how far away the location was and provided step-by-step instructions on how to get there. She found herself relying on the faceless voice with the impeccable directions often as she became more involved with her CASA responsibilities.

Beverly typed Riverfront Rehab into Google. The address was about twenty minutes away, in a part of town Beverly was unfamiliar with, but she had no trouble finding it, thanks to the array of satellites hurtling unseen overhead that linked her with the rest of the world.

It was a concept that still amazed her.

The only problem she encountered along the way was from a source she should have anticipated. The nursing facility was in East Toledo, so to reach the destination meant crossing the Maumee River. Naturally the GPS chose the shortest route, leading her to the Cherry Street Bridge.

Had she been two minutes earlier she might have missed

the lake freighter heading downriver to the grain elevators. As it was she sat in the line of cars backed up by the opening of the drawbridge ahead, sitting the long minutes it took for the massive ship to pass through, occasionally glancing at the Skyway Bridge only a few miles from her position. The structure – still less than ten years old – soared above the river, allowing even the tallest of vessels to pass under with ease. Though not the most direct route to her destination, it provided an uninterrupted drive across the river.

The detour would have saved her time in the long run, but for now all she could do was sit patiently in her car and wait.

Riverfront Rehab was a series of a half-dozen one-story buildings, reminding Beverly more of an old motel than a care center. There seemed no rhyme or reason to the placement of the structures, but rather a haphazard arrangement that had no doubt grown through the ages whenever time, and money, allowed for expansion.

The exterior could have used some work. The lawns, though not untidy, were plain and austere. A few small shrubs eked out an existence with what appeared to be a minimum of attention from the grounds-keeping staff. The paint on the walls was faded, the colors muted and dull.

Beverly was left with the impression it was a struggle for Riverfront to maintain its existence.

The interior was moderately better. The linoleum in the front hallway was cleaned and polished. The walls were painted with bright blues and yellows. Murals of trees and clouds adorned several panels. It was an attempt at cheeriness that invited you to enter after passing through the doors.

The nurse at the front desk wore the world-weary expression of medical personnel everywhere, those who strive for excellence in care while dealing with the constant cut-backs and long working hours encountered in their work environment.

She was sympathetic to Beverly's errand and, as luck would have it, familiar with the CASA program.

Beverly knew from experience that this wasn't always the case. Sometimes she found herself wasting time establishing her credentials in an effort to talk with the people she needed to see. With all the government rules and regulations, the constant bombardment of HIPAA laws and privacy concerns and the accompanying paperwork associated with bureaucracy, it was often confusing, not only for lay people but for medical personnel as well, to know who was permitted access to patient information. The court order Beverly carried opened a lot of doors for her, but often the people she encountered were slow in responding to it.

Beverly was led to a private visiting area, a glassed-in compartment with a sofa and small table. The room had a homey feel to it, and would have been a pleasant atmosphere in which to visit someone other than the fact that its only view was the hospital rooms outside, the only people in sight uniformed nurses and robed patients. It served as an oasis in a desert of troubled souls.

As Aleisha Turner entered the room Beverly stood to greet her.

The young woman spoke first. "Who are you?"

The tone conveyed not anger, but rather exasperation, as though here was a person distraught and tired of dealing with things. At one time she must have been an attractive woman. Beverly understood now where six year old Nataya got her good looks. But the years had not been kind to Aleisha. Her entire body seemed to slump, as though giving up the fight. Her eyes drooped, lending her a sleeping look that made her appear lazy. The corners of her mouth turned downward in a perpetual frown, a scowl that gave the woman a mean sort of countenance. Her hair, curly and stringy, refused to be constrained by the simple band at the top of the young woman's head. The strands struggled to free themselves, resulting in a disorderly arrangement that presented the appearance of neglect.

And the hands. They were old hands. Not soft and supple like the hands of youth should be. They were wrinkled and worn, a testimony to years of hard living.

"I'm Beverly Johnson. From the CASA office."

"What's that? The CASA office?"

"I'm a Court Appointed Special Advocate. Lucas County has assigned me to be the guardian for your children."

No answer came, the young woman staring and saying nothing. Beverly couldn't decide whether she was confused with the whole affair or merely apathetic.

"I'm responsible for looking after the welfare of your children."

"You mean you here to take my kids away from me." Aleisha said it not as a question, but rather as a statement of fact, from someone who had dealt with the government hierarchy in the past and had a deep mistrust of its dealings.

"No, Miss Turner. Not at all. I'm here to insure that your children are being well cared for while they're away from you, until such time as reunification is possible."

"Reunification? What's that mean?"

"It means the court wants all children to remain with their parents if at all possible. We understand you're going through a difficult time here. We want to see you get yourself better, so you can be there for your children and they can be returned to your care."

Aleisha made no reply, as though this new information required further contemplation before she could commit herself to it.

"So why you here, then?" the young woman asked at last. "Why ain't you visiting my kids?"

"I have visited with Willard and Nataya already. They're both beautiful children."

She made no reply. Beverly expected some sort of acknowledgment for the compliment paid to her children. Or maybe a query concerning the baby. But it seemed Aleisha Turner's mind was in a faraway place, focused on her own personal concerns, rather than on any considerations regarding her family.

"So how are you doing, Aleisha?"

"I don't feel good. The medicine they givin' me – Buprenorphine, or somethin' like that – just make me feel sicker. Ain't medicine suppose to make you better?"

"Sometimes it takes a while until your body adjusts to it. I'm sure the doctors are doing everything they can for your recovery."

"My doctor's an asshole. Come in here with his highfalutin' ways like he know all about my life an' all about my problems an' he gonna fix everythin' just like that. What he know about my life? What he know about my problems? Like he know what it like to wonder where your next meal comin' from? Just lookin' at him you can tell he ain't never missed a meal in his life."

"I'm certain he has your best interest at heart. I'm sure he wants to see you doing better."

"He ain't interested in nothin' but the money the state gonna pay him for takin' my case. He ain't interested in me or my problems."

"I'm interested, Aleisha. If there's anything you want to tell me – any questions you have or anything I can find out for you – just let me know."

"I just needs to know when I can go home."

"When you're ready, Aleisha. You've been through a lot. Everyone wants to see you feeling better."

"Sure they do. They just thinkin' about me, ain't they? And now they sayin' I need to take some classes."

"What classes?"

"I don know. That fella from Children's Services what was here. Patrick somethin' or other. Says I got to start takin' some classes or I won't never get my children back."

"That would be Patrick Zimmerly," Beverly informed her. "He's the case worker from Children's Services. He must be talking about parenting classes. To help you cope and understand how to better provide for your family."

"Nobody needs to tell me how to provide for my fam'ly. I do what it takes to see they taken care of. They got a roof over their head, ain't they? They don't never go to sleep hungry. I do just fine with my fam'ly and nobody gonna tell me otherwise."

Aleisha's initial hostility had failed to abate as they spoke. Rather, she seemed to be more worked up as the conversation continued, as though talking about things only made the matter worse for her.

Beverly had to concede that the young woman's belligerence was understandable. To a point. She had survived a harrowing experience, and now found herself isolated from her normal routine and cut off from the people in her life. She was no doubt frightened for the future.

But that gave her no right to lash out at someone who was trying to help her. Aleisha Turner should have realized by now what she was doing to herself. And to her children.

Beverly struggled to control her emotions. A string of thoughts ran through her head, things she wanted to say to express her feelings regarding the matter. *Are you taking care of your children when you're walking the streets at night, Aleisha? Or how about when you're strung-out on heroin? Is that being responsible? Does that behavior make you a good mother?*

Instead she remained silent, as she focused on the undiminished glare of defiance on Aleisha's face. Behind the facade was the fear of the future, the uncertainty of what lay ahead, the unspoken questions regarding the road to recovery she was navigating. She had been through a lot already, but the journey to come was still a hazardous one with a variety of potential pitfalls along the way.

Beverly forced herself to remain calm. "I want to see you get better, Aleisha. I want to see you get yourself cleaned up. But my primary concern right now is those three children of yours. And their future. And what's best for them."

Beverly pushed herself away from the table as she stood, gathering her papers together.

"You can sit there and complain all you want to and never see your children again. Or you can be an adult about it and cooperate with the people who are trying to help you. Do the hard work involved to turn your life around. It's your choice.

"But whether you like it or not I'm one of the people you're going to have to work with. So you better get used to it."

Beverly sat in her car, fighting back the tears. She hadn't meant to speak so harshly. It was so unprofessional of her to behave the way she had.

But she hated to see someone waste their life away like that. It wasn't good for Aleisha. And it wasn't good for her children.

Chapter Nine:

BEVERLY WAS STILL PARKED IN FRONT OF Riverfront Rehab when her cellphone rang, the vibrant tone surprising her with its sudden clamor. The name Mary Bradley registered on the readout.

"Hello," she answered, reverting to her CASA personification. "This is Beverly Johnson."

"Hi. This is Mary Bradley. Michael's Aunt."

"Yes, Mary, I know who you are. Thank you for returning my call."

"I just don't understand what this is about," she began, her tone immediately defensive. "I've already spoken with Patrick from Children's Services. I thought everything had been arranged regarding the baby."

"I understand your confusion. But I'm not from Children's Services. I'm from the CASA office. My role is a bit different from the Agency's. But I think this would be easier to explain in person. Maybe if I could stop by this evening...?"

"I don't know. I just got home from work and I'm pretty worn out. What with the baby and all. I'm just not used to all this running around. It takes me an extra forty-five minutes in the morning to get him dressed and drop him off at daycare. Then there's extra time in the evening as well."

"Of course. But I need to see Michael sometime before

the end of the month."

"Is that really necessary?"

"Yes it is. I'm required to visit with each of the children I'm assigned to at least once a month. I was able to see Willard and Nataya yesterday. But if today isn't convenient perhaps some other time would be better for you?"

The voice on the other end of the line hesitated, obviously considering her options. "No. We may as well get this over with." The tone was similar to the one used when discussing a dentist appointment, or something else equally unpleasant.

"Good," Beverly responded. "I have your address, and I'm pretty familiar with the area where you live. It will take me about thirty minutes to get there. Does that work for you?"

"That will be fine."

Beverly was about to say more but the line had already been disconnected.

The apartment complex appeared well maintained, with a neatly manicured front lawn and miniature flowering trees scattered throughout. There were several buildings facing the parking lot, each identical to one another, down to the faux wood shingles sheathing the walls and the bright green awnings adorning each window. A lighted area behind the parking lot sported a tennis court. Two figures cavorted on the black top in what appeared to be a spirited match, the occasional thud of the tennis ball hitting the asphalt surface exploding in the still air and then echoing between the buildings. The sound initially startled Beverly until she was able to determine the cause of the disturbance.

It appeared to be a quiet area, which surprised Beverly considering the location. Just down the road was a Wal-Mart, with a slew of restaurants and fast food establishments around the corner. These amenities were no doubt convenient for the people who lived at the apartments, and one would have expected more traffic in the area because of the retail establishments. But the place seemed distanced enough from the main strip that this wasn't the case.

Mary Bradley lived in a second floor apartment. A flight of stairs led to a miniature balcony, which gave access to the private entrance to her living area.

The woman who answered the ring at the door was much younger than Beverly had expected, looking barely older than a teenager. She had a youthful vitality to her, that fresh look of the adult newly on her own and discovering the wonders of the world. Though hidden just beneath her features lurked a layer of exhaustion.

She ushered Beverly into the apartment and immediately began to move about, as though she contained an excess of energy she needed to relieve herself of.

"Excuse the mess," she began, rummaging through a pile of papers on the table. She appeared to be doing little more than rearranging the stack. "I had a long day at work and I didn't have a chance to clean up yet."

"Where do you work, Miss Bradley?"

"At the Hair Express in Starbeam Plaza," she supplied, not bothering to look up. "Six straight hours on your feet cutting hair can be a killer." She faced Beverly, managing a smile. "But you can call me Mary."

She had the papers stacked in a neat pile now, and moved them to a spot on the counter behind her. Grabbing a cloth from a drawer beside the refrigerator she made a casual swipe of the kitchen table.

"So you say you're with the CASA office?"

"That's right."

Beverly explained in a few quick sentences the role she played in the proceedings.

"That's nice that you take the time to help out the way you do," Mary remarked.

"It's worth it, knowing I'm helping the kids through a tough time."

"But you're not here to see me, are you? Have you met Michael yet?"

"No I haven't."

"He's a doll. When he's not tired, anyway. Then he can be a regular terror."

She smiled with the comment, an infectious display that Beverly couldn't help returning, thinking back to what life had been like raising two little ones.

"I just put him down for a nap before I called you," Mary continued. "He always seems cranky when I pick him up from daycare."

She made a motion to leave the room but Beverly interrupted.

"Let him sleep for now. There's a few things I'd like to talk to you about first. How are you dealing with having a little one around the house?"

She paused to consider a moment. "I have to admit it's more work than I anticipated. It's different than what I'm used to. You know? I've never really been around children much. They bring a real change to your routine."

"It's great that you're willing to take your nephew in."

"Well, somebody had to. I think Children's Services considered my parents, but I don't think that would have worked out very well."

She paused suddenly, as though caught saying something she shouldn't have. Lingering silence hung on the air for several seconds.

"Is there a problem with your parents?" Beverly asked at last.

"No. Of course not." The answer came a bit too rapidly, as though it was a forced reply. "It's just that they both work full time. And they're getting older now. Been a long time since they had to take care of a baby. I just think it was the best thing all around that I stepped in."

"Of course."

Mary Bradley rushed on, as though anxious to leave the matter behind. "But I'm up to this. I really am. I know I have a lot to learn, but it's getting easier every day. As long as it's only for a few months I should be okay."

"And if it's longer than a few months?"

She paused, considering the question. "You think it will be?"

Beverly plowed ahead. "These things generally take a year or so to resolve. Sometimes longer. Depending on the severity of the case."

"Really?" As if the information was a revelation to her Mary stopped in her motions. Pulling a chair out from beside the kitchen table she sat down, staring at her hands for a moment as they rested on the tabletop. "I guess I could do that. If I had to. But it's not what I was expecting."

Beverly sat down, facing Mary more directly. "These things take time. A lot depends on how Aleisha does with her recovery."

"I wouldn't hold your breath waiting on that. She's pretty mixed up. From the sounds of it, she has been since before my brother met her. I don't know what Mark sees in her."

She stopped, as though questioning herself whether to say more. Beverly remained silent, giving her time to sort her thoughts. Most people liked to talk about themselves. And their problems. Sometimes the best way to get information was by being a good listener.

"Actually, I take that back," Mary announced at last. "When she's cleaned up Aleisha's pretty attractive. Or at least she was when Mark first met her. She's let herself go a bit since then. And I suppose she's good in bed. She's certainly had enough experience with that sort of thing."

"You don't think much of Aleisha, do you?"

"How can I? The girl's a mess. She doesn't take care of herself. Doesn't take care of the kids. Mark sees more of those kids than their mother does."

"Then tell me about your brother. Is he good with the children?"

"I guess. As good as a guy can be with these things. I mean, he's no Mr. Mom or anything. But he gets by."

"I'm still a bit confused about the day Aleisha had her overdose. About what actually happened...."

"Just stop right there. I'm sure whatever Mark did was motivated by anger over his situation. His wife comes home high on heroin – after being with some other guy, no doubt – what was Mark supposed to do? I think he's been pretty patient with her for far too long, all things considered. He puts up with a lot from Aleisha."

Beverly found the conversation headed somewhere she wished to avoid and felt it best to change the subject. "So has Mark seen the baby since all this happened?"

"A couple times. He stops over to say hello and check on how things are going."

"Do you know if he's had contact with the other two? Willard and Nataya?"

"Why should he? Let's face it. They're not his kids. They're not his responsibility. They're just another burden Mark doesn't need in his life. Like their mother."

The awkward silence that followed Mary Bradley's proclamation was broken by the shrill sound of crying coming from the other room.

"That's Michael. Guess he's ready for his bottle."

Beverly rose from her seat. "Do you mind if I get him?"

"Well.... The bedroom's sort of a mess. I left in a bit of a hurry this morning."

"That's okay."

*****

Beverly zeroed in on the sound of the baby's crying, turning the corner into a hallway and heading for an open door on the right. At least Mary had been honest about one thing. The room was a mess, with clothes scattered everywhere. Some obviously belonged to the baby, but the majority of them appeared to be Mary's. The bed was unmade. The dresser top was cluttered with hair brushes and sprays and lotions and loose earrings.

Taking a quick look around in an effort to determine whether this was indeed a safe environment for an infant, Beverly was at least satisfied that the clutter was, even with all the mess, just clutter. Nothing looked dirty and dingy. There were no empty dishes, or day old piles of food, laying around. Nothing had the look of having sat in the room for ages. Rather it looked like the bedroom of a young woman without enough time on her hands, struggling to keep up with things and getting further behind all the time, burdened with a sudden responsibility she was having a hard time adjusting to.

Welcome to Motherhood, Beverly mused, as she stepped into the room.

Beverly wandered over to the crib. The baby was a tiny thing, with thin arms and spindly legs. His diaper seemed to hang on him, like it was intended for a larger child. He was much smaller than Beverly had expected, though it had been a while since she'd been around an eight month old infant. They grew so fast maybe she was just forgetting how small they started out.

Michael was pale in color, nothing like his mother except for the small patch of hair that appeared to be coming in the same black as hers. His tiny fists waved in the air as he exercised his lungs, a piercing scream that, while not loud, tended to grate on the nerves.

Beverly reached into the crib and lifted the child, pulling him toward her and resting him upright against her chest in the classic position for burping. Though it had been years since she had held an infant – her youngest grandchild was nearly seven, after all – it all came back to her in a flash. Without even being aware of it she began a gentle rocking motion back and forth, a movement that the child seemed to respond to.

By the time Beverly carried him into the kitchen the tears had stopped.

Mary looked over from the counter where she was preparing the bottle, a smile of approval on her face. "You look like a pro doing that."

"I guess it must be like riding a bicycle. Some things you never forget."

"I can take him if you want."

"No." Beverly shifted the infant's position, letting him rest in the crock of her elbow while she sat down. He seemed so fragile, so defenseless, that Beverly felt an overwhelming urge to hold him and protect him. Her gaze remained locked on Michael's face, studying the delicate features. "I don't mind holding him a while."

After handing Beverly the bottle, which the baby eagerly accepted with the greediness prevalent with infants, Mary took a seat at the table. "I don't want you to get the wrong idea here. I feel bad for Aleisha's older kids. I really do. I guess, in a way, I feel bad for Aleisha too, even though she caused a lot of her own problems.

"But it's not my brother's concern anymore. Or, at least, it doesn't need to be. And it's certainly not mine, either. I'll do what I can for Michael. And I hope everything works out for the family. But we all have our lives to lead. Aleisha needs to live with the choices she's made."

Chapter Ten:

$\mathbb{S}$IX PEOPLE SAT IN THE ROOM. THEIR chairs were formed into a circle, so they were facing one another. Harking back to the tradition epitomized by the legendary Knights of the Round Table, each of them had equal representation in the group, for the simple fact that there was no head position.

Or such was the intention of the arrangement. In truth, it was obvious by their demeanor who was in charge.

Dr. Antonio Bargalony held a notebook in his hand, sitting ramrod straight in his chair as he lorded over the meeting. Even though he permitted the participants to speak freely, allowing the conversation to cover a multitude of topics, he managed with his manipulations to control the general themes they discussed. Years of conducting such sessions had made him an expert at the task.

Occasionally he would interject an observation, or ask a pointed question, thereby steering the conversation in the direction of his choosing. Sometimes his comments were placed in a deliberate manner to maintain the flow of a topic, or often presented to allow one of the others in the group to be included in the discussion. At other times he would force the dialogue in an attempt to gather more information, eliciting more detail concerning something he considered important.

The notebook in his hand was referred to from time to time as he occasionally made a notation on the page. He performed the act as unobtrusively as possible, though the others present in the room never failed to notice the deed. Five pairs of eyes riveted on his pen as each spectator wondered what was being recorded.

Aleisha had sat down directly opposite the physician, with two others on either side between her and the doctor, but she still felt too close to him. He was an intimidating presence, and had been from the first moment she met him.

Aleisha felt leery of the current situation, as though she was being finely scrutinized. She felt as if each word she said was being analyzed for some hidden, dark meaning, and she had to be cautious in case something she inadvertently said would come back to be used against her at a later date. She had a mistrust of authority. And in this room, at this time, Dr. Bargalony was the ultimate authority.

Judging by the appearance of the others in the room they all felt much the same as Aleisha. There was an inherent nervousness to the group, with a reluctance to express themselves. When they spoke it was in whispered tones, as though afraid of voicing too loud an opinion.

They were all young adults, except for one gray-haired woman with a spinsterly look that was obviously much older than the rest of the group. There was one male, besides the doctor, and he seemed pretty quiet and withdrawn. She knew his name was Bryan, because they had each introduced themselves at the start of the session, but other than that he was a mystery, offering little to the conversation. Just another stranger in a room full of strangers.

The group members apparently knew each other from previous sessions. There was a degree of friendliness among them, at least in so far as familiarity could be advanced in such a rigid setting, though she doubted any of them would be construed as friends to one another. Aleisha was the new kid in town. She felt awkward, as though she didn't belong with these people, having nothing in common with them other than the fact they must have all been messed up in some way or other or else they wouldn't even be here.

There was only one member of the group Aleisha felt any kind of connection with.

Janelle seemed much like Aleisha, a black girl perhaps a few years younger than her, who said things – and implied things – that made Aleisha feel that here was a kindred spirit. Without even knowing Janelle's history Aleisha felt she could relate to the young woman, as though they shared a common heritage. Without even understanding the reason why she felt less alone in the room knowing Janelle was there.

Mandy, a pale faced girl with stringy blonde hair and an inclination to fling her head back from time to time to keep the loose strands from covering her eyes, was talking now, rambling on about something or other that had happened at home. Though old enough to be on her own she apparently still lived with her parents, in a household that from the sounds of it was rigid and unforgiving.

Aleisha wasn't really paying attention to what the girl had to say. Part of her treatment required her to attend the group session. That didn't mean she had to participate.

At a break in the girl's narrative Dr. Bargalony spoke up. "So, Aleisha. What do you think about what Mandy was saying?"

Aleisha shrugged.

"Do you see any parallels between her experiences and yours?"

"Not really."

The doctor chose to ignore Aleisha's indifference to the proceedings.

"A common enough response. On the face of things we're all different from one another. That's usually the first thing we notice when we meet new people. Rather than embracing our commonality we focus on the attributes that keep us apart.

"But I'm sure you can find something if you look deeply enough. Though each of us is unique in our own ways, we can employ our common similarities to bring us a better understanding of one another. Mandy comes from a big family. Six children, was that right Mandy?"

The girl nodded.

"Six children. Which gives her a lot of closeness, being part of a group. But it also denies her some of the private time she would like to have. Which makes her feel she is missing out on things."

Mandy nodded in agreement. "I just feel trapped sometimes. Like I'm being watched. And judged. And nothing I do is ever good enough for them."

"I think we can all understand those feelings," Bargalony continued. "We all have the desire to fit in, yet still maintain our own persona. How about you, Aleisha? Did you ever experience anything like that growing up?"

Aleisha answered immediately, not bothering to consider the question. "No. Nothin' like that."

"Didn't you ever feel the need to strive for your parent's approval?"

She shook her head, muttering under her breath. "My folks weren't really much involved with us kids. They never paid us much attention."

"Then why don't you tell us something about your family?"

"Not much ta tell."

"Let's start with the basics. How many brothers and sisters do you have?"

"Three brothers. One sister."

"Are you close?"

She hesitated, considering her answer. She felt obligated to reply but didn't relish the thought of opening up in front of a bunch of strangers, all of whom were staring at her as though she had something important to say. "We wasn't ever really that close."

"You used the word wasn't. As if your family was a thing of the past, rather than part of your present life. Would you say that's accurate?"

"Yeah. I suppose."

"Do you keep in touch with them?"

"Jus' Kareen. She a couple years older than me. We still talk. Once in a while. Ain't seen the rest of the fam'ly for a long time now."

"Then tell me about Kareen. Have you talked to her since you arrived here at rehab?"

She shook her head a silent no.

"Why not?"

"Wouldn't do no good. Ain't nothin' she can do to help me. Besides, she'd just wanna lecture me and tell me what a mess I made of my life, anyway. She always been good at tellin' me what I been doin' wrong. I'm sure she wouldn't have nothin' good to say to me now."

"How do you know that?" The question came from the elderly lady, who had introduced herself earlier as Linda. She actually leaned forward and placed her hand on Aleisha's knee as she asked the question. It was no doubt meant as a gesture to show closeness but Aleisha found the touch to be uncomfortable. It was an invasion of her personal space, an unwanted gesture from a total stranger.

"Maybe your sister would like to come visit you," Linda suggested. "Maybe it would be a good chance for the two of you to grow closer." And then, in a faraway tone, more to herself than to the others in the group, she added another remark. "At least you got somebody out there you can talk to."

Mandy picked up on the inflection, the tone of loneliness that permeated the voice. "You sound so negative, Linda. So depressed. Like you're all alone. You must have someone in your life?" Mandy suggested.

"Nope. Don't nobody want anything to do with me. Not after the way I treated them."

Silence held the room for several seconds, with everyone present reluctant to break the mood. Even Dr. Bargalony seemed content to wait, allowing the moment to linger.

Finally Linda continued, her eyes downcast. "It's my own fault. After my knee surgery two years ago the doctor had me on Vicodin, for the pain. It was all that got me through the day. And after a while it was all I could *think of* to get me through the day.

"When I needed money to buy some more pills, and didn't have none of my own, I took it. Took it from my husband. Took it from my kids. Anyone I could find what I could sneak some money from their wallets. Didn't matter to me who I was hurting because all that mattered to me was getting more Vicodin."

Aleisha, pushing the hand from her knee, spoke up. "At least I never hurt nobody. I earned the money I needed. I never stole nothin'."

Mandy asked the question on everybody's mind. "How'd you earn it?"

A spark of defiance entered Aleisha, daring her to say anything, giving her a willingness to speak out. If these people expected honesty she would give them honesty.

"By fuckin'."

She expected some sort of reaction, perhaps a show of shock on the faces around her, but none came. It was as though the people assembled in the room had heard it all – had done it all – and nothing could surprise them anymore. Where she had expected the revelation to make her feel more powerful the opposite had occurred.

Feeling suddenly vulnerable, like she had exposed herself too much, Aleisha rushed to say more.

"Men are such assholes anyway. Do all their thinkin' with their dicks. So if some guy wants me ta spread my legs for him. And is willin' ta pay me fifty bucks ta do it. Why shouldn't I? They get what they want. I get me some spendin' money. And nobody gets hurt."

Until now Janelle, the other black girl, had remained silent. But apparently her interest had been aroused with Aleisha's revelation. "Aren't you afraid? With all the creeps out there?"

Aleisha shrugged. "I been roughed up a bit. Got a black eye once. But you learn quick ta recognize the lowlifes. If they looks funny ta me I don't even get in the car with 'em. It's as easy as that. And it beats workin' a real job. I name my own hours. Go ta work when I want and where I want. And don't got no asshole of a boss tellin' me what ta do."

"Sounds like you got it all figured out."

Aleisha nodded in agreement. "That's right."

"Then what are you doing here?"

Chapter Eleven:

BEVERLY STONE ENJOYED THE PERSONAL satisfaction she received from working as a CASA volunteer. She felt like it gave purpose to her life; a reason to get up in the morning. This had been especially true in the beginning, after Russell's death, and had helped her to deal with the loss of her husband.

The long months following the accident had been a difficult time for Beverly. Her children had been wonderful through it all. Jennifer and her husband Thomas had stopped by constantly the first few months, so much that they almost became an annoyance. Joey and his wife Teri didn't stop in as often. Whether they were just too busy, or merely felt they shouldn't pry into her personal life, Beverly couldn't say. When they did visit they always brought the grand kids, which was a treat regardless of Beverly's mood.

Spending time with the grand children only intensified Beverly's desire to participate in the CASA program. Not all the children out there had the comforts her kids had grown up with. And while she couldn't provide for the children she dealt with in her CASA cases the way she had done for her own children – spoiling them rotten, Russell liked to chide her – at least Beverly could do her part to insure that someone had their best interest at heart.

But there was one aspect of being a Court Appointed

Advocate that Beverly still struggled with.

Writing the court report.

Early in each assignment, usually within the first month of receiving a case, the court held an Adjudication Hearing. This was to determine whether the allegations truly represented a case of child neglect or abuse – she had yet to receive a case where it didn't – and further to come to a decision on how to proceed in resolving the issues facing the family. To assist the court each CASA had to present a report, detailing not only the events leading up to the allegations but what the volunteer had personally discovered in their investigation after visiting with the children and interviewing family members.

The writing itself didn't bother Beverly. Thirty years as a teacher had more than prepared her for that. Rather it was the implications of what the report meant that troubled her. The magistrates based their decisions largely on the information they received from the case workers and the CASA volunteers. Incorrect information, or important information missing entirely, could therefore lead to a faulty ruling.

Beverly took this responsibility seriously and often found herself spending more time preparing the court report than was probably necessary, agonizing over the minutest morsels of information. She was working on the preliminary report, organizing her findings and detailing what she had learned so far, when she heard the quick buzz of the doorbell from the front of the house. The sound preceded the opening of the door, followed immediately by approaching footsteps.

She surmised it must be her daughter Jennifer, a guess that was proven correct when Beverly heard the familiar voice calling.

"Mom!" The voice emanated from the front of the house, in the shrill tone Jennifer traditionally employed to insure her voice was heard. "Are you home?"

"In the kitchen, Dear."

Jennifer entered the kitchen as she entered every room, like a hurricane on a path of destruction. She bulldozed her way through life, plowing through any obstacle with fierce determination and an urgency to succeed. She seemed to never slow down, but rather lived a whirlwind existence with her job and family and juggling half-a-dozen things at once. Somehow she managed to keep her life on track, her goals firmly in mind, though to an outsider it must have seemed a preposterous undertaking. She had been a precocious child when young and her attitude hadn't changed in the intervening years.

Jennifer threw her purse on the table then proceeded to grab a glass from the cupboard. After helping herself to some orange juice from the refrigerator she sat opposite her mother and began rummaging through the papers on the table, shifting through them as though expecting to mine some valuable information. Beverly doubted her daughter was even interested in what she was looking at. With Jennifer it had always been a fear of being left out of things. She wanted so much to belong that she plunged into anything for the opportunity to fit in.

"What's all this, then?" Jennifer asked at last.

"My latest CASA case. Just trying to get things organized."

After a few more seconds looking at the information she seemed to lose interest, much as her mother had surmised would happen. "You're still doing that?"

"Of course I am."

"You push yourself too hard, Mom."

The statement sounded ironic, coming from her frenzy-paced daughter, but Beverly said nothing.

"Why don't you just enjoy life instead of getting yourself all worked up over things like this?"

"But I enjoy *this*. It gives me satisfaction, knowing I'm being useful."

"So what kind of loser you dealing with this time?"

Beverly scowled in reply.

"What? They are losers, aren't they? Otherwise they wouldn't be in the situations they're in." She recited the statement as though it was the most obvious notion in the world.

"Just because they're having problems doesn't make them losers. I prefer to think of them as...." Beverly paused a moment, searching for the appropriate term. "Misguided individuals," she finally managed.

Jennifer offered a weak chuckle. "So what are your *misguided individuals* up to this time?"

"Three kids. Two boys and a girl. And the little one's just adorable. You should see him."

Jennifer waved her hand with a show of impatience. "Yeah, I get it. All children are adorable. But what did the parents do? I mean, they had to do something or you wouldn't be involved. Right?"

As much as she loved her daughter, Beverly often was taken aback at Jennifer's attitudes. She was opinionated about everything, regardless of whether or not she understood the topic under discussion.

In spite of herself Beverly plunged on, knowing full well she was setting herself up for a lecture from her daughter.

"The mother has an addiction problem. She overdosed on heroin and wound up in the hospital."

It sounded so simple, a few words to describe a person's life, but Beverly realized there was nothing simple about what Aleisha Turner was going through.

"Loser," Jennifer re-iterated, interrupting her mother before more information could be provided. "You may as well cut your losses and move on to the next case."

"How can you say that? You know nothing about the woman. Nothing about the life she's living and what she's had to put up with."

"And you do?"

"Not yet," Beverly admitted. "But I'm learning. That's a lot of what this job is all about. To dig deep and discover what's behind the problems. I'm sure there's some good in her. There's good in everyone."

Jennifer stood and walked over to her mother's side, placing her hand on Beverly's shoulder with a gentle rubbing motion. "That's one of the things I love about you, Mom. Your optimism."

Beverly responded to the compliment with a smile.

"But sometimes you're just too naive," Jennifer continued. "I've read about these people. In newspapers. Magazines. Once they get hooked they stay hooked. The only thing they care about is getting their next fix. It's all they think about. And if they have to cheat, or lie, or steal, to get that next hit, then that's what they're going to do."

"You make them sound like a lost cause."

"Maybe that's what they are."

"I don't believe that. I refuse to believe there isn't some good in everyone."

"I just don't want to see you get hurt, Mom. I know you. You let your optimism control things and pretty soon your expectations are sky high. And that's a long way to come down from when things turn sour."

"I'm a big girl, Miss Jennifer." The term was one Beverly and Russell had used on their daughter when she was little, every time they felt she was getting a bit too big for her britches. It seemed appropriate for the present situation.

Jennifer smiled at the verbal reprimand. "I know you can take care of yourself. God knows you've been through a lot the last few years. I just don't want to see you set yourself up for a fall."

"I'm not the one you need to be concerned about. It's the children in the case you should worry about. They're the ones we have to look out for."

"Then it's lucky for them they have someone like you on their side." Leaning down, Jennifer delivered a hug to her mother. "You always were a great Mom. You were there for me and Joey when we were growing up. Seeing to our needs. Anticipating our wants. If you're half as concerned about these kids as you were about us then they have nothing to worry about."

"Don't forget your father. He spent his whole life going off to work every day to put a roof over our heads. So Joey could play soccer. And you could have your piano lessons."

Jennifer, detecting the familiar faraway look that entered her mother's eyes as she reminisced, hugged Beverly a second time. "You miss him a lot, don't you?"

There was no reason to even consider the question. The answer was an obvious one. "Of course I miss him. Every minute of every day." She sighed. "It just isn't the same without your father here to share things with."

"I think Dad would be proud of you, Mom. The time you devote to helping these kids is great."

Beverly failed to respond, her thoughts obviously focused on something else.

Jennifer recognized the signs from her mother and felt again the helplessness that had overwhelmed them after her father's death, as her mother withdrew into herself, searching for a solace from her loneliness that none of them could deal with. As bad as the loss had been for Jennifer, she could only imagine the heartache of losing someone you had shared a life with for over forty years. Her mother was so much stronger now, and coping so much better with things. But it still wasn't easy for her. At times it still hit her hard.

Jennifer pulled away, forcing herself to laugh, hoping to ease the tension. "Piano lessons. Of all things. You know I never wanted those lessons. I don't know why you guys wasted the money on them."

Beverly jerked slightly, as though awakening from a daydream, and smiled at her daughter. Her eyes glowed from the remembrance of raising her children. "Because that's what parents do, Dear. They spoil their kids."

Jennifer offered a mock look of indignation. "So now I'm spoiled, am I?"

"We were no worse than you are with your daughter. Where is Emily, anyway?"

"She spent the night at Melinda's. They've got a swimming pool over there and the kids practically live in it. I expect Emily to come home with gills one of these days."

Jennifer took another drink from her glass, draining the remainder of the juice. She then rinsed the glass in the sink and set it on the counter.

"Anyway, I've got to be going. I just wanted to be sure everything was all right."

"You're a dear for checking up on me."

"Hey, maybe it's time you got some spoiling for a change."

The two exchanged a goodbye kiss, Jennifer departed, and Beverly returned to her case notes.

Chapter Twelve:

SITTING ON THE EDGE OF THE BED IN HER tiny room, her hands twisting themselves into knots while her feet beat an unconscious rhythm against the floor, Aleisha stared straight ahead at the blank wall before her. She could hear sounds from outside – murmuring voices, the shuffling footsteps of someone's slippered feet, even once a hint of laughter, sounding incongruous considering her location – and as before each of the noises seemed to assault her, forcing its way into her brain with an irritation akin to fingernails across a chalkboard.

She could use a hit right now.

Just the thought of it eased her mind. How great it would be to escape into the blissfulness of heroin's embrace; how wonderful to succumb to the overwhelming peace that always accompanied using, as the euphoric feelings drove away all of life's problems. She tried to recall the sensation, the heightened awareness of the event, the wonderful feelings that lifted her into a state of ecstatic bliss.

But the memory failed her, serving as a poor substitute for the release she craved, causing her apprehensions to grow as her nervousness increased.

It just didn't seem fair. She didn't belong here. Yes, she grudgingly admitted to herself, something had gone wrong following her last rush. Maybe Pete had given her too large a dose. Or the shit had been mixed improperly. But it had never happened to her before. She was certain it wouldn't happen again. Now that she was aware of the consequences she would be more careful.

She hoped they let her go home soon. She wanted back in her familiar surroundings. She wanted to be able to come and go as she pleased, instead of being caged up like some kind of animal. Who were these people, anyway, to tell her how to live her life? She wasn't hurting anyone. She just wanted to enjoy life on her own terms and do the things that brought her pleasure. Why didn't they just leave her alone?

As she pondered these thoughts Aleisha became aware of someone standing in the doorway, making no sound, wordlessly watching her as she struggled with her inner emotions. She turned toward the figure and realized it was Janelle, the other black girl from the group session.

Feeling as though her privacy had been violated Aleisha snapped a greeting. "What do you want?"

"Just wanted to see if you were okay."

"Why wouldn't I be okay?"

"I don't know. You seemed pretty angry during therapy. Like something was bothering you."

"What do you expect? You want I should be happy them makin' me stay in this shitty place?"

"It's for your own good."

"You really believe that?"

"Of course I do."

"Honey, you got a lot to learn 'bout things. Don't you know nothin'? People don't never do nothin' good for nobody else. Not unless they gonna get somethin' in return. That's the way the world works."

"Well, I don't agree with you." Janelle voiced the statement as a declaration of fact, as though harboring no doubts concerning her convictions. "I think there's a lot of good people out there. Doing a lot of good things."

"Well, I guess you're 'titled to your opinion."

"It's not just an opinion, Aleisha. I know it's the truth."

"Is that so? And how do you know that, Miss High-And-Mighty?"

"Because two years ago I was right where you are now. Doing some of the things you've been doing. Feeling the same way you're feeling about yourself. Lost. Confused. Angry about my freedom being stripped from me. Afraid to return to life on my own again."

"I ain't afraid of nothin'. I could leave here right now and do just fine."

"I don't believe you. It's okay to lie to me, Aleisha. Once we get out of here we won't never see each other again. But don't be lying to yourself. If you can't be honest to yourself then this place won't be doing you no good."

"It's not gonna do me no good anyway. It's just a waste of time."

"It doesn't have to be. It's all what you make of it."

"That sounds like the same crap Bargalony's been preachin'."

"I know he comes on strong sometimes, but Dr. Bargalony is a good man. He can help you, Aleisha. I know he can because I've been through it myself. I've been clean now for twenty-five months. And it feels great."

"Then tell me this, Janelle. If you doin' so good how come you're back in this place?"

The girl standing in the doorway immediately became silent, her eyes lowering to stare at the floor. The burst of enthusiasm she had shown moments earlier, in an effort to convince Aleisha of the merits of the surroundings, evaporated in an instant. It was as though a switch had been thrown, turning off everything around them and allowing her to retreat to a private haven in her mind. Even Aleisha, as involved as she was in her own concerns and fixated as much as she was on her own issues, noticed the change in the young woman.

"I'm sorry," Aleisha managed at last, though she wasn't certain what for.

"No. That's okay. It helps when I talk about it. It really does."

Still she hesitated, as though fighting with herself on how to proceed.

"Why don't you come in and sit down?" Aleisha suggested.

Janelle accepted the offer silently, seating herself on the room's only chair and staring at the floor at her feet. For a few moments she said nothing, obviously gathering her thoughts together. After a deep breath she began to talk. The tone was introspective, as though she was saying the words for her own benefit, and Aleisha just happened to be a casual observer to the event.

"You should have seen me three years ago. I was hooked. Bad. I used to have a good job. My boyfriend and I were doing all right, then, financially. Had a nice apartment. We both had a new car. If we had been smart we would have set some of that money aside, saving for the future.

"Instead we pissed it all away. With the extra money we had I used to go on splurges. Anything to make me feel like I was enjoying life. It started out drinking with the girls, late night parties where the fun just never seemed to end. We were young and excited and full of life."

Her face lifted, looking Aleisha directly in the eye for the first time since entering the room.

"And we were stupid."

Again she turned away, drawing into herself once more.

"One night my friend Carol offered me some smack. You know, I didn't even know what it was at first. But I knew right away I liked it. It made me feel omnipotent. Like anything was possible. Like nothing could stand in my way.

"And the more I used the stronger the feeling got, to where I couldn't think of anything anymore but getting my next fix. Know what I mean?"

Aleisha nodded wordlessly, though Janelle, involved with her recitation, failed to notice.

"After a while chasing the dragon became a full time occupation with me. There wasn't time for anything else in my life. I lost my job. I nearly lost my boyfriend."

She paused. Aleisha waited, expecting the young woman to continue, but after a long minute of silence felt the need to prod Janelle into continuing.

"What happened?"

"The dragon turned on me. They found me passed out in a ditch – unconscious – with no recollection of how I got there. Couldn't remember a thing, except feeling like all I wanted to do was die."

Her voice quieted with the next words.

"I ended up here."

"I hear you. In fuckin' prison."

"It's not like that, Aleisha. This is a good place. The people here are generally concerned with your welfare. When I arrived I was about as low as a person could be. But they never gave up on me.

"Neither did David."

She paused, lost in a memory.

"Is David your boyfriend?"

"He was. And he was simply wonderful. He never voiced a negative comment about my behavior. It was all such a surprise to him that I managed to live the life I did right under his nose without him suspecting a thing. I think he even felt guilty, as though the whole thing was his fault. Like he had let me down or something."

She laughed at the thought.

"Can you imagine? Here I was being a holy terror. Going through money like it was water. Alternating between being so high I was floating on Cloud Nine and so low that some days I had to struggle to get out of bed, dragging myself to the bathroom to puke my guts out and try to get over the sickness that had hold of me.

"And David felt like *he* let *me* down.

"He was wonderful. This place was wonderful. Oh, I was like you at first. I fought it. I struggled against it. But finally I woke up to the fact that my life had become a pile of crap and if I didn't do something about it soon I may never get another chance."

She stood, a smile of triumph gracing her face. "And I did it. I gave up on the Jolly Pop. That part of my life is over. And I'm never going back there."

Janelle approached, clasping Aleisha by the hands in a show of confidence.

"You can do it too, Aleisha. I know you can. It won't be easy at first. You have a long road ahead of you. But if you want to do it. If you fight to do it. You can turn your life around."

Aleisha was uncertain how to respond to the other woman's enthusiasm, embarrassed that she lacked Janelle's strength. She remained sitting on the bed as Janelle turned to leave the room.

Her visitor was just passing out the door when a new thought occurred to Aleisha.

"Wait a minute."

Janelle stopped in her tracks, turning around to face the room.

"If you're doin' so damn good, and ain't never goin' back to the skag again, then what the fuck are ya doing in this place?"

The gleam evaporated from Janelle's eyes, the light of triumph replaced with the somber look of failure.

"Two weeks ago there was a fire at our apartment. The family next door left a hot plate on or something, I don't know. I guess it don't really matter how it happened, does it? Just that it happened. I was gone at the time. David wasn't."

She took an extremely deep breath, then forced herself to continue.

"I never even got to say goodbye to the person who saved my life. The person who meant everything to me. He was taken away and it felt like my whole world just fell apart.

"I couldn't handle it. Not after everything else I'd been through. I wanted to just escape from it all."

Tears were in her eyes by now, memories of the recent past flooding in with an overwhelming torrent of guilt and shame.

Her next words were a whisper, barely audible across the room.

"I ended up here."

An awkward silence pervaded the small space until Aleisha decided to speak. "I'm sorry, Janelle. I had no idea."

"You just don't realize, Aleisha. All you're thinking about now is how much you're missing your dope. But I'm missing something a lot more important than that. Something that was taken from me that I can never replace. And I know, no matter what happens, I can never get it back."

She turned, leaving the room without another word.

Chapter Thirteen:

IT STILL GAVE BEVERLY AN uncomfortable feeling to venture into some of the neighborhoods where the CASA children grew up. It wasn't any personal concerns that bothered her, for she no longer felt unsafe visiting the areas. That had been an issue in the beginning, when she first began the program. She had felt like an intruder then, an outsider, someone who didn't belong in the neighborhoods she called upon. But with time her concerns had lessened and she'd grown to accept the way things were.

She had been traveling the city for several years now while performing her volunteer duties, seeing many parts of Toledo she had been completely unaware of previously, and in all that time she had never been approached in any manner she felt inappropriate, leaving her with the conclusion that people were people, no matter where they called home. The families she dealt with were no different than her or her neighbors, except they lived different lives in different situations and surroundings.

What did perturb Beverly was the squalor she was exposed to, and the utter disregard some people appeared to have concerning cleanliness. As far as she was concerned being poor was no excuse for being dirty. Personal pride should have been a requisite for anyone, especially for those raising young children in their households.

She understood the realities of the situation. Not everyone

had the money to afford expensive upkeep on their homes. But she had assisted many clients who, while possessing little more than the bare necessities, at least managed to be appropriate in their appearance while making the attempt at keeping their houses presentable. Many were the places she had set foot in with old walls, and worn carpeting, and furniture that was obviously cast off from someone else. But the walls shined, a testimony to the elbow grease employed in scrubbing them. The floors were tidy and well-swept, as if they had just received a thorough vacuuming. The furniture was displayed proudly, as a token of what the families had, not as a gesture to what they were lacking.

These places were truly homes to the people who lived there. You could tell by their demeanor they appreciated what they had. Beverly felt honored to be permitted to visit.

The address she had been given for Aleisha Turner did not fit this category. Located on a dead end side street near the very end of the block, it had suffered much in the way of neglect, presenting a forlorn look bordering on abandonment. Boxes were piled high on the front porch to the point they left barely room for passage to the door. A corner was missing from one of the front windows. Someone had bothered to cover the hole with a piece of cardboard, but shattered shards of glass still lay on the porch, just beneath the window, forgotten by everyone.

Two vehicles occupied the driveway. The pickup in front – a black Chevy with one green fender and one yellow one – appeared to have found a permanent resting place. Or, perhaps more accurately considering the looks of things, a permanent rusting place. It looked like it hadn't been moved in ages.

The Impala behind the truck hadn't fared much better, a multitude of dents and scratches attesting to the abuse it had suffered over the years. Its back end was in the air, supported by jacks, with both rear tires removed and sitting on the ground next to the car. A bumper sticker on the back of the vehicle had the word FORD emblazoned on it, followed by the explanation Fix Or Repair Daily, an obvious testimony to the owner's preference in car manufacturers.

Beverly pulled to the curb, shut off the engine, retrieved her ID badge, and exited the vehicle.

It was only as she was walking toward the house that she noticed the young man at the side of the Impala. He squatted beside the vehicle, intent on his business, grease-stained hands manipulating parts that Beverly assumed had something to do with the car's brakes.

For a moment she stood in silence, watching the man work. He had a leisurely way to him, his movements deliberate and steady, as though he had all the time in the world ahead of him. While he appeared to know what he was doing it was obvious he had no intention of rushing through the procedure. He seemed preoccupied with the activity, oblivious to anything around him.

Beverly drew closer, clearing her throat to attract his attention.

He turned to face the distraction.

"Good morning," Beverly began.

He nodded a curt reply and continued with his mechanical work, effectively ignoring her in the process.

"I'm looking for Mark Bradley."

He finished tightening a bolt before placing his wrench on the ground and standing up. He was a good looking young man with long blonde hair and muscles that rippled beneath his shirt. He seemed out of place, like he should have been on a beach in California, chasing down a wave or perched on a lifeguard stand, ready to spring to action, rather than changing a tire on a rundown Toledo street.

Though, when she considered it, Beverly came to the conclusion that it would be difficult to see the young man exerting himself any more than necessary. As a surfer he would have given up after the first spill. Anyone swimming with him on guard duty would have taken their life into their own hands; from the looks of his lackadaisical motions she doubted he could ever make it off the lifeguard stand in time to rescue a drowning victim.

"I'm Mark," he answered at last. His voice had a slow, lazy drawl to it, a tone that perfectly suited his appearance. "What do you want?"

His manner, though not impolite, bordered on the offensive, as though Beverly's presence was a major intrusion in his life.

"I'm here about Aleisha and the children."

"Great. Somebody else from Social Services. Can't you people just leave us alone?"

"Actually I'm here from the CASA office. I've been appointed by the court to investigate on behalf of the children's welfare."

By this point he had finished wiping his hands on a soiled red cloth, what looked to be half of an old t-shirt. He discarded the material, allowing it to fall on the ground, and it blew under the car and out of sight.

"The children's welfare? What's that mean?"

"It means my priority is your children. I'm here to insure they are in a safe environment and being taken care of. And while I'm concerned about Aleisha's well-being – and yours, Mr. Bradley – my focus is Willard, Nataya, and Michael. They are my number one priority."

He made no reply, content to wait until she was ready to continue.

"Do you mind if we step inside to talk some more?" Beverly asked at last.

He glanced at the porch, as if seeing it for the first time.

"I haven't had the chance to clean things up, with Aleisha gone and all. Not that she was ever that concerned with keeping the place up, anyway. She left most of the household chores for me to take care of even when she was home."

"Don't worry about the mess," Beverly assured him. "I'm not here to see the house."

Which wasn't exactly true, but she didn't want to tell him that. An important part of her responsibilities was to determine whether the children she represented had appropriate living conditions. She knew the children wouldn't be returning to the house anytime in the near future. There were too many issues to resolve before that could take place. But, in the event the case plan was followed and the family was reunited, Beverly felt it necessary to see what the children had to contend with.

The interior lived up to the expectations presented by the outside of the place. Clutter was everywhere. Empty bottles and pop cans. Dirty plates with dried traces of food clinging to the surfaces. Soiled clothes were ubiquitous; resting on the floor, covering the furniture, dangling from the banister of the stairs, the articles giving the impression they had waged war on the place and won.

Looking down a hallway Beverly spied the kitchen area, which if anything was more of a disaster than the rest of the place. Dishes and pots and pans overwhelmed the available counter space and spilled onto the simple wooden table. A dirty stain covered the majority of the old linoleum flooring. Beverly tried not to consider what had caused the blemish.

Mark Bradley led the way into a room that appeared to be the focal point of the living area, as evidenced by the 52 inch television that dominated the environment. Mark plopped onto the sofa, seemingly oblivious to the chaos surrounding him, and grabbed a can of beer from an end table. Beverly couldn't help wondering how long the beer had sat there.

"Sit down if you want," he offered, taking a swig of the brew as he propped his feet up.

Beverly took a quick glance at the choices available to her

and elected instead to remain standing.

"I visited with Aleisha a few days ago. At rehab. She seems to have a lot of anger."

He shrugged. "That's just 'Leisha. She's always pissed off about something or other. After a while you get used to it."

"So you don't think it has anything to do with her addiction?"

"I suppose it could. Just hadn't thought much about it."

"How long has she had a drug problem?"

"I wouldn't exactly call it a drug *problem*."

"Oh? What would you call it?"

"She uses occasionally. That's all."

"And that doesn't bother you?"

"Of course it bothers me. I've told her to stop. That what she's doing ain't good for her. But she has a hard time dealing with things sometimes. I guess she's always been that way. But it's not like she does it all the time."

"How about you, Mark? Do you use drugs?"

"Of course not. Do I look like an idiot or something?"

"But you're okay with Aleisha using?"

"No. I'm not *okay* with it. I've told her before she needs to quit." Then, as an afterthought, "If not for her sake then for the kids."

Beverly was left with the distinct impression he added the disclaimer for her benefit, to show what a good parent he could be, rather than through any genuine concern for the children.

"I understand you struck her the night she ended up in the hospital."

His reply was slow in coming, as though he was considering his words carefully. "Where'd you hear that?"

"It was in the Police report, Mark. There's no sense in denying it."

"I'm not trying to deny it. I just think things were blown way out of proportion. 'Leisha comes home late, all strung out like that.... Hell, she wasn't even aware what she was doing. On top of that, she has the nerve to tell me she's been out walking the streets.

"How's a guy supposed to react when he hears something like that from his wife? I was angry, that's all. I shouldn't have hit her but I was angry."

"Have you seen her since then?"

He shook his head. "The case worker says we shouldn't see each other until after the hearing next week."

"And then what?"

"I don't know. Guess that depends on 'Leisha, don't it? If she cleans her act up I guess we'd try to make it work."

"And if she doesn't?"

"Then we go our separate ways."

"What about the children?"

"What do you mean?"

"If you and Aleisha go your separate ways. What happens to the children? Who's going to raise them?"

He paused to consider, as though the thought had never entered his mind previously. "I suppose I could take Michael. I'm not really good with babies but I guess I could learn. But the other two...."

He shook his head.

"No. Willard and Nataya are 'Leisha's children. They're all right, I suppose. As kids go. But I'm not ready to be a single parent of three children. Plus my job don't pay that well. Things are pretty tight around here as it is."

"Where do you work, Mark?"

"O'Henry's Auto Parts. On 17th. Do you know it?"

"I've been past it, before. Guess that explains why you know so much about cars."

"I get by. Brakes and things. The simple stuff. I do okay with that. Sometimes I can even pick up some extra money by helping my friends out."

Beverly began moving for the door, satisfied there was nothing more to learn from the visit. "Well, I just hope things work out for you. For *all* of you."

"I'll be okay," he remarked, as though trying to convince himself. "I don't know about 'Leisha. I hope she can get her shit together. For the kid's sake, if nothing else.

"But hey, there's always somebody looking for kids. Right? I'm sure they'll find a home somewhere."

Chapter Fourteen:

ALEISHA FELT AS THOUGH SHE WAS sitting through a rerun of a bad television show. The same characters sat in the same chairs and, as far as Aleisha was concerned, talked about the same issues and annoyances they had talked about a week ago. It all seemed so pointless and non-productive.

They sat in a circle as always, Dr. Bargalony presiding over the group. It seemed the doctor said less now than he had before, allowing the others to fill in the gaps in the conversation. Aleisha of course had no way of knowing this was by design, with the therapist encouraging increased interaction between the patients as they became more familiar with one another and better accustomed to speaking their minds.

Aleisha had noticed another discrepancy from earlier group sessions, though if asked to describe the variance in words she would have been hard pressed to do so. It had been apparent from the start that they were all different from one another. It wasn't only a physical difference, though that had a lot to do with it as well. Or something in their backgrounds, their life stories, that separated them from one another.

Every one of them was a unique individual. They each had different views and opinions – often extremely contradictory to one another – that manifested themselves into occasionally heated discussions as they voiced their disagreements.

Yet as the sessions had progressed, and an intimacy began to grow between the participants, without any of them being aware of it the members of the group found themselves focusing more on their similarities than on the things that had kept them apart. How each of them felt isolated, even when they were in the company of others. Or how they all wrestled with feelings of inadequacy; that no matter what they did, or how hard they tried, they could never rise above their present situations and cope with the stresses of everyday life.

These thoughts were never openly voiced, but Aleisha felt the connection nonetheless.

Some aspects of the sessions, however, seemed to never change.

Mandy still tended to drone on about matters, with a seemingly endless litany of complaints and problems. "Life is so unfair" seemed to be a pet phrase of hers. She resorted to it often while talking. Yet, from Aleisha's point of view, the girl had it made. She lived in what sounded like a mansion in Sylvania. Her father was some sort of big shot lawyer who handed the girl anything she could ever want. Her childhood couldn't have been any different from Aleisha's if they purposely attempted to find someone to contrast with her.

But there were similarities as well. They both shared the feeling of being overlooked while growing up, Mandy because her parents were always working too much to pay attention to their daughter, while Aleisha's folks were always so busy trying to stay ahead of the creditors, always scrounging for the next meal, always attempting to finagle their way through life, that they had no time for their youngest daughter. Both girls had fallen in with the proverbial bad crowd. Aleisha's peers had introduced her first to marijuana then, with the progression of time, to the heroin that had been the cause of her present circumstance. For Mandy the drug of choice had been alcohol. It didn't matter how it came; a six-pack of beer, a bottle of

Smirnoff, or shots at the local watering hole.

Aleisha became aware of a voice intruding on her thoughts as Dr. Bargalony stood from his chair to address the group.

"As I'm sure you're all aware, today is the final session for one of our members. Janelle will be going home today."

Linda, sitting beside Aleisha, began clapping her hands. Soon the rest joined in, though it was a half-hearted demonstration at best. The departure of one of the group only served as a reminder to the others that they would be left behind; that they had yet to resolve the issues in their lives and had more work ahead of them toward recovery.

The physician continued. "Do you have anything you would like to say to everyone, Janelle?"

She hesitated, obviously at a loss for words, then stood slowly. "I want to thank you all for being here for me. I mean that sincerely. I know we'll probably never see each other again. And that's okay. Because for a little while, anyway, I had somebody to talk to. So I didn't feel so alone. Just remember this. What you're going through isn't unique to you. We've all been there."

She paused, sniffling slightly. "I've been where you are. I know what it's like. And it gets better. Believe me. It gets better."

Eventually the session ended. Dr. Bargalony departed first. Being the only one in the group with an actual time-table for the day he didn't have the inclination to linger. There were rounds to be taken care of, and office visits scheduled for later in the afternoon, and the perpetual pile of paperwork and correspondence to review in the evening. He said his goodbyes and hurried away.

No sooner had the therapist left the room then Linda and

Mandy formed a miniature swarm around Janelle, the two double-teaming her with their goodbyes. Maybe their sincerity was genuine, but to Aleisha it all seemed so phony. They talked like they were losing an old friend, reminiscing as though they had shared good times together rather than a few minutes in a room full of strangers. Eventually they ran out of things to say and took their departure.

Bryan, more reserved than the others, said a simple "So long" and left. As the only man in the group he seemed to be at a disadvantage when trying to get his share of attention, though Aleisha suspected it would have been the same had the group been composed solely of males. Though Bryan had been there longer than Aleisha he seemed even more reticent than her to open up to the group.

At last it was only the two girls, Janelle standing in the doorway where she had said her goodbyes, Aleisha still sitting in her chair, the location unchanged from the space occupied during the session. When Janelle turned to smile Aleisha felt an instant of hope, like she was viewing the face of freedom.

"Looks like you made it, girl," Aleisha began. "Fin'ly gettin' outta here."

"That's right." Janelle drew closer, a smile of encouragement on her face. "But your day's coming, too, you know."

"It don't really matter none. It's not like I got somewhere to go anyways."

"How about your sister's? What was her name? Karen?"

"Kareen," Aleisha corrected.

"That's right. Have you spoken to her yet?"

"No."

"Why not?"

"Didn't see no point in it."

"Don't do that to yourself, Aleisha."

"What? What am I doin?"

"Sitting there feeling sorry for yourself, that's what. Sure you've got problems. We all got problems. You don't have to tell me about problems."

Aleisha made no reply.

Janelle walked over, choosing to sit down on the chair beside the other woman.

"You came in late to the group, Aleisha. You never heard my whole story, did you?"

"I didn't want ta pry. Figured it weren't none of my business, anyway."

"That's where you're wrong, Aleisha. You're not prying. It helps when you talk about things. I guess that's something you still need to learn. It's something I've finally discovered, but it took me a while to figure it out.

"You need to understand, David was my whole life. He saved me, when no one else was there. He looked after me. Saw me through the bad times. And then, just when things were looking good...."

She paused, emotion stifling the words.

"It don't seem fair, what happened," Aleisha observed.

"You're right. It wasn't fair. But I guess it's like they say. Life's a bitch and then you die. And that's the way I felt. Like I just wanted to end it all. All I could think of was how to escape. The old way. Just find someplace to take a hit. Just keep myself so buzzed that I couldn't think of nothing else."

Her gaze locked on Aleisha's eyes, as if seeking a kindred spirit that would understand what she had gone though.

"I felt my life was over. And what did it matter anyway? What did anything matter anymore? The days following David's death were a blur to me. I still don't recall what happened, or how I managed to get through it all."

She paused, considering her words.

"That's not quite true. Theresa. My little sister. That's how I got through it. She was by my side the whole time. I moved back in with her and my mother. They knew I was hurting. They knew how vulnerable I had become. They didn't want me doing something I would regret.

"They realized how hard it had been for me, breaking my habit. And knew how easy it would be for me to fall back. So they kept an eye on me, making sure I wasn't anywhere near where I could score any heroin.

"But they didn't realize how devastated I was after David's death. How totally desperate I had become."

Aleisha watched the young woman's body shiver, as if an intense chill had enveloped her.

"I got hold of some prescription sleeping pills my mother had. Don't know how many I took, but I figured it would be enough.

"It seemed like such a good idea. Just lay down on my bed. Close my eyes. Drift away. And that was it. I remember thinking it was taking too long, and wishing I could just get it over with. Just get away from my pain.

"But then something else happened."

She moved her chair closer, clasping Aleisha by the hands. "It was the strangest thing. I never saw it coming. But all of a sudden I got scared. I began to doubt what I was doing. I thought of all the things I was throwing away. All the good times I wouldn't have because of a stupid bottle of pills.

"But, by then, it was too late. I wanted to just get up but I couldn't. I was telling myself to get out of bed but my body refused to listen to me. I wanted to run to the bathroom, puke my guts out, do whatever it would take to get those damn pills out of my system. But I had waited too long. I couldn't move. I couldn't speak. I was beginning to feel like I couldn't even breath.

"I felt my mind racing in a thousand different directions at once. It was pure agony. That peaceful slumber I had been expecting wasn't there for me. Instead I was in hell. And I was trapped there, imprisoned because of my own stupidity. And there was just no turning back."

Janelle lowered her head, her breaths slow, her hands trembling against Aleisha's fingers.

"That's all I remember before I blacked out."

Silence gripped the room. The quiet breathing of the two young women overpowered everything else. Voices from outside the room were lost in the distance, resonating with a vagueness akin to a forlorn whistle in a late night fog.

"How'd ya end up here?" Aleisha asked at last.

"I was lucky. My mother had gone out for the night to do some shopping. She had only been gone a little while when she remembered she left something at home. Isn't that funny? I don't even recall now what it was she had forgotten. She came home early – much earlier than she should have – and found me passed out on the floor.

"I don't remember the ride in the ambulance. Or them pumping my stomach. Or my mother sitting awake at my bedside the entire night, afraid to leave me out of her sight. I found out about those things afterward. I only remember waking up. And thinking how glad I was to be alive. How *lucky* I was to be alive."

Janelle stood up.

"Don't give up on yourself, Aleisha. The way I did. Fight to make yourself better. There are good people out there willing to help you through this. Let them help. Don't think you have to do it all by yourself. Okay?"

Aleisha merely nodded a meek reply.

Janelle turned for the door, took three steps, then paused. A counter along one side of the room held magazines and books. Worn paperback romance fictions. Picture books of animals and exotic places. Readers Digest, National Geographic, and an assortment of crossword puzzle books. Janelle tore a page from one of the magazines, grabbed a pencil from the shelf nearby, and scribbled down some information.

"Here." She handed the slip of paper to Aleisha.

"What's this?"

"My mother's address. It's where I'll be staying. I want you to come visit me after you get out, so I can see how you're doing."

"You sure you want me ta?"

"Of course I'm sure. You're always welcome. And if you need anything. Anything at all. Don't be afraid to ask."

Aleisha watched, speechless, as Janelle turned and walked out of the room.

Chapter Fifteen:

T HE DAY OF THE HEARING CAME AT LAST. Drinking her morning tea, looking one last time at the printed copy of the report she had completed and subsequently filed with the court, Beverly considered the progress in the case so far. The children had somewhere to live, people taking care of them, and from what Beverly had seen they were all in safe environments for the time being. She couldn't have been more pleased concerning the children's situations.

Aleisha was still in rehab, but it wouldn't be long and she would be on her own again. Once released she needed to continue with her recovery program, among other things. She would attend further counseling sessions and see her doctor on a regular basis. Aleisha would also be required to drop a urine sample whenever instructed to – by either the case worker or by Beverly herself – to verify she was no longer using drugs. Beverly would continue to check in on Aleisha from time to time, to gauge how her recovery was progressing, while maintaining the monthly visits with the children.

Mark had his goals as well, completing anger management and parenting classes as set forth in the case plan.

All these things would be reviewed at the hearing, as well as setting specific times and dates for supervised family visits. Once the court agreed with everything then it became a waiting game, with the children living disjointed lives for however long it took for Aleisha to pull her life back together. The young woman was the key to the family's future.

Beverly still wasn't adjusted to court time. The hearing was set for 9:30 in the morning. Early as usual, by 9:20 she sat alone in one of the hard plastic chairs outside the courtroom awaiting the arrival of the other participants.

Lucy Lemly, the attorney for Aleisha Turner, showed up at 9:35, followed moments later by Mark Bradley's attorney, an elderly gentleman named Carl Hemmings, whom Beverly had met on a previous case. Both attorneys, accustomed to the downtime at the courthouse, sat down and immediately began perusing documents from their work piles.

Mark showed up next, looking presentable in a pair of clean slacks and a polo shirt. He nodded to Beverly then sat down to confer with Carl.

The minutes ticked by. It was nearly ten by the time Aleisha Turner arrived, led in by Patrick Zimmerly, the case worker from Children's Services. Following on their heels was the attorney for the County, Mark Anochevsky.

Beverly was impressed with the change in Aleisha. She still looked tired, as though she wasn't getting the proper rest. Her movements were slow and deliberate, as if uncertain where she should go and what was expected of her. Her face presented an appearance of apprehension, a look that told Beverly the young woman was still confused and fearful for her future.

But there was a strength to her now, a certain dignity of bearing, as though she had weathered through a storm and was moving on to better things. Her color looked improved. Gone was the sickly pallor she had worn in the rehab center the day Beverly had first spoken with her. Aleisha had also managed to put on a little weight, enough to remove the sunken look to her cheeks and give her limbs a less ungainly attitude from what Beverly had noticed on their first meeting. The attractive young woman that had been hidden earlier was beginning to emerge once again.

Beverly stood to greet them. "Hello Aleisha."

"Miss Beverly." Her words were spoken softly, a distinct difference from the anger her tones conveyed when last Beverly had seen the young woman.

The case worker presented his hand in greeting. "Patrick Zimmerly."

"Beverly Johnson." The two shook hands. "From the CASA office. I feel like we've met already, from your emails. How do you feel the kids are adjusting to things?" Beverly inquired.

"Good," Patrick acknowledged. "We're setting up visitations for Tuesday and Thursday afternoons at Children's Services for both parents. That way all the siblings can see one another. Does that sound okay to you?"

It made Beverly feel good to be included in the process, like she was an integral part of what was happening in the case and not just someone hanging around to do busy work. "That sounds fine to me," she replied.

They would have spoken more but at that moment the courtroom door opened and a clerk stepped into the hall. "Magistrate Peterson is ready to see you now."

As they were moving forward Aleisha paused, placing her hand on Beverly's sleeve to arrest the forward motion.

"Miss Beverly? I want ta apologize for my behavior the other day."

"There's no need to...."

"I was rude ta you," she continued, forcing the words. "There was no reason for me ta be like that. I know you're only tryin' to help my kids. And I appreciate that."

"That's okay, Aleisha. I know you're going through a lot right now."

"Still ain't no excuse. I guess I just been so involved in my own problems – so concerned with what I been going through – that I forgot all about what I was doin' to my kids. I guess it took you remindin' me. To make me see all the hurt I been spreading around."

Beverly found herself speechless, excited to hear Aleisha's self-revelation but uncertain how to respond.

It didn't really matter, as the young woman resumed without a pause. "I want to do whatever it takes to make things right. My fam'ly deserves that. I love my kids, Miss Beverly. I want you ta know that."

"I'm sure you do, Aleisha."

With that said they turned and followed the others.

The courtroom seemed much larger than necessary, as far as Beverly was concerned. The front portion was dedicated to a large wooden desk that occupied the full width of the room. Here Magistrate Paulette Peterson presided. Beverly had appeared before Peterson on a previous case and admired the woman's demeanor. Though a no-nonsense individual that conducted her proceedings in a businesslike fashion, she always took the time to consider the participants of the case, setting their minds at ease by carefully explaining anything that could be confusing to someone unaccustomed to the dealings of the court.

Three tables, each with a pair of chairs facing the bench, occupied the center section of the courtroom. To the right sat the representatives for the county, Patrick Zimmerly and Mark Anochevsky. Aleisha sat at center with her attorney while Mark and his lawyer were on the left.

The rear of the room had a series of chairs set up against the wall. This was where Beverly sat, by herself and feeling a bit out of things. She knew she was an important part of the proceedings. Or, at least, that's what she reminded herself, reviewing in her head what they had taught her to believe during the training for the position. Though at times – like now, sitting alone and apparently forgotten – she wondered about the truth of the matter.

Magistrate Peterson, speaking into a microphone from her desk, asked each of those in the courtroom to identify themselves. It was another of the formalities. Beverly was the last to answer. "Beverly Johnson," she announced. "CASA guardian for Willard Turner, Nataya Turner, and Michael Bradley."

The proceedings continued from there, Children's Services presenting the allegations of child neglect due to Aleisha's use of heroin and Mark's violent behavior around the children. Neither parent protested the allegations. From time to time Aleisha's attorney would whisper something to her client, who would nod in a halfhearted way as the discussion continued. When Patrick Zimmerly had finished the magistrate faced Aleisha directly.

"Do you understand the allegations presented against you today, Miss Turner?"

"Yes, Your Honor."

"Do you have anything to add in your own behalf?"

She shook her head silently and her attorney spoke up. "No, Your Honor," Lucy Lemly answered in a firm voice. "My client agrees that the facts as stated by Children's Services are accurate and truthful."

The Magistrate, a smile on her face, addressed Aleisha directly. "I need to hear it from you Miss Turner. Do you have anything you want to present to the court on your own behalf?"

"No, Ma'am."

"Thank you. Mr. Bradley." Peterson was facing Mark now. "Do you understand the allegations against you today?"

"Yeah. I do."

"And do you have anything to add in your own behalf?"

"No. Nothing."

"Then the court rules that this case will be entered into the permanent records of the State of Ohio as one of child neglect against the parents, Aleisha Turner and Mark Bradley. Mr.

Zimmerly, I understand the children have been placed in suitable homes?"

"Yes, Your Honor. Willard and Nataya Turner are currently residing in a Foster residence. Michael Bradley is living with a sister of the father's. We submit that Legal Custody of the children be given at this time to Lucas County until further notice, while maintaining the current temporary living arrangements."

"Are you agreeable to that, Miss Turner?"

"Yes'm."

"Mr. Bradley. Are you agreeable to the child placement arrangements?"

"Yes I am."

"Very good. Miss Johnson. As the court appointed Guardian to these three children are you in agreement with the living arrangements decided upon for the children under your supervision?"

"Yes I am, Your Honor."

"Is there anything else you feel the court needs to be aware of at this point, Miss Johnson?"

"Nothing, Your Honor."

"Very well."

It appeared she was about to move on when Carl Hemmings, Mark's attorney, spoke up. "If it pleases the court?"

"Go ahead, counselor."

"Considering Miss Turner's background and some of her past actions, we would like to submit that Mark Bradley be subjected to paternity testing to determine if he is indeed the father of Michael Bradley."

"Miss Lemly? Does your client have any objections to Mr. Bradley being tested for paternity of the child?"

"No objections, Your Honor."

Beverly couldn't help wondering if this was truly the case. No sooner had Mark's attorney broached the subject then Aleisha shot her husband a scathing look. The magistrate apparently chose to ignore the ramifications of the glance, abiding with what the young woman's attorney had stated.

"Then the court agrees to paternity testing. Mr. Zimmerly, has a case plan been prepared for the parties involved?"

"Yes Your honor."

He went on to detail the specifics, all things Beverly was aware of. Continued rehabilitation for Aleisha. Parenting classes for Aleisha and Mark. A review of the visitation schedule for seeing the children.

Considering everything concerned, and the fact that these proceedings directly affected the future lives of at least two of the people present as well as the three children absent from court, it was a relatively short affair. Less than fifteen minutes after entering the courtroom all parties were dismissed.

Aleisha accosted Mark the moment they were outside the room. "What's with this paternity testin'?"

Mark looked embarrassed, an expression that didn't seem to fit his build or character. "We just want to be certain Michael is really mine."

"I tol' you he was, didn't I?"

"You told me a lot of things, 'Leisha. Like you told me you weren't using heroin anymore."

"I made a mistake, Mark. That's all. But Michael is your child. I promise you."

Lucy Lemly leaned closer to her client. "It's in your best interest that Mark is tested, Aleisha. This way we'll know for certain and there won't be issues later if it comes to providing child support."

"Michael is your child, Mark. I swear."

Mark said nothing as he turned to leave. As he departed Beverly couldn't help noticing that Aleisha appeared to have lost some of her earlier strength. Her shoulders slumped. She stared ahead with a dejected look.

Patrick Zimmerly approached. "Come on, Aleisha. I need to take you back to Riverfront."

Beverly, at a distance, followed them down the stairs and moments later was outside.

Chapter Sixteen:

"THE STATISTICS PRETTY MUCH SPEAK for themselves," the young woman at the front of the room was saying. "In 2013, 8,257 people died in the U.S. of a heroin overdose. Here in Ohio drug overdoses caused 1,914 deaths in 2012."

She paused, taking time to glance over the more than two dozen people sitting at the tables facing her, aware that she had their undivided attention.

Among those listening to the presentation was Beverly Stone, who sat on a hard plastic chair in the middle of the room. She shared the table with a young man casually dressed in a pair of jeans and a t-shirt featuring the Bat-Man logo. Beverly's pen was poised above the ink-scribbled paper in front of her, halted now as she listened to the words addressed to the group.

Beverly was attending the day's session as part of her CASA requisite to continue her education by enrolling in periodic training sponsored by the CASA office. She had signed-up for the all day training months ago. It had sounded interesting enough, though at the time she saw little more to it than professional curiosity concerning a subject she knew nothing about.

Her feelings had changed since taking the case involving Aleisha Turner and her three children. She was now connected personally with a family involved with drugs and she had first-hand knowledge concerning the complications arising from their misuse. She had seen the ravages inflicted upon Aleisha Turner through the young woman's drug use, had visited her in the rehabilitation center and seen the worn and exhausted body of what had once been a lovely young woman. She had seen the anger in the eyes, heard the tones of resentment and frustration in the word's she spoke, but had also felt the fear and pain behind that anger, and recognized the feelings of hopelessness and helplessness that had overwhelmed Aleisha.

All due to a drug that corrupted minds as it manipulated bodies by controlling the person's free will.

Beverly focused her attention once more on Alexis Rawlings, who continued to speak from the front of the classroom.

"Let me put this another way," Miss Rawlings continued, glancing at the clock on the side of the room. "It is now one-thirty in the afternoon. So five hours ago would be...." She paused for some quick mental calculations. "Eight-thirty this morning. How many of you have been awake since eight-thirty this morning?"

Within seconds every hand but one was raised in the room, the lone dissenter looking very much like he had indeed just crawled out of bed moments ago and dragged himself to the training session.

Rawlings continued. "I've been up since well before eight-thirty myself. Of course I had to drive in from Columbus this morning. But the point I want to make is this. In the time all of us have been awake...." She looked once more toward the sole participant who had failed to raise his hand. "All of us but one, anyway. In that time somebody else, right here in the state of Ohio, has died of a drug overdose. Because, statistically speaking, once every five hours someone in this state will succumb to this horrible epidemic.

"And it is an epidemic. Make no mistake about that. It is

a devastating plague that grows worse every year, as the presence of drugs grows ever more prevalent on our city streets.

"But don't make the mistake of thinking this is only an inner city problem. Far from it. Illegal drugs are just as much a problem in the suburbs as they are in the heart of Ohio's cities. And it's not just heroin. Each day in the United States 44 people die from an overdose of prescription painkillers. We're talking legal medication in many cases illicitly obtained and wrongfully administered."

She paused in her recital, taking a deep breath as though to control herself. And for the first time Beverly detected the trace of weariness in the speaker.

Alexis Rawlings had introduced herself at the beginning of the training session as part of a task force administered through the offices of the governor of Ohio. It was a task force created with the purpose of finding solutions to the drug problems facing the state. Miss Rawlings had revealed that she had served in her present capacity for nearly five years, gathering information and statistics concerning the misuse of drugs in an attempt to halt the widespread effects of opiates and other potentially harmful drugs. That she was a dedicated civil servant determined to do whatever she could to find solutions was obvious from her energy and enthusiasm and the passion of her oration.

That she was frustrated and exhausted and overwhelmed with the task that still lay ahead of her was obvious as well, if you took the time to look behind her facade and read the signs she strove to conceal.

Beverly found herself feeling sorry for the woman. In her short time dealing with Aleisha Turner, Beverly had found frustration and disappointment already. She couldn't imagine living with the hard realities of the drug problem on a daily basis.

A voice spoke up from the other side of the room.

"You make it all sound so helpless. Isn't there something

that can be done about all this?"

Alexis Rawlings' response was immediate. "Of course there is. A big part of the solution is to make people more aware of the realities of the situation. People like you, who are taking time out of your busy lives to attend this training and listen to what we have to say, can make a big difference. I'm certain some of you have medical backgrounds and can relate to a lot of what we're discussing today. Or perhaps you are involved with the issue through the courts, as an attorney or a CASA volunteer or as part of a foster parenting program.

"Some of you, unfortunately, may have first hand experience concerning how these drugs can ravage a person, both mentally and physically, having witnessed the devastating affects on a loved one. It can leave you with a feeling of inadequacy and total helplessness.

"To all of you I can only say this. There is no easy answer. But there are things that can be done.

"Participation in medically sanctioned detoxification programs, to wean the abuser away from their drug of choice, is an obvious starting point. Therapy sessions with skilled counselors, to endeavor to ascertain the underlying reasons that drove the drug user along their path of destruction, are a crucial component of the healing process. Often some life changing incident, or incidents, is responsible for the low self-esteem that pushes the user into a life of abuse, situations relating to stress induced trauma that leads back to childhood. Therapy is essential in getting to the root of the problem.

"An important component of any successful drug rehabilitation program is the willingness to recognize that we can't just turn our heads and ignore the plight of those suffering with a drug addiction.

"Help is out there, through community services and medical personnel and through agencies such as the task force I am proud to be a part of. We can make a difference. Even if it's just to turn one person's life around. Change has to start somewhere."

A hand went up on the side of the room, from a middle-aged woman wearing colorful scrubs featuring animals and rainbows. She had a weary look to her, as though she had just come from an all-night session in the Children's Ward at one of the local hospitals. "What about Narcan? Is it effective?"

Alexis nodded in firm agreement as she focused on the woman. "Absolutely."

She then turned to address the rest of the class.

"Opioid Drugs such as heroin and many prescription pain killers affect the body by slowing a person's breathing, often to the point where they cannot be revived. The drug she's talking about – Naloxone, which is sold under the brand name of Narcan – can be administered as an injection or a nasal spray to quickly restore normal breathing patterns in someone who has overdosed."

Images flashed through Beverly's mind, of Aleisha Turner unconscious and unbreathing following her overdose. It seemed hard to believe that an incident such as the one that nearly took the young woman's life away could be prevented by a simple injection.

"Is it safe?" Beverly asked.

"Medical professionals and emergency personnel have been using Naloxone for more than forty years. It has no potential for abuse. Its only function is to reverse the effects of opioids to prevent overdose death.

"The only down side – and I hesitate to even label it as such – is that Naloxone has a shorter half-life than the opiods it is designed to counteract."

A bevy of confused glances greeted the announcement.

Alexis was quick to explain.

"What this means is that by the time the beneficial affects of the Narcan have worn off the user may still be experiencing symptoms from the drug, or drugs, that caused the respiratory failure in the first place. That's why it is so vitally important that medical attention should be sought, even after administering Narcan. Because there is still the chance the victim may relapse into an overdosed condition.

"The good news in all this is that Narcan is in common use here in Ohio. There is even talk that very soon it will be available without a prescription. An act as simple as walking into your neighborhood Kroger and picking up some Narcan might mean the difference between a loved one's life or death."

Chapter Seventeen:

WILLARD TURNER WAS EXCITED.

He and Nataya would be visiting their mother today.

It had been over four weeks since the accident at the house, when his mother had fallen down the stairs and the ambulance had taken her to the hospital because she was sick. This was the longest he and Nataya had ever been away from their mother, and it had felt like an eternity to him. That was too long of a time to be away from her, as far as Willard was concerned.

He missed everything about her. He missed the nights when his mother would tuck him into bed, and read him a story, and lean over him as she adjusted the blankets around him – smelling that wonderful smell that he couldn't help wondering if all mothers had – and kiss him goodnight. It hadn't happened like that every night. As a matter of fact, the nights Willard recollected were few and far between. But they occurred often enough, and were special enough, that they had left an indelible memory in the child's mind.

He missed their lunches together, with Michael perched in his little yellow seat on the counter, and Willard and his sister sitting at the table when his mother brought over the hot dogs. Or the Spaghetti-Os. He liked the kind with the little letters the best. Sometimes, if she had enough time, his mother would make them grilled cheese sandwiches.

But that wasn't very often. His mother was usually too busy for that. Or too tired. He didn't know what his mother did at night, when she left the house, but he knew it must have been important or else she wouldn't leave them at home like that with Mark. Sometimes she wouldn't get back until after they were in bed, and Willard and Nataya wouldn't see their mother until she woke up late the next morning. A lot of times they didn't see her until they got home from school in the afternoon.

Which meant they spent a lot of time with Mark. Which wasn't that bad. Mostly Mark just ignored the kids, so they were left on their own to find things to do by themselves. They got to watch a lot of television that way. Once in a while Mark would let Willard play video games with him. On the big television in the family room, too! Minecraft was Willard's favorite. The game didn't make a lot of sense to him, but he liked that you got to blow things up once in a while. The hard part was trying not to fall into the lava.

"Willard? Are you ready to go?"

He turned at the sound of the voice and saw Mrs. Kale enter the room. She seemed like a nice lady. She fixed them dinners at night. And sometimes, when she was feeling in a good mood, she would pop some pop corn and they were allowed to take it to their room to eat while they were watching cartoons. She never yelled at them either, or made them do chores, or criticized them for doing things.

She mostly just left them alone.

She was a lot like Mark in that respect.

"I'm almost ready," Willard announced.

"Well, make it quick. Mr. Zimmerly will be here any minute to take you to see your mother. You don't want to hold him up."

She left the room and Willard, moving at the sedate pace he always managed, followed her into the front of the house. Nataya was already there, an eager excitement painting her face as she sat on the couch. She held her dolly, Miss Jasmine, combing the plastic hair with a small brush, quietly involved with her own actions.

"Will Michael be there, too?" Willard asked.

"I would imagine. Do you miss your little brother?"

"I guess. Sort of. He's all right when he's sleeping. But sometimes he seems to get a lot of attention."

"He's a baby," Nataya announced, not bothering to look up as she continued primming Miss Jasmine. "All babies need attention."

Mrs. Kale approached Nataya. "And how do you know so much about babies?"

"Mommy told me. Mommy knows everything."

Just then the front doorbell rang, the chiming audible throughout the house.

"That's Mr. Zimmerly, children. Time to go."

The drive to where they would see their mother was a short one. Mr Zimmerly asked them questions on the way over, like how they liked their new home. The question didn't make sense to Willard. Living with Mr. and Mrs. Kale wasn't like being home. It was like visiting someone you didn't really know. What did it matter whether they liked it there or not? His mother must be doing better now. Maybe she wasn't sick anymore, and they could all go home – to their *real* home – together.

So it didn't matter whether he liked living with Mr. and Mrs. Kale or not. He wasn't going to be there long. He had no intention of getting accustomed to living with them.

The car came to a stop in a parking lot, and from there it was almost a block walking along the crowded city streets to the big red building Mr. Zimmerly had pointed out to them as they drove by.

Willard was surprised to see a policeman standing inside the door, on the other side of a low table. The revolver holstered at the man's hip seemed about the most exciting thing Willard had ever seen, a fearsome object that held a fascinating attraction to an eight year old boy. A roped area led to where the officer stood, the cords herding those who entered the building toward a metal doorway with no door.

"What's that thing?" Willard asked.

The case worker smiled at the youngster. "Have you ever heard of a metal detector?"

"I guess. Like on airplanes?"

"Sort of like that. They just want to make sure everyone in the building is safe. That nobody brings in something they aren't supposed to."

The announcement puzzled Nataya. "What sort of things?"

"Like guns," her brother informed her, a mischievous smile on his face, his eyes once again focused on the police officer's service revolver.

Nataya came to a halt, a look of panic entering her eyes. "Do I have to?"

"There's nothing to worry about," Mr. Zimmerly assured her. "It doesn't hurt."

She shook her head violently back-and-forth, gripping tighter to her dolly. "Miss Jasmine doesn't want to."

"Then leave your doll out here," Willard suggested, fully aware his sister wouldn't agree to the proposal.

"No. Miss Jasmine is scared by herself. She don't like to be left alone. I'm not goin'."

"If you don't go in then you don't get to see Mom," Willard pointed out.

"I don't want to see Mom." Nataya was nearly in tears by now, horrified by the sight of the imposing metal doorway towering above her. "I want to stay out here. With Miss Jasmine."

Mr. Zimmerly held out his hand toward the little girl, at

the same time bending down to speak with her at eye level. "I can go in with you. Would that be okay?"

"No."

Any further discussion was delayed with the approach of a uniformed police woman. She looked neat and proper in her uniform, but – to Willard's way of thinking – not at all what a girl should look like. Her hair was cut short, giving her an almost manly appearance, and her face displayed a hard-edged expression, like she wasn't the type of person you wanted to disagree with.

But when she smiled at the children her eyes seemed to light up, and Willard forgot all his apprehensions. He liked her immediately.

She brushed past the case worker and stopped next to Nataya.

"Is that your doll, young lady?"

The tone was friendly. Reassuring.

Nataya nodded.

"What's your doll's name?"

"Miss Jasmine."

"Jasmine? Like in *Aladdin*?"

She nodded once more.

"That's her favorite movie," Willard proclaimed. "When we were at home we used to watch it over and over again."

"It's no wonder," the police woman replied. "It's my favorite movie too."

The little girl's eyes opened wide, with an expression akin to astonishment. "Really?"

"Really. My favorite part is the big blue guy."

"That's the genie. He's funny. But I still like Jasmine the bestest."

"And that's why you named you're dolly Jasmine?"

She nodded, a smile lighting up her delicate features.

"But don't you think Jasmine would like to go visit your

Mother?"

Nataya considered. "Prob'ly. But she don't want to go through the metal de...." She looked back at Mr. Zimmerly. "What was it called again?"

Willard flashed his sister a look of disbelief. "It's a metal detector."

"Miss Jasmine is scared."

The police woman smiled a knowing smile. "Well, we can fix that. Follow me."

Taking the young girl's hand, which Nataya offered with no hesitation, the woman walked over to the side and unhooked the rope, presenting an opening through the barrier and around the detector.

"We can go this way."

"You sure it's okay?"

"Of course it's okay, sweetie. As long as I say it is."

The two passed through the opening in the rope, which was then secured behind them, while Willard and Mr. Zimmerly strolled through the detector. The eight year old paused once they were on the other side, gazing back with a marked degree of disappointment registering on his face.

"Was that it?"

"Afraid so, Willard."

"I didn't even feel nothing."

By this time they had joined up with Nataya, who reluctantly released the officer's hand.

"It was nice meeting you, young lady. You be sure to take good care of Miss Jasmine."

"I will."

Mr. Zimmerly smiled at the young girl's escort. "Thank you for helping me out with that."

"My pleasure."

"Come on, guys. Let's go meet your mother."

Chapter Eighteen:

$\mathbb{I}$T FELT GOOD TO BE GETTING OUTSIDE, even if it was only for the thirty seconds it took to walk from the back door of Riverfront to the utility van the facility used to transport its patients. A gentle breeze wafted across the paved parking lot, bringing with it the aroma of freshly mowed grass mingled with the smell of tar from a nearby street. A maintenance road crew toiled on the concrete, adding the harsh racket of machinery and the pungent odor of diesel fuel to the early afternoon.

The sun shone from a clear blue sky, though failed to deliver the warmth the sight seemed to promise. It was beginning to feel more like autumn already, the heat of summer forgotten now. The leaves on the trees were starting to turn, presenting a palette of reds and oranges and yellows, an overwhelming display that greeted Aleisha as she stepped into the afternoon sunlight. The last time she had been outside – not counting the court appearance, which had been such a whirlwind experience of nerves and apprehension for her that she failed to recall any particulars of the day – was the day she had stopped at Pete's.

The day she had overdosed.

It had been cool that day. At least she remembered that much. And she had ended up at Pete's with a mark, though she couldn't have described the guy if her life depended on it. Just another faceless customer in a string of meaningless encounters.

She still didn't understand what had gone wrong. She had mainlined before. Not a lot, but frequently enough to know what to expect from the experience. There was nothing unusual that day; nothing inherently different from the other times she had injected. She vividly recalled the sudden jolt as the heroin hit her vein, along with the instant feeling of euphoria that overwhelmed her and transported her away from every trouble, every care, every concern she could ever imagine. Each time was like a new beginning, like she was living life to the fullest and nothing could ever top how she felt.

And each time when it was over, and she found herself confronting the crash that ultimately followed, she could think of nothing else but how to get her next hit.

She still craved it, mentally at least, the wonderful feeling of having no cares in the world. But her physical symptoms had abated. She no longer felt sick in the evening. She managed to sleep most nights, much better than she had in years, and the days were less tiresome than she was accustomed to.

The van pulled away with its single passenger, Aleisha's thoughts dwelling on her past as they drove crosstown to the Juvenile Center. Her children were waiting to see her there, anxious to greet her after what they could only understand as her sickness. What could she tell them? How could she explain what she had been through?

She doubted Nataya would even question her mother's absence. She was still at that glorious age of life when each day was a new adventure. Each experience a new stimulus to enjoy. As long as she had her dolly with her there was little that seemed to upset her.

Willard was another story. Even at his sister's age he had been different, more aware of his surroundings, more attuned to what was going on around him. Aleisha had heard that was the way with first born children, and maybe that explained some of his behavior. He struggled with the burden of trying to grow up too quickly. He was protective of his sister, looking after her with a wisdom of someone many years older. And though he said little, keeping his thoughts to himself, she suspected he noticed a lot more than he let on.

Perhaps it was Aleisha's fault, after all. She thrust responsibility on her son, expecting far more from the child than a mother should. Willard no doubt knew Michael better than she did herself, having been burdened with the care of the infant the long nights when Aleisha was away, haunting the streets, searching for an escape from her own troubled yearnings.

Aleisha pushed such thoughts aside. She loved her children. She would do anything for them. Maybe it was about time she started to prove that to them.

"Mommy!"

Nataya ran to the door, greeting her before she could even enter, and with the child in her arms Aleisha walked into the visitation room at Children's Services. It was a plain, simply adorned area, the antiseptically clean type of environment institutions set aside for the use of a multitude of people. It was inoffensive to anyone who entered, to the point of being barren and devoid of personality to all. A few prints hung on the wall, close-up renderings of wildflowers that were no doubt meant to inspire but instead, in Aleisha's mind, served only to portray life as cold and barren and sterile.

She shook these forebodings from her mind to concentrate instead on the reason for her being there; the children. Setting Nataya down she grabbed Willard, who had wandered to her side, and received an equally enthusiastic greeting from her son.

"It's good ta see you both."

The children beamed, their joy at seeing their mother obvious. "It's good to see you Mom," Willard announced. "I missed you."

"Me too." Nataya clung to her mother's side. "I missed you too."

"So tell me what you've been up ta."

"Nothing." The reply came simultaneously from both children, as if they had rehearsed the answer.

"Nothin'?" She scowled at them with a mock look of disbelief. "I don't believe that. You been away from me all this time and you ain't done anythin'?"

Willard merely shrugged in reply.

By this time Aleisha had maneuvered the children over to the plain brown sofa in the room, where she sat down between the two of them. She glanced over at the doorway. Patrick Zimmerly stood there, watching them, and offered a meek smile before speaking. "I'll be right outside if you need anything."

He left the room, but maintained a position in the hallway where he could observe their interaction. The wall facing the hall was comprised of floor to ceiling windows, allowing an unobstructed view into the room. It made Aleisha feel like she was on display for all the world to see. It made her feel uncomfortable, like she was afraid to even interact with her children. It made her feel self-conscious, aware of every movement she made.

It made her feel angry.

What the hell did they think was going to happen that made them think they had to scrutinize her so closely? She wasn't a monster. She was a mother spending time with her children. Why couldn't they just leave her alone and let her live her own life?

"Are you feeling better now?" Willard asked, disturbing her reverie.

She smiled at her son. "Mommy's a lot better than she was, Willy."

"Does that mean we can all go home now?"

She forced a smile, realizing it would be difficult for the

children to understand why things were taking so long, but not wanting to upset them. "In a little while. Mommy's still not feelin' good as she should be."

Nataya tugged at her mother's sleeve to get her attention. "I miss my toys."

"Ain't you got toys where you at?"

"Not my toys."

"Well, when we go home your toys will all be there, waitin' for you. Won't that be nice?"

She nodded in reply, looking down at the dolly in her arms as she fidgeted with Miss Jasmine's hair.

Through the window, approaching from behind Patrick, Aleisha spied a figure walking closer, carrying a baby. It took her a moment to realize the woman was Mary Bradley, Mark's sister, and the baby was hers.

She grabbed Michael the moment they entered the room.

"He's so big!" She rocked him back and forth in her arms, feeling how heavy he was. "I guess he been eatin' all right."

"He's got a good appetite," Mary agreed, turning to face Willard and Nataya. "Don't you have no hellos for your Aunt Mary?"

"Hello Aunt Mary," Willard answered, while Nataya merely flashed a weak smile.

"Where's Mark?" Willard asked.

"My brother couldn't make it, Honey. But he says hi."

"Just as well," Aleisha observed. "I don't think I want ta see him, anyways." She considered a moment. "Not after what he pulled last week."

Mary was still in the process of unloading the diaper bag, finding a clean bib and a bottle for the baby, and she finished the task before responding. "What's that supposed to mean?"

"You know what I'm talkin' 'bout. Sayin' he got to have testin', ta make sure he the father. This baby's his. I already tol' him that."

"He just wants to make sure."

"So you on his side too?"

"I don't want to be on nobody's side, Aleisha. I just want to make sure the baby is taken care of."

"Well, I do appreciate you lookin' after him. He seems ta be doin' good."

"He is. He's sleeping good at night. He had a bit of a cough the other day, but the doctor said it weren't nothing to worry about."

"You took him ta see the doctor?"

"I had to. But he's okay. So when you getting out of rehab?"

"They ain't told me yet. I hope it's soon. All I do is stare at them same damn walls all day long. I need ta get outta there."

"Are you going back home? With Mark?"

She answered immediately, like she had already deliberated on the point and reached a firm conclusion. "I don't think I'm ready for that. I spoke ta my sister. Kareen. Her apartment's tiny, but she says she can make room for me."

"That's good. At least you'll be with family."

"But not *my* fam'ly."

She glanced at Willard and Nataya, the two children each busy now with their own tasks. Willard had found a puzzle in the room and was laying on the floor, feet in the air, trying to assemble the thing. Part of it was completed, revealing the face of a kitten smiling up at him from what appeared to be a wicker basket. Nataya looked on, her fingers twisting Miss Jasmine's hair into knots as she watched her brother struggle with another piece that stubbornly refused to fit against any of the other pieces.

Aleisha sighed. "I just want ta go home."

Chapter Nineteen:

IT WAS RAINING WHEN SHE WOKE UP, THE type of heavy autumn downpour that raises puddles on the lawns and causes streets to overflow and sewer drains to back up. Lightning flashed occasionally, searing the heavens with jagged streaks that lit up the landscape then disappeared, only to be followed by the grumbling of distant thunder. It was a cold rain, and Beverly felt the chill deep inside as she scurried from the front porch to the car, an old plastic grocery bag thrown over her head as hastily devised protection against the inclement weather.

She really would have preferred staying home. After all, that's what retirement was about; not having to rush off in the morning to do someone else's bidding, but rather for lingering in your own home however long you desired. She had left that hustle and bustle world behind her when she retired from teaching.

But she had different obligations now.

Driving slowly down the street, the wipers beating against the downpour yet failing to keep the windshield clean, Beverly considered the importance of what she was involved with. She had told herself she would be an advocate for children, looking out for their welfare, and she took the responsibility seriously. If that meant having to drive downtown on a rainy September afternoon then that's what she had to do.

The rain had let up some by the time she reached her

destination, though she managed to get soaked none-the-less while walking to the Juvenile Center. She knew the routine by now, and found the meeting room reserved for the 2:30 conference with no problem.

Children's Services held monthly meetings at their offices concerning the families they were involved with, gathering whoever was available to discuss how the case was progressing and making certain there were no issues that needed to be addressed. Beverly tried to make every meeting, in a sincere attempt to stay abreast of any new information. She had time now, and the inclination, and she felt it was the best way to represent her clients.

Patrick Zimmerly was there already, along with Judy Dencher, a coordinator from the department.

"Hello, Beverly. I'm surprised you weathered the storm to come down here."

"Good afternoon, Patrick." She shucked off her jacket, shaking it several times, and draped it over a chair. "I hope I'm not too late."

"No. I suspect everyone will be running behind, what with the weather. You know Judy, don't you?"

"Of course. We've met several times. Hi Judy."

"Good to see you, Beverly. How do you think things are progressing so far?"

"The kids seem in a safe place. And that's good. After visiting where they used to live I'm thinking it would be hard to ever send them back there."

Patrick took over the conversation. "I hear you. It isn't the most pleasant of surroundings for raising children, is it? Unfortunately, we can't enforce the way people choose to live. As long as they aren't neglecting or abusing their children – as long as they provide a roof over the kids' heads and see to it that they're fed and clothed and attend school on a regular basis – then there's not much we can say about how they choose to live."

"It is one of the frustrations of the job," Judy agreed. "But if we can make people more aware of things, through parenting classes and such, maybe they can develop better living habits along the way."

Beverly glanced at the clock. "Is anyone else coming?"

"This could be it. Dr. Bargalony said he would try to stop in, if his schedule allows."

"That's Aleisha's therapist, isn't it?"

"That's right. Have you met him?"

"Not yet."

"I think we'll give him a few minutes more."

"By the way," Patrick interjected, "the test results came back."

"What test?"

"Paternity testing. Mark is Michael's father."

"That's reassuring. I was afraid the aunt might give up on the little boy if she discovered she wasn't a relation."

"I've seen it happen," Judy added. "Then it's back to finding adequate housing for the child."

As they spoke another person entered the room, a short man wearing a brown suit and a scowl on his face, his pointed beard betraying a trace of rain that meandered down the whiskers to form a steady drip emanating from his chin.

"Sorry I'm late."

He threw the remark out to the room as he deposited some folders onto the conference table. A moment later he was seated, rifling through his paperwork.

Beverly immediately surmised the newcomer would rather be somewhere else. He acted as though he was obligated to be there – like attending the funeral of a distant relative – rather than that he had the desire to participate. Though perhaps Beverly was being unfair. The pace of life was hectic anymore for most people. The fact that he took the time to show up at all indicated how concerned he was about the welfare of the people he was dealing with.

After suitable introductions were exchanged Dr. Bargalony proceeded with his observations. "Aleisha Turner is responding well to therapy," he informed the group. "She seems to be connecting with people in a more positive manner than her previous interactions indicated."

Beverly felt the need to speak up. "She seems to have a lot of anger."

He nodded in agreement. "That's true. But you must understand, Beverly, that the resentment she holds has been generated from years of disappointment. She is a child of the social system, born and raised in a household struggling just to obtain the basic necessities of life. Things have never been easy for her.

"Yet even with all the adversity she's had to face she has managed to develop a certain amount of independence. A fierce determination, if you will, to sustain herself, no matter the cost. Even her choice to prostitute herself can be seen as a manifestation of her strength."

Beverly found herself taken aback with the statement. "I hope you're not condoning her behavior."

"Heavens, no. Her behavior is destructive, a ruinous lifestyle that, ultimately, can only be dangerous. Not just for her, but for her family and those around her. But I feel her choices in life were driven from desperation, an urge to escape, while at the same time greatly influenced by the low self-esteem she cultivated from years of destitution."

Patrick leaned forward to broach a question. "But she's learning to deal with things now. Correct?"

"Absolutely. I think she's made tremendous strides the last few weeks. So much so that I plan on releasing her from Riverfront soon."

"Where will she go?" Beverly asked.

"I understand her sister has agreed to let her move in for a while."

"That would be Kareen Turner," Patrick supplied, as he ruffled through a stack of papers. Finding what he was seeking, he passed a paper over to Beverly's side of the table. "Here's the address."

"Thank you," Beverly responded, copying the information while Dr. Bargalony continued.

"Aleisha's having to deal with some tremendous issues in her life. Things she's never considered or contemplated before. But she's making tremendous strides in her recovery. With continued counseling I hope to see her assurance grow to the point where she can turn her life around."

"That would be wonderful."

"Don't get too excited just yet. It's a long road ahead, Beverly. Erasing a lifetime of conditioning doesn't come overnight. But with continued support I think Aleisha Turner will do just fine."

Chapter Twenty:

MARK BRADLEY SAT ON THE COUCH, THE
baby resting on the cushion beside him, as his sister worked in
the kitchen, clearing the dishes from their evening meal.
Looking at his son, examining the tiny fingers and delicate
features of the infant, he felt like he was seeing the child for the
first time. He had always assumed Michael was his but, at the
same time, a certain part of him had questioned the fact. He
realized Aleisha had a troubled past. He knew that when he first
met up with her, but had accepted it as part of her nature. In
some respects it made their relationship more exciting; like she
was a wild creature that couldn't be tamed. It brought a fiery
intensity to their lifestyle.

Somewhere along the line things had cooled down
between them, as they had settled into the everyday existence of
just surviving, and he had grown to accept living with Aleisha
and her children. That was how he always thought of them. As
her children. Willard and Nataya were of course hers
exclusively, a memory of the past she kept hidden away from
him. When Michael came along he just seemed another part of
her brood.

But it was different now. Now he *knew* he was the father.
There was an absoluteness about it that nearly terrified him.

He realized he couldn't count on Aleisha to be there for

her children. She certainly had exhibited nothing in the past that demonstrated her ability to be a loving mother. She could barely take care of herself, let alone nurture and protect those in her charge.

Which meant, for better or for worse, Michael was his responsibility now.

It was a situation he hadn't anticipated and it left him confused and bewildered.

Mary's voice issued from the kitchen. "So have you seen Aleisha yet?"

"No."

"And why not?"

"I'm just not ready for it."

"Well, you know what I think, don't you?" She entered the room drying her hands on a dishrag. She threw the cloth on the counter as she left the kitchen and failed to notice that it managed to slip to the floor. "I think this was all for the best. You're better off without her so you may as well cut your loses and get on with your life."

"You never cared much for 'Leisha, did you?"

"Can you blame me?"

Mary scooped up the baby from the couch, holding Michael in her arms as she sat down in the chair opposite her brother. The television had been on since they got home but she felt the need to grab the remote and turn the volume up, the endless chatter of the voices on the screen providing a discordant background to their conversation. Neither of them seemed to notice the distraction.

"Aleisha's a piece of shit, Mark, and you know it."

"She's not all that bad."

"Yes she is, and it's about time you realize that. I'm sure she's great in the sack – probably knows every position in the book – but is that really what you want from a wife?"

"She has her good points."

Then, as an after thought, he amended the comment, more for his own sake than anything else. "At least she *had* her good points."

"That's the thing, isn't it? How long has this been going on, anyway? The drugs? Her walking the streets at night. God knows what sort of trouble she's been messed up with. And she's only getting worse, Mark."

"Maybe this time will be different."

"Quit fooling yourself. Addicts don't change. All they can think of is getting high. And thinking of their next hit. They don't give a shit about the people around them." She glanced down at Michael, as though noticing him for the first time. "Or their families."

"Maybe the rehab will do her some good."

"Get real."

"No. I mean it. I think the overdose was a wake up call for her. Showed her the kinds of chances she's been taking. Hell, she's been clean now for weeks. I think that's saying a lot for her."

"Of course she's been clean for weeks. She hasn't had a choice, has she? She's got people watching her twenty-four hours a day. She probably can't take a piss in that place without someone taking note of it."

Mark ignored the comment as he continued. "She gets out tomorrow. Maybe she'll do okay."

"You're just fooling yourself. You know that?"

He failed to reply.

"Why's this so important to you, anyway? You should be glad she's finally out of your life."

"She'll never be out of my life." His eyes diverted for a moment to look at his son. "Not as long as Michael's around. We're his parents."

"So all of a sudden you're the All-American Dad and

you're going to have this picture perfect family life?"

"I know it's not like that. But...." He hesitated, searching for the words.

"But what?"

"Leisha's been through a lot. If she gets out and stays clean, and she's willing to work at this, then maybe she deserves another chance."

"I still think you're fooling yourself."

Any comment he could have made was interrupted by the sound of the front doorbell. The two siblings exchanged puzzled glances.

"Expecting somebody?" Mark asked.

"No." Mary nodded toward the baby in her arms. "Can you grab that for me? I sort of got my hands full."

Mark stood up from the couch, stepped past the dining room table and through the tiny kitchen, and was to the door moments later. The sight of the woman standing outside in the light tan jacket took him by surprise.

"Mom?" His tone grew colder with the recognition, though his mother either failed to notice or chose to ignore his manner. "What are you doing here?"

"Can't I even stop in to visit my grandson?" The words flowed in hesitation, betraying an underlying embarrassment with the situation.

He made no attempt to move from the entrance.

"So are you going to let me in or do I have to stand out here all night?"

"Where's Dad?"

A casual toss of her head indicated something behind her. Mark shifted position slightly to see his parent's car in the parking lot. The driver's window was cracked open, and in the fading light he could just make out the puff of smoke that drifted from the vehicle's interior. The red glow of a burning cigarette showed briefly, but nothing could be seen of the man behind the wheel.

Mark hesitated still, uncertain how to react.

Mary, her voice calling from the other room, decided the issue. "Might as well let her in."

Their mother entered with faltering steps, as though she was a stranger and didn't belong there. Without a word she approached where Mary sat on the couch, stopping to stare at the little figure in her daughter's arms. A smile graced her lips.

"May I hold him for a minute?"

Mary turned toward Mark, and it was only after his slight nod of approval that she stood and relinquished Michael into the arms of his grandmother. The older woman seemed uncomfortable holding the baby, as though the situation was an unfamiliar one for her. But her eyes sparkled as she gazed into the youngster's face.

Sylvia Bradley turned toward her son. "He has your nose, doesn't he?"

"You never said anything about that before. Why the sudden interest?"

She made no reply, avoiding the adults in the room as she concentrated on the child.

"Or maybe you just didn't want to believe before that Michael really was my son. Now you can't ignore the fact, can you?"

"I just wanted you to be happy. That's all I ever wanted. That's all your father ever...."

"Leave my father out of it!" His exclamation stopped her words, his outburst leaving no doubt about his anger. "He made it clear a long time ago how he felt about 'Leisha and her kids. But 'Leisha's a part of my life, Mom. She's part of who I am."

"You can't mean that. Not after what she's been up to. The things that have been going on."

"It's none of your business, Mom. You were never

interested before, so don't go pretending it means something to you now."

"But you must realize...."

"Just drop it!"

The shouted words startled the baby, who instantly began waving his arms and kicking his legs as he began testing his lungs. Mary grabbed the child and the two disappeared to the back of the apartment.

Sylvia stared at her son as though he had just ripped away part of her life. "That's not fair. I've tried to be there for you. But your father...."

"Don't be pulling that on me. As bad as Dad is, at least he's honest enough to say what he feels. He made it plain from the start that he didn't want anything to do with my wife and my kids. But you. You pretend that you care, but you're no better than he is."

"But I tried, Mark. I wanted to be there for you. Really I did." Reflexively she folded her arms, rubbing her hands up and down her shoulder, feeling the dull pain hidden beneath her jacket, trying hard to ignore the bruises she'd somehow managed for years to conceal from the outside world. "You just don't understand."

"I understand enough."

He walked past her, opening the front door, and stood defiantly to the side.

"I think it's time for you to go."

She nearly replied, nearly spoke up in protest, then thought better of it. Without a word she left the apartment.

Her husband said nothing as Sylvia stepped into the car. Shifting into gear, he pulled from the parking lot and took the turn onto the main road. After traveling for several minutes Frank Bradley crushed out his cigarette in the ashtray, his eyes focused on the road ahead.

"Did you get to see the brat?"

"I saw our grandson, if that's what you mean."

"You know goddamn well what I mean. And I sure as hell don't want to hear you calling him my grandson."

"But it's true, Frank. He's Mark's little boy."

"That may be. But I sure as hell ain't calling him my grandson. That goddamn whore your son married is nothing but a damn drug addict. Strung out on heroin. Contaminating her children with that filth she fills her body with. She's no damn good and I don't want anything to do with any of them."

He pulled his eyes away from the road ahead for a moment, glaring at his wife. "And I don't want you having anything to do with them either. Understand?"

Sylvia kept her thoughts to herself, realizing there was nothing to be gained by discussing the matter further.

Five minutes down the road a shopping plaza came into sight. The store on the corner had a green neon sign with the bold letters KELLY'S glaring out at them. Below that, blinking off and on in red neon, was the single word LIQUOR.

Making a turn at the last minute, Frank Turner pulled in front, maneuvering into a parking space.

"Wait here," he commanded.

Sylvia sat in silence, watching her husband enter the liquor store. She observed him through the barred windows, patrolling the aisles, deciding on his selection for the evening. Finally, the choice made, he carried several bottles to the front counter.

She said nothing as the courtesy light flashed back on, announcing his return to the car. Two bottles, in plain brown wrappers, went carefully into the back seat. Frank Bradley got behind the wheel, started the engine, and they resumed the journey home.

She tried in vain to hold back the tears as she stared out the window at the dark night around them.

Chapter Twenty-One:

IF ASKED A MONTH AGO HOW SHE FELT about Riverfront Rehab Aleisha would have been adamant about her viewpoint. To begin with, the place was a monumental waste of time, with endlessly dull routines serving no purpose other than to entertain the patients or fill the pockets of the administrators running the place. It cut her off from life. It isolated her from family, and friends, and all the activities she enjoyed doing. There was no personal freedom to be found within the highly structured confines of the establishment. You were expected to conform and adapt to fit the mold they designed for you, rather than be permitted to express your own individuality. It was little better than a prison.

That was how she had felt a month ago.

But now, sitting in the tiny room that had been her home for the past few weeks, waiting for Kareen to pick her up and take her away from the facility, her attitudes had altered. She felt frightened about the future, uncertain what to expect on the outside. She didn't want to leave her haven of safety. It was a shelter from all the stress and hassle and confusion prevalent in the world. She found she had connected somehow, even though she had fought the notion, with the people in her therapy group. She realized she still had to face the world on her own, and may never see these people again in her life, but even so there was a certain reassurance to be found in the fact that what she was going through wasn't unique to herself. There were others who shared the same apprehensions; the same fears and forebodings. It made everything seem somehow easier to cope with.

But there were other fears, other concerns, that had cropped up lately, developing with an awareness Aleisha had never experienced before.

What would she do once she was back out *there*? She had never considered her future beyond how to make a few bucks and score another hit. No long range plans had ever figured in her life, no calculations for where she would be five, or ten, or twenty years from now. Every day – no, every moment of every day – had been greeted with no consideration of what would happen next, with no regard for the consequences of her actions. Events happened, she reacted to them, in either a positive or negative manner, then she moved on to other things, discarding any knowledge or experience she gleaned along the way. It was the way she had been raised, the way she was used to behaving, and anything else was unknown to her.

The time in rehab had forced her to take a good look at her situation, reassessing things in her life she had never stopped to consider before. Pregnant at age fifteen, forced to drop out of school to take care of Willard, she had struggled the last ten years of her life merely to get by, watching the kids she grew up with move on to better, more fulfilling lives while she agonized over a day to day existence that brought her no joy and even less contentment.

Many of her former friends had succeeded beyond her wildest imaginings. True, there had been a handful like her, those too bitter to fight for something better or just too lazy to push themselves forward, who had succumbed to the same lackadaisical lifestyle Aleisha had fallen into. They still lived from day to day, those lucky enough to find a job scrounging from paycheck to paycheck, with no concern for the future other than facing things as they came and making the most of the situations once they got there.

Several people she had grown up with had already paid the ultimate price, losing the final battle though drugs or alcohol or, in one instance, a senseless killing driven by juvenile pettiness that had escalated into something much more dangerous.

It was a penalty Aleisha had nearly fallen to herself.

And it all seemed such a pointless existence to her now.

But what would she do? The only skill she had, the only profession she had ever managed to make money at, was selling herself for a few bucks to the next asshole that came along, using her body as a means to get through life.

For a long time she had told herself there was nothing wrong with what she had been doing. Nobody was being hurt. The guys got what they wanted. She made a few bucks out of it. And if the Johns didn't come to her they would just hook up with someone else anyway. It wasn't going to go away. Why not take advantage of the easy pickings her physical attributes brought her way?

But she had never really believed that. Each time she entered a cheap motel room with a stranger, or laid down on a filthy mattress with an overweight egomaniac who considered himself God's gift to womankind, or snuck into an alley for a quick one just to squeeze out a few more bucks for that next hit, she had left behind a bit of herself, a lingering feeling of worthlessness encompassing her and tearing away still further at what little self esteem she had.

She had no desire to return to the lifestyle.

And what of her children? How unfair had she been to them over the years? Could she ever make up for all the wasted hours and days she had spent away from them?

She couldn't change the past, but that didn't mean it wasn't too late to affect the future.

But how? How do you modify a lifetime of routine? How

do you turn your back on your old life and start fresh when you have nothing new to work with?

Kareen arrived in the early afternoon, bringing with her an old suitcase for the meager belongings Aleisha had accumulated during her sojourn.

"I bet you're excited about getting out of here?"

"It will be nice ta get outside again."

"God, I can't imagine how you could stand it cooped up in this place. Would drive me batty."

"It was all right. Once you got used ta it. Weren't really that bad."

"Well, it's all behind you now."

The suitcase was packed by this time, the simply furnished room looking empty and forgotten as they turned their backs on it. Kareen carried Aleisha's things, hefting the meager items easily as they headed to the front desk. Aleisha spied a few patients standing just outside the community room, staring at her with a mixed look of envy and sorrow.

"Give me a minute. Ta say goodbye."

"Well, make it fast. I still got to get home to make supper and Leroy don't like to be kept waiting."

Mandy and Linda stood with Nicole, a new girl who had joined the sessions after Janelle's departure. As Aleisha left her room the trio crossed the hallway, intercepting her halfway.

"I'm so happy for you," Linda began. "I hope everything works out for you."

"I'm sure it will." Mandy, ever the optimist when it came to other people's lives, chimed in. "Just don't give up. Okay?"

Aleisha nodded a meek reply. "You guys take care now. I'm sure you be outta here in no time yourself."

Nicole, still a relative stranger to her, offered a meek so long and drifted away with the others.

As she turned she saw Bryan, standing alone, leaning

against a wall, staring at her with a confused look on his face. Of all those in the group she had connected the least with him. She had seldom related with men in the past, other than on a sexual level, and Aleisha had never considered that to be anything more than a necessary obligation. No doubt her ambivalence toward Bryan could be attributed to their differing genders.

But there was more to it than that, Aleisha realized. While the others – including herself – had grown to the point where they could communicate openly with one another, Bryan continued to maintain a stoicism that kept him apart from the group. A reluctance to speak out had left him isolated. She felt, even after hours of group therapy together, that she didn't even know him.

Aleisha wandered over. "Bye Bryan."

"Bye."

They stood there, an awkward silence gathered around them, until Aleisha decided at last to turn away. She had taken a single step before he spoke up.

"Thank you."

She paused, wondering if she had heard correctly, before turning to face him.

"What?"

"Thank you," he repeated.

"For what?"

He shrugged. "Just for being you, I guess. For not judging me. For being honest about things. It made me feel...." He struggled with the words he was searching for. "More normal, I guess."

"But I didn't do nothin'."

"You did enough."

He stood there, looking lost and forlorn, as though his best friend was about to walk out the door. She didn't understand it. They had hardly spoken to each other. In all their time together, he had never expressed any interest in her, not even the desire to strike up a conversation.

Several times in the last few weeks she had seen him sitting alone, like he was suffering some sort of self-imposed isolation. He seemed to desire that, steering from crowds, avoiding conversations, many times turning and heading the opposite direction at someone else's approach. Maybe he was just shy, or uncomfortable with human contact, but whatever possessed him it drove him away from people.

She felt suddenly overwhelmed with his isolation. As alone as she felt, here was somebody that was in an even worse condition than she was.

On a whim she reached out, hugging him, leaning to bring her mouth close to his ear and whispering. "Good luck Bryan."

As she left he turned quickly away, wiping a tear from his eye, and then he was out of her life.

Chapter Twenty-Two:

I⊥T WAS OBVIOUS THE APARTMENT HAD never been designed for a family. The kitchen was tiny, with not even room enough for a small table. Merely opening the refrigerator door used up most of the available space. The living room served as the dining area, a folding table in one corner with two collapsible chairs comprising the dinette set, while a worn sofa and chair on the other side of the room faced the television. Down the hallway the bathroom door stood ajar, with the single bedroom at the end of the hall completing the floor plan.

"This is it," Kareen announced, as the two women entered.

Aleisha had never visited her sister's apartment before. She was startled with its small size. "There's not much room, is there? I feel like I'm gonna be in the way."

"Don't you worry 'bout it. You're my baby sister. We'll make it work."

"And your boyfriend ain't gonna mind none?"

"Leroy's just gonna have to get used to it. It's my name on the lease, not his. 'Sides, he's gone most the time anyways. Won't be no problem. But you'll have to sleep on the couch."

"That's 'kay. It's just nice ta have somewhere ta stay."

Kareen sat down. "So what happens now?"

"What do you mean?"

"What are your plans? I don't mind you hanging out here

for a while. I really don't. But take a look at this place. We'll be bumping into each other constantly."

"I didn't realize I was bein' such an inconvenience ta you. Maybe I should just find somewhere else ta go?"

"Now don't go getting pissed off about it. All I'm saying is you need to start thinking about your future."

"You think I ain't been thinkin' 'bout it?" Aleisha nearly sat down but she felt too much nervous energy to do so. She contented herself instead with pacing the small room, a maneuver that was difficult in the cramped quarters. "I don't know what to do. I'm scared, Kareen."

Kareen stood, walking over toward Aleisha to halt her pacing. There was a marked family resemblance between the two, especially noticeable when they stood next to one another, though Kareen was a stockier, more heavily built version of her little sister. There was also a harder edge to her, like this was somebody you didn't want to be on the bad side of. Aleisha had always been somewhat intimidated by her older sister, and now that she was dependent on her for a place to live that feeling was only stronger.

"Let's get a few things straight," Kareen began. "You've screwed up your life enough already, Aleisha. It's about time you started to set things straight. Number one, I don't want to see you bringing no men back here."

Aleisha felt suddenly on the defensive, having to explain a situation she hadn't even considered before her sister brought it up. "I weren't planin' on bringing no men here. I wouldn't do that."

Kareen flashed a quick look of disbelief and continued. "I'm not finished. No drugs. Unless it's something your doctor prescribes for you to take. And even then I want to know what it's for and when you supposed to take it."

Aleisha was starting to feel the anger grow. "Anythin' else?"

"As a matter of fact there is. You stick to your case plan and see it through. Don't go missing none of your appointments. Make sure you visit them kids on a regular basis. You do what you supposed to be doing."

"I didn't expect ta be gettin' a lecture."

"Well, you better get used to it. I'm not gonna let you ruin my life the way you nearly ruined yours. I only want the best for you, Aleisha. You're my sister, and you're important to me. But I can't live your life. There's things you gonna have to do on your own. I know it's gonna be lots a hard work. And I'll help much as I can. But if you can't work at it too you can't expect nobody else to be there for you. Understand?"

Aleisha nearly blurted something out, criticizing her sister for trying to run her life and not minding her own business.

Then she recalled something they had talked about in group session. That before you criticize someone you should consider where they were coming from; why they were saying the things they were saying, or doing the things they were doing.

Aleisha took a deep breath, to calm herself, and considered her sister's words.

Kareen was right, though it was a grudging admittance on Aleisha's part to think that. Her life was messed up due to the poor choices she had made over the years. By all considerations she was lucky to even be alive. If things had gone differently that night at Pete's her life would have taken a completely different turn.

She had been given an opportunity to set things right. Starting right now.

Aleisha swallowed her pride before replying. "You won't get no trouble from me, Kareen."

"Good."

Anything further that needed to be discussed was interrupted by the sound of a quick knock on the front door. Before either woman could respond Kareen's boyfriend entered the apartment, walking into the room like it was the most natural thing in the world for him to be there.

Leroy Jackson's presence made the already small apartment seem even more cramped. He was a big man. He looked like he could have played basketball in high school. He certainly had the height for it. He carried himself with the swagger of confidence, projecting an easy attitude of authority about him.

He walked past the two women, giving them a cursory glance before heading into the kitchen. He returned with an opened can of beer in his hands. "Who's this?"

"My sister Aleisha. I told you she was gonna be staying here for a bit."

"She do look like you, don't she?" Leroy gave Aleisha a thorough visual examination while proclaiming the words. Aleisha felt uncomfortable with his perusal, like he was lingering longer than he should have on certain of her features, though Kareen failed to notice.

And maybe she was only imagining things anyway, Leroy's next words portraying the fact that his attention was elsewhere. "So when do we eat?"

Kareen headed toward the kitchen area. "I'll get right to it."

Chapter Twenty-Three:

W HENEVER SHE VISITED THE CHILDREN in her CASA cases Beverly made it a point to spend some time with them in their own rooms. She felt the children were more likely to be at ease in familiar surroundings, with their belongings close by, and it would give them an opportunity to open up to her. Plus it gave them the chance to be away from their current authority figure. In the case of Willard and Nataya this would be the foster parents, Robert and Peggy Kale.

The children she dealt with were going through so many changes in their lives already. They deserved some time to just be themselves, lingering in surroundings they were comfortable with. Beverly wanted them to see her as a friend, not as an intrusion.

She no longer viewed children the way she had before entering the CASA program, as innocents living a carefree existence. Many of these kids had been exposed, at an extremely early age, to circumstances and events that Beverly had never even considered before in her life. Drug abuse. Domestic violence. Inadequate housing and insufficient food. They needed to grow up rapidly in their world or they wouldn't grow up at all. Of necessity they often developed a hardened shell, as protection against all the bad that surrounded them. It was a shell that proved difficult for an outsider to penetrate.

Beverly considered an important aspect of her job the

147

need to break through that exterior and find the real child beneath.

In some respects the amazing thing was that so many of the children she dealt with carried on as children were meant to; playing with toys, watching television, doing the normal routines and activities children should grow up with. The difference being these children were burdened with other cares, problems and responsibilities that her own children certainly avoided growing up in their suburban household.

Beverly spent a few minutes talking with Peggy Kale before seeing Willard and Nataya. She had yet to meet Robert Kale, who always seemed to be working when Beverly came to visit. Peggy appeared considerate of the children, concerned for their welfare, but didn't seem the easiest person to warm up to. It all seemed like just a job to her, something she did out of necessity and not for any love for the children she sheltered. She carried herself with a certain coolness, an aloof attitude of efficiency that Beverly couldn't help but notice during their conversations.

"So everything is going fine?" Beverly asked.

"Of course. Though sometimes the kids just seem so bored. I try to get them to go outside to play but they'd rather sit in front of the television. It's all they ever want to do. I suspect they were left alone at home a lot and never learned anything else to do."

"Do you interact with them much?"

"We try. We've taken them to the zoo a couple of times, but they didn't seem too interested. They liked the new Aquarium but were pretty much bored with the rest of it.

"We insist on a family dinner each night, at the kitchen table, so we can all spend time as a group. Saturday is movie night, where we watch something together. Try to make it feel more like a family for them. Though it's tough finding a movie we can all agree on. David's fifteen now, you know, and he's not too keen on watching the stuff Nataya likes. But we change it up once in a while so everyone gets a say in things. It seems to work."

"Have they been seeing their mother?"

"Of course. I make certain they're ready to go, right on time, whenever Patrick needs to pick them up. A few times I've even dropped them off myself when he's been too busy. Their mother's been good about showing up as well. Not that she's had any say in it. After all, the people from rehab bring her there and take her back afterward. Now that she's out of Riverfront I don't know how it will be."

"Any health concerns?"

She considered a moment. "Not that I can think of. They seem to eat okay. Neither one has a particularly hearty appetite, but that doesn't appear to affect them in any way. I suppose it's just their nature."

"I'd like to see them now if I could."

"Of course."

Peggy Kale knew the routine by now. She led Beverly to the back of the house, where Willard and Nataya were in the room they shared, the two of them sitting on the bed and watching the small television in the corner of the room. They acknowledged Beverly's arrival, seeming neither excited about her being there nor bothered by her presence. For them the monthly visits was just another part of their current routine.

Beverly waited until she was alone with the children to begin. "So how are you guys doing?"

Nataya never bothered to answer, or even look in Beverly's direction, though whether it was from her natural shyness or from her attention being captivated with the activity on the television was difficult to say.

Willard, who seemed to have a bearing and nature far beyond that which his young age dictated, managed a simple greeting. "Hello, Miss Beverly."

"What are you watching?"

He shrugged. "I don't know."

She moved closer, catching a glimpse of the show in front of them. "Oh, I recognize that. My grandchildren watch this all the time. That green guy's funny, isn't he? What's his name again?" She knew the answer but was using the question to initiate some sort of interaction with the children.

"Mike Wazowski," Willard supplied. "The big furry guy is Sulley."

"And the little girl's name is...?"

The question seemed to catch Nataya's interest. "That's Boo."

"Of course. She doesn't seem scared of those monsters, does she?"

"They're friendly monsters," Nataya offered, her tone that of someone remarking on the blatantly obvious. "And they're silly."

"I can see that."

By this point Beverly had pulled up a chair and sat down, focusing her attention on the children while half-watching the movie on the DVD.

Nataya slipped off the bed to approach Beverly, leaving her dolly behind as she did so. "Guess what grade I'm in now at school?"

"Well, let's see. You are getting pretty big. Must be sixth grade."

The response brought a chuckle from the child. "No, silly. I'm in second grade."

"That sounds like fun."

She nodded in agreement. "So is Mommy done being sick now?"

The change in conversation caught Beverly slightly off guard. "Why do you ask that?"

"She says she won't be in the hospi..." She paused,

struggling with the word, before looking at her brother for assistance. "What's the name of the place?"

"Hospital," he offered, his attention still focused on the television as he answered the question.

"That's it. The hostipal. She says she's done at the hostipal. So she must not be sick no more."

"You're mother is doing a whole lot better than she was. And we hope she won't be getting sick any more."

"Does that mean we get to go home soon?"

Beverly didn't want to lie to the child, but she also didn't want to fill her with false hopes and expectations. She knew the child's mother had a long recovery ahead of her. "Not for a while. Your mother still has to get feeling even *more* better. But you'll get to visit with her more often, now. So that will be nice, won't it?"

"I guess." No enthusiasm showed in her reply. Nataya frowned, her disappointment obvious.

"But this is a nice place to stay, isn't it? Don't you like it here?"

"It's okay," she conceded. "But I still miss home."

"What do you miss about home?"

"I don't know. Stuff."

"I bet you miss you're baby brother."

"He cries too much," Nataya admitted. "Keeps us up at night."

"That's what babies do. He can't help it."

No reply came from either child.

"So what is it you miss?"

Willard, eyes remaining firmly focused on the television, answered for his sister. "She misses Mark." Then he added an afterthought. "So do I. We haven't seen him since we came here."

"I'm sure Mark misses you guys, too."

"So when can we see him?" Nataya asked.

"Well, I don't really know. But I'll be sure to tell him you guys miss him. Okay?"

They both nodded, apparently satisfied with the answer, and Nataya jumped back up on the bed, grabbed Miss Jasmine from where she had been deposited, scooted over beside her brother, and the two resumed their movie viewing.

Chapter Twenty-Four:

ALEISHA SAT ON THE BENCH AT THE SIDE of the road, wondering how much longer she would have to wait for the coming bus. Children's Services had provided her with a pass, which allowed her to use the city's public transit system, but even though it was better than walking it was still inconvenient. It was a ten minute walk from Kareen's place to the stop, easily twenty minutes crosstown on the bus, then another five minutes to the doors of the Free Clinic. Once she was done at the clinic she still had her two o'clock appointment with Dr. Bargalony – which of course was on the other side of town – so that meant another walk to the bus stop and another twenty minutes on the bus.

It seemed all she did anymore was waste time going from place to place.

She hoped it wouldn't take too long at the clinic. She had never been there before, but she realized in the months ahead it would become part of her weekly routine. Patrick Zimmerly, the case worker from Children's Services, had stopped at Kareen's apartment the previous afternoon. He had brought with him instructions for Aleisha to have her urine tested within twenty-four hours.

She couldn't refuse the summons. Part of her agreement with the court was to go for a drop anytime it was requested of her, from either Children's Services or the CASA office, to determine whether she was using heroin since being released from rehab. Failure to comply was as much as an admission of guilt on her part, which could jeopardize her standing with the court, delay her reunion with her family, and ultimately – depending on future determinations – send her to jail instead of back to rehab.

She didn't want to lose her family. She didn't want to lose her personal freedom. She didn't want to lose what little shred of personal dignity she had yet remaining. She knew it wouldn't be easy, but it was the path she needed to follow for her future. So, the drop summons firmly ensconced in her purse, she was on the way to the Free Clinic.

Eventually the bus arrived and she suffered through the interminably long journey to her destination. After disembarking a brisk walk took her to the front door of the Lagrange Free Clinic, a drab three story brick building that had no doubt been ultra-modern in 1950 but, like so many things in Aleisha's life, hadn't weathered the years well.

The front foyer was plastered with posters, all pertaining to the troubles young individuals – particularly young women – could get themselves into. If you have a drug problem seek help. If you are a victim of domestic violence seek help. If you are pregnant and have nowhere to turn seek help. There were so many posters they overlapped one another, contesting with their neighbors for what little space the walls could afford them. Phone numbers were provided for those in trouble, which seemed ridiculous to Aleisha since half the people she knew didn't even have a phone. Besides the information hot-lines, addresses were included of the various clinics, agencies, and departments that dealt with whatever particular trouble arose.

Aleisha scurried past, barely noticing the advertisements after her initial observation, and found her way to a front counter. After waiting in line for five minutes she was greeted by an elderly woman with Betty on her name tag. Betty presented the cool efficiency prevalent in bureaucratic employees everywhere. "Number?"

"What's that?"

"What number are you?"

Aleisha was confused. "I don't have a number."

Betty sighed in exasperation and pointed to a roll of paper with tear off numbers. "Everyone takes a number when they get here. We'll call your number when it's your turn."

"But I didn't know."

"I'm sorry. You have to have a number."

"Look, I been in line almost ten minutes already. Can't you....?"

"We have to take everyone in the order they arrived. That's the rules."

"But...."

"Please take a number and have a seat, ma'am. We'll get to you when it's your turn."

Lacking any further recourse, Aleisha took a number and found a place to sit. She had been seated for less than two minutes when a young woman approached her.

"You're Aleisha, ain't ya?"

"Yeah." She scrutinized the new arrival – the black hair cropped short off her forehead, the pair of silver rings in the upper lip, the expanse of tattoos that covered both arms – but failed to recognize her. "Do I know you?"

"Sure ya do. It's Veronica. We met at Pete's. About a year ago."

"You don't look familiar."

"Well, you were pretty out of it that night. I guess I was too, but not 'till later. That was some nasty shit Pete was passing around that night. So what ya been up to?"

Aleisha hesitated, wondering how much she wanted to reveal about what had happened to her. It was embarrassing to feel she had lost control of her life and her actions were dictated now by whatever the court decided. Her personal freedom had been violated and she was still getting used to it. But hours of therapy sessions had made it easier to talk about her problems; so many people knew already what she'd been through it wouldn't make much difference to tell somebody else.

"I just got outta rehab," she admitted at last.

"Bummer. We'll, at least you're not stuck in there no more."

"How 'bout you?"

"I'm okay. They grabbed me last winter, threw me in jail for three months for solicitin'. Weren't so bad, though. I didn't have me no place to live so the city actually done me a favor. Otherwise I probably would of froze my ass off walking the streets."

"So what are you here for?"

As soon as she asked the question Aleisha felt like she was sticking her nose into somebody else's business. Too much time at rehab had made her accustomed to speak her mind, asking anything she was curious about. It was a habit she would need to be careful with, Aleisha reflected, now that she was out with *normal* people again.

Veronica didn't seem to mind, answering with no hesitation, as though her personal issues were common knowledge and she could see no sense in hiding anything. "Think I picked somethin' up from one a them scumbags I been rollin' around with. My clit's all swollen and red and itches like hell."

"That's too bad," was all Aleisha could manage in reply, though the other girl failed to notice the lackluster response.

"But I got me a sweet deal going on right now," Veronica continued, leaning closer in confidence. "Pete's offered to let me be a tester for him."

"A tester? What's that?"

"You know. When he gets some new shit in someone gets

to try it out for him. See whether it's any good or not. So I get as much as I want without paying a fucking cent for it. Is that a sweet deal or what?"

Before Aleisha could respond a voice interrupted from the front of the room. "Twenty-seven!"

Veronica looked at the slip of paper in her hand. "That's me. Gotta go." She took two steps away, then turned for a moment. "We should get together sometime. Me and you."

"Sure. We'll do that."

As the young woman walked away Aleisha looked at the number on the printed paper in her hand. Forty-two.

"Damn."

She slumped into her seat to resume the long wait.

At last her number was called, and Aleisha found herself talking to Betty once again.

"So what are you here for?"

Aleisha presented the written summons to appear for a urine drop.

Betty took one look at the paper and shoved it back across the desk to Aleisha. "You're in the wrong place. Take them stairs to the third floor and check in at the front desk. They'll tell you where to go."

Before Aleisha could respond Betty was calling the next number.

The girl manning the counter on the third floor was more pleasant than Betty, but only marginally so. She took down the necessary information and instructed Aleisha to wait until she was called.

It only took twenty minutes this time, and at last Aleisha found herself being escorted down a hallway by a lab-coated young woman with blonde hair and a brisk demeanor.

"We'll need you to wash your hands first," she was

instructed, "and then we'll give you a paper cup to fill. Understand?"

She nodded.

"Be sure to catch the beginning of the stream. If you have too much to fill it stop and pull the cup away. And if you can't fill it completely that's okay too. Any questions?"

It all seemed ridiculously straight-forward. Aleisha couldn't help wondering how many people were confused with such simple instructions.

She entered the bathroom, noticing the single toilet and hand basin. Metal bars were on either side of the toilet, apparently for assistance if people were handicapped. A wooden bench was situated on the other side of the room.

She was about to close the door behind her but the technician resisted, moving into the room. "You can't be alone. I have to witness you voiding."

"What do you mean?"

"It means too many people try to pull something in here. We have to be certain the specimen we get is yours, and it was taken today." She handed over the paper cup, which Aleisha had set on the sink upon entering the room, then sat on the bench. "So go ahead."

Aleisha nearly said something, pointing out how demeaning the whole thing was, then realized the futility of it all. This was how the system worked so this was what needed to be done. Besides, what was the big deal anyway? She'd taken her pants off plenty of times in front of strangers before. One more time couldn't hurt.

Chapter Twenty-Five:

$\mathbb{B}$EVERLY HAD REALIZED EARLY ON IN her CASA career that there was only so much she could accomplish in her position. She wasn't going to change the world. It wasn't even certain that she could change the small group of participants in the cases she was involved with. Though that didn't mean she couldn't try. One never knew what the future held, or what the ramifications from her participation in the program would bring.

But her primary role as Guardian was to oversee activities, performing as an extra set of eyes for Children's Services, monitoring the lives of the children in particular, to be certain their needs were provided for.

She also interacted with the parents on a regular basis, in so far as she would meet with them to gauge their progress and determine whether they were following the guidelines set down by their individual case plans. In most cases the mothers were the ones receiving most of the attention. This wasn't a sexist view of the world, but rather the hard realities of the situation. Often the fathers weren't involved with the children at all or, as in the case of Willard and Nataya, were an unknown entity. In so many of the cases brought before the court the burden of raising the children fell to the mother.

As a result the mother's progress was key to the successful completion of any case. Her recovery was of paramount importance when it came to the future of the children. So in addition to her monthly visits with the CASA kids Beverly made it a habit to check in, on a regular basis, with the mother in each of the families she was involved with.

Beverly arrived at the apartment at 3:30, the time Aleisha had agreed upon for their meeting, and was greeted by a woman who could have been Aleisha's twin. She was immediately struck by the resemblance between the two sisters.

"I'm Beverly Johnson. From the CASA office."

"Yeah. Aleisha said you was coming. I'm Kareen. Her sister."

Beverly smiled at the remark. "That's pretty obvious. You look a lot like her."

"Everyone says that. I just wish I was as skinny as my sister." She laughed casually at the remark, as though she had used it before in the past.

"Is Aleisha here?"

Kareen took a quick glance around, as though seeing the apartment for the first time. "Ain't nowhere for her to hide in this place." The smile on her face as she voiced the reply attested to the fact that she made the comment in jest. "She ain't got back yet from her appointment," she added, by way of explanation. "But she should be here soon."

"Is it okay if I wait inside for her?"

"Not much room, but come on in if you want."

Beverly was struck by how small the apartment was. She could have practically fit the whole thing in her living room. She felt immediately guilty, to think of all the comforts she had in her own life compared to how people like Aleisha and her sister lived. Then again, she and Russell had worked hard over the years. Everything they had they earned. There was nothing she needed to feel guilty about.

Though sometimes it didn't make sense why some people had so much while others had so little.

Was it a denial of opportunities that left them in such a condition, or did they merely lack the drive to push themselves to succeed? Her daughter Jennifer would have called it laziness, but Beverly had seen enough to realize that wasn't always the case. Things were never that simple.

Perhaps the most disturbing aspect of the poverty she encountered as a CASA volunteer was that it seemed to be a self-perpetuating system, each generation of poor and under-privileged people raising children who fell themselves into the same system. The same lifestyle. The same bleak way of living with seemingly no way out of their circumstances.

Beverly firmly believed what she was doing was one way to break the cycle. By giving the children hope, and showing them there were other alternatives in life, she was doing her part to enhance the future of the coming generation.

Beverly pulled her attention away from such thoughts to examine her surroundings, which while tiny and cramped managed in spite of that to portray a welcoming attitude.

A blanket and pillow occupied most of the couch. Kareen scooped the articles up, throwing them casually into a corner of the room.

"Sit if you likes."

"Thank you. I will."

Beverly was pleased to see that the place looked at least maintained. Space was obviously at a premium, but somehow they managed to make it appear uncluttered. A few dishes could be seen in the kitchen, sitting on a towel on the counter to dry, but otherwise things seemed to be organized and tidy.

"Must feel crowded when you're both here?"

"It does. But we manage to find our own space somehow."

"So how's Aleisha adjusting to things?"

"Okay. She getting a bit restless, but she managing."

"Any problems?"

"There better not be. I already told her I weren't gonna take no bullshit from her. She screwed up her life enough already, she better not go fucking up mine."

Beverly grimaced inwardly at the language. Though not a prude by nature, she was still unaccustomed to the frank ways the people she dealt with found to express themselves. Knowing it wasn't her place to judge, she ignored the expression Kareen had used and continued with her questions. "How do you two get along?"

"All right. I guess. We sisters, so what can you expect? For a long time Aleisha wouldn't have nothing to do with me. Said I deserted her so I should just stay out of her business. But that weren't the way it was."

She paused a moment and Beverly remained silent. Whatever was on Kareen's mind, it seemed she was preparing to say more.

Beverly had noticed before, with the people she dealt with during her CASA investigations, that they were forthcoming with her, discussing the most personal of events in the most straight-forward of manner. It had surprised her initially, to see how willing people were to talk about what they were going through, and how casually they often discussed the most intimate of details.

Beverly had finally reached the conclusion that they appreciated having a sympathetic ear to listen to them. The violence that often lurked just outside their doors, the drugs that controlled the streets they lived on, the need to scrounge for anything that came their way, these were all just everyday facts of life they had learned to live with. They talked about their troubles in the same nonchalant ways that the people in Beverly's family talked about the weather or a local sporting event. And for the same reasons. It was there, plain and simple, and there wasn't anything you could do to change the way things were.

You just had to deal with it.

Kareen continued after a brief pause.

"Things was never good for us, growing up. My father was a bastard, plain and simple. He'd steal the shirt off your back if he thought he could make a profit on it.

"But that weren't the worse of it. He'd beat my mother, any time a the day or night, for no reason, Just 'cause he were a son-of-a-bitch. At seventeen I had enough of it. I left and never looked back."

"And Aleisha?"

"Well, she were five years younger. Didn't have much choice but to hang around."

"Couldn't you do something? Call Children's Services or...?"

Kareen shook her head. "Can't tell you how many times the police come knocking at our door. But it didn't never change things. If anything it made it worse, cause Pa would be pissed off when they left and take it out on us kids. Believe me, things was easier all around if we just kept our mouths shut and put up with his trash.

"That's when things broke down 'tween me and Aleisha. After I went out on my own. Guess she figured I deserted her or something. But weren't nothing I could do about it. I had to look out for yourself."

"You're helping her now. Maybe that's a step in the right direction for the two of you to reconcile."

"I suppose. Long as Aleisha don't go doing nothing stupid."

"So what happened to your parents?"

"Pa got shot about nine years back. Got himself mixed up in some sort of drug deal that went bad and didn't have sense enough to get outta there in time."

"And your mother?"

Kareen paused, a thoughtful look on her face, as though it

was a question that needed some consideration. "Don't rightly know what happened to her. Were shortly after Pa got it that Aleisha took off. She were pregnant by then, and I guess she moved in with one guy after another for a while. None of them didn't never seem to work out. We both sorta lost track a the rest of the family after that. I suppose Ma might still be out there. Somewhere. I just ain't heard nothing and I ain't been interested enough to find out."

Aleisha arrived shortly after that, looking worn out from her day's activities. Without a word Kareen disappeared into the back bedroom, allowing Beverly and her sister the opportunity to take advantage of what little privacy was available in the cramped space of the apartment.

"I guess things going okay," Aleisha answered, when Beverly asked how she was doing. "Got me running 'round so much don't hardly got time for nothing else."

"Dr. Bargalony seems pleased with your progress."

She shrugged. "It is what it is."

"That sounds pretty noncommittal. Don't you see any changes?"

"I guess. He just keep goin' over the same shit every day. I gots ta start feeling good about myself. Gots ta start plannin' for my future. How can I do that when they got me attending therapy, and parenting classes, and all this other bullshit? And couple times a week I'm goin' to the clinic for a drop. Ain't got time for nothin' else."

"This is temporary, Aleisha. The classes won't last forever. And stay clean, so you only drop negative at the clinic. That can only help you at the next hearing."

"I ain't had nothin' ta do with no drugs since I been out. I'm stayin' away from that shit."

"I'm glad to hear it. And you've been seeing your kids twice a week, right?"

"That's right. But it goes too fast. I wish I could see more of 'em. It don't seem fair ta me. Mark gets ta see Michael whenever he wants."

"Mark's situation is different from yours, Aleisha. He wasn't using heroin. The court sees you as more of a risk to your children. They don't want anything to happen to them."

"So how long do I has ta wait? I just want ta spend time with my kids."

"Be patient, Aleisha. You're proving yourself right now. You're showing everyone how responsible you are and that you're working at changing your life. With time you'll have longer visits with the children. You'll be able to start doing more activities with them."

"Don't know when I'll have time for it. I got ta find me a job, too, start earning some money." She glanced around the apartment, taking in the cramped space around her. "I can't stay here forever. Need a place of my own."

"Have you considered moving back in with Mark?"

"I'm not ready for that. I'm still pretty pissed with him 'bout that paternity business."

"Chances are that was his lawyer talking, not him. They like to cover all the bases."

"I guess I should think about it. When I get me some free time, that is."

"Just keep doing what you've been doing and everything will work out. I'm sure of it."

Chapter Twenty-Six:

W HEN BEVERLY ARRIVED SEVERAL days later for her monthly visit with the baby Mark was at his sister's apartment. The two adults were watching television, apparently captivated by the antics of the guests on some sort of talk show, while Michael sat in his swing. The gentle click-clack as the seat moved back and forth competed with the other sounds in the room, though Mark and his sister seemed not to notice. It must have proven to be a soothing sound for the baby. He was asleep, leaning to one side, as the swing continued its steady rocking motion.

"He's grown a lot since I first met him," Beverly exclaimed.

"And he's getting into everything," Mary added. "He's scooting around so much I can't even walk out of the room for a minute without wondering what he's getting into. I never realized a baby could crawl so fast."

"But that's a good thing. You want to see him growing and learning new skills."

"But it's too soon! I was just getting used to having a baby and now I almost have a toddler on my hands. I don't know if I'm ready for this."

"Has he seen much of his brother and sister?"

"Only at Children's Services. We all show up at the same

time so Aleisha can see all the kids at once. And, of course, the children get to see each other as well."

"How about you, Mark? Do you join them?"

Beverly noticed a hesitation before he spoke. "I haven't yet."

"Why not?"

"I just think I would feel too uncomfortable. From what Mary says the case worker watches them all like a hawk."

"I'm sure that's not true."

"Well," Mary chimed in, "he keeps close by."

"He's concerned about the children. That's all. He has to be. But he wants to see the family reunited. That includes you too, Mark."

Beverly felt suddenly like a matchmaker; like she was trying to push Aleisha and Mark back together again. She had no idea what their relationship had been like in the past, though she suspected the stormy incident that brought them to the attention of Children's Services wasn't the first of its kind. Maybe they were better off away from each other, living separate lives, and it wouldn't do either of them any good to get back together.

But there was more involved than just the two of them. There were the kids to consider. Not that she wanted to see any couple together merely for the kids' sake. That wasn't healthy for anyone.

Aleisha Turner had major problems to contend with. How she dealt with them – and, perhaps more importantly, how she didn't deal with them – would have a strong influence on the future of her children.

The kids were apart already. It was certainly feasible that things wouldn't change in that respect. Mark Bradley could end up having custody of the baby while Willard and Nataya went their own way, either with their mother or, depending on Aleisha's condition, with someone else.

But it would be good for Aleisha to have someone in her

life that cared for her. Whether Mark was that someone was difficult to say, but Beverly was pretty sure it wasn't Kareen. The sisters had seemed okay with their present living arrangement, but Beverly had felt a tension beneath the surface, as if they both would rather the circumstances were different. It was too confined of a space to expect it to be anything other than a temporary situation.

"Willard and Nataya were asking about you, Mark," Beverly announced, deciding to hold her tongue no longer.

Mark turned from the television to face her, as if this was a revelation he hadn't expected. "Were they?"

"Sure they were. Stop to consider what they're going through. The home life they were adjusted to has been disrupted. They no longer can rely on the things they were accustomed to. They're having to learn to deal with new people. New sets of rules. A new way of living. It has to be frightening for them, when you stop to think about it.

"It might not be so bad if their mother was around more. But she's been taken from them as well. When it comes down to it there isn't much in their life that *hasn't* changed, other than the fact that the two of them are still together. You could be a positive influence in their lives, Mark. The person that helps them maintain a healthy outlook."

He made no reply, keeping his thoughts to himself, and Beverly left with no clear idea in mind what he thought about things.

Beverly drove home in silence. Often she listened to the radio while in the car, enjoying the music she and Russell had shared together, but sometimes she preferred the silence. It gave her time to be pensive.

The case with Aleisha and her family, like the other cases Beverly had handled in the past, had reached an almost stagnant phase. In the beginning was the hustle and bustle of preliminary activity; researching the particulars, investigating the participants, preparing for the first court hearing. Toward the end of an assignment the goal was in sight. When you could see all your hard work coming together as an accomplishment you could be proud of, satisfied that you had been there for the children under your care, it made all the work and effort seem worthwhile.

In the middle – those long months in-between – things were different. Certain aspects of the case, like the recovery time for a person with a drug addiction, couldn't be rushed. You had to have a lot of patience, which was a thing Beverly grudgingly had to admit was not always her strongest characteristic. Time crept forward, until the next visitation, gearing up for the next hearing, waiting and wondering if something would happen to disturb the outcome and hoping only positive changes were ahead.

As hard as Beverly worked she was fully aware that her influence on the outcome of the case could be nominal. Some families grew closer, the bonds between them strengthening their desire to stay together. Others grew apart, discovering in the process that things weren't going to get better and the only solution, for the sake of the children involved, was to move in different directions from one another.

It was a hard reality of life that often made her work frustrating.

Chapter Twenty-Seven:

$\mathcal{S}$HE AWOKE IN THE MIDDLE OF THE NIGHT, startled, for a moment confused about where she was. The room was dark, save for a small green dot of light on the front of the television that stayed on constantly. It wasn't nearly enough light to provide illumination, though it was just enough to serve as a source of irritation when she was trying to get to sleep each night.

The window in the kitchen looked out onto a parking lot behind the apartment. The area outside was well lit, the glow of the streetlamps entering past the curtains, projecting the design of the muntins on the window into a tic-tac-toe design that splashed onto the wall above the sofa. Laying on her back, staring at the shadows, she could almost make out X's and O's on the stuccoed texture of the wall.

She stood and made her way to the kitchen, retrieving a glass from the cabinet, and after allowing the sink to run for several seconds poured herself a drink of water. The liquid failed to quench her thirst. She felt hot and sweaty all over, and found herself gasping for breath, as though she had just completed an exercise routine. She wanted it to stop. She wanted the aches to go away. She tired of the constant feeling that all she wanted to do, more than anything in the world, was to scream at the top of her voice over the injustice of it all. She felt like laughing and crying at the same time, questioning her emotions and wondering why the nights had to be so difficult.

She told herself things were getting better. Life was improving. She was getting stronger every day. In time this would all be behind her.

She slunk back to the couch, collapsing on the cushions, reminding herself that it wasn't all just one big lie. And finally, after tossing and turning late into the night, Aleisha at last succumbed to sleep.

Chapter Twenty-Eight:

T HE DAYS WERE GROWING COLDER. THE leaves on the trees were present in their full autumnal glory, brilliant colors displayed for the world as they heralded their approaching departure. Many had already succumbed to the season, the fallen leaves blowing in small eddies that accumulated against chain-link fences and collected beside houses and buildings. The days were growing shorter, losing a few precious minutes of light at the start and finish of each day. Already the afternoon sun was sinking noticeably toward the horizon, throwing lengthening shadows from the downtown buildings to darken the streets beneath.

Aleisha noticed none of it as she stepped off the bus. She was running late, a routine that had plagued her the entire day, having slept in longer this morning than she should have. It was a fitting start to a day filled with late appointments, missed buses, and wasted time as she scurried through her daily activities. She hadn't even managed time for lunch, which was just as well because lunch was a luxury she could barely afford.

She glanced at a clock in the window of an office she passed, noting the time.

"Shit. I'm late."

Aleisha sprinted the last two blocks, huffing for breath as she made it through the doors of the Juvenile Center. Throwing her purse and some loose articles from her coat pocket onto the table for examination, she made the customary pass through the metal detector. Once cleared she gathered her belongings, stuffing everything into her pockets in a frantic manner, then rushed toward the elevators.

She attempted to relax inside the lift, willing herself to calm down as the elevator took her to the third floor, but picked up the pace again while navigating the maze of hallways interweaving themselves through Children's Services.

Her children were waiting and she had nearly been late to see them.

It didn't surprise Aleisha to have Nataya run out to meet her; her daughter's constant enthusiasm always brought a smile to her mother's face, no matter how trying of a day she was experiencing. She gave her daughter a hug and a kiss – delivering a peck on the plastic cheek of Miss Jasmine as well, at Nataya's insistence – and the two of them entered the family viewing area hand in hand.

What Aleisha hadn't been expecting – and what made her pause just inside the doorway, unconsciously brushing a strand of loose hair to the side of her face – was to see Mark in the room holding their baby.

He looked up, greeting her in the exaggerated juvenile talk grownups habitually use around the very small. "Look who's here!" Holding Michael propped up against his chest, the toddler's tiny legs dangling from the seat Mark's arms provided, he approached his wife. "It's Mommy. Say hello to Mommy."

Aleisha moved closer, pulling the baby from Mark's grip, then drawing the child toward her. She delivered an enthusiastic hug to her son, wondering as she did so what was fueling her emotions. Was it joy at seeing her baby? Or the elation she felt from Mark's presence?

She buried her face against Michael's cheek, allowing

herself a moment to become more composed, before addressing Mark.

"I didn't expect ta see you here."

"It's all right, isn't it?"

She nodded. "Yeah. It's good."

Aleisha felt a tug against her arm and looked down to see Willard standing against her.

"Look what Mark give me."

It was only then that she noticed the miniature car her son held, a bright red die-cast model.

"What you got there?"

"It's a race car. See what it does?"

Willard bent down, pulling the car backward against the floor, then released it and watched as the tiny vehicle propelled itself forward. Moments later it disappeared under one of the chairs, managing to elude him before he had time to grab it to halt its forward progress. "Oh, oh" was all he could manage before looking at his parents for assistance.

Mark shrugged. "It's your car, Sport. Better crawl under there and get it."

He wiggled his way beneath the chair and Aleisha and Mark sat down, beside each other, on the couch.

"It's nice to see you, 'Leisha."

She remained silent, not trusting herself to say the right thing.

"You look better," he continued. "Then the last time I saw you."

"I would hope so. Last time you seen me I was in pretty bad shape."

"Let's not talk about it. That's all behind us. Right?"

When Patrick Zimmerly entered forty-five minutes later she couldn't believe her time was up and the visit was over. It felt like she had just walked in the door.

The case worker, all business as usual, approached Aleisha. "Don't forget, you have Drug Court next week."

"I remember," she replied, a look of distaste on her face.

"What's Drug Court?" Mark asked.

"A monthly review of the court's current case load," Patrick informed him. "Regarding those people currently within the system that are working on rehabilitation over drug issues. It gives us the opportunity to keep up with how everyone's recovering and make sure there's no problems before they become major issues."

Aleisha apparently regarded the matter differently. "Just another way of prying inta my life. Sos I don't get any privacy. Sos I don't get to thinking I'm an actual human being."

"You can't look at it like that, Aleisha," Patrick admonished. "Think of this as a positive thing. We know what you're going through is difficult. We want you to get the most from your recovery, and return to a normal life with your family. The court wants to reward you for all your hard work by showing we're on your side."

Aleisha merely scowled in reply.

"Should I be there?" Mark inquired.

"You can come if you want. For moral support. But it's not necessary."

Patrick escorted Willard and Nataya from the room after the children said their goodbyes, while Mark gathered up the baby's diaper bag and other belongings. As they departed Aleisha, carrying Michael down the hallway toward the elevator, turned to face Mark.

"Drug Court. Just some more a the bullshit I got to put up with."

Mary was waiting outside when Aleisha and Mark left the building. "Hope you guys had time to catch up on things."

"You know," Mark pointed out, "you could have come up

with us."

"That's okay. I had some shopping to do."

Aleisha wondered what kind of shopping she could possibly have done in the downtown business district but she kept her thoughts to herself. She suspected Mary had only used this as an excuse to give the family some time together.

By this point the group had reached the parking lot, where Mark's Impala squatted beside the tiny foreign car parked next to it. As Mary maneuvered the toddler into his car seat in the back of the vehicle Aleisha and Mark stood beside one another. An awkward silence hung between them, like they were strangers to one another with nothing to discuss.

Finally Mark spoke up.

"So what are you doing the rest of the day?"

"Heading back to Kareen's. I could use a nap after the day I been though. I catch the bus on the corner."

"I can drop you off if you want."

"Don't want to be no bother."

"We don't mind. Really. We've got nothing going on right now anyway."

Aleisha glanced into the back of the car, the compartment overwhelmed already with the car seat, diaper bags, and what looked to be some groceries, but decided she could squeeze in. "Beats waiting for that damn bus," she pointed out as she climbed in.

They rode in silence. The only contribution coming from anyone was the series of gurgling sounds Michael made in his car seat while he chewed on a plastic rattle. Occasionally the Impala made a grinding sound, from somewhere in front.

"I think the tie-rod's starting to go," Mark informed them. "I'll have to pick one up." Aleisha knew he'd have no problem getting the parts he needed at the auto parts store where he worked.

The rest of the journey to Kareen's place was a quiet one.

Arriving at her sister's apartment Aleisha stepped from the car, started the walk to the front door, then turned to face Mark. "Thanks for the ride."

After a moment's hesitation she continued. "Will I see you again?"

Mark answered immediately. "Yeah. Count on it."

Chapter Twenty-Nine:

Walking into drug court was a surprise to Aleisha. She hadn't really thought about it much, but she had assumed it would be like the earlier hearing, a short affair with a small group of people in a simple room.

The reality was far different.

Drug Court was held in an actual courtroom, the type of place she had only ever seen before on television or in the movies. The judge presided from a large bench in front. Several tables faced the bench, then came a wooden railing that separated the back half of the room. Seats were provided in the rear.

Aleisha was momentarily taken aback with the number of people in the room. Apparently, she found out later, the sessions were open to anyone who cared to stop by, a notion that put her immediately on the defensive. There seemed no privacy involved. She would be required to stand in front of everyone and answer whatever questions were directed at her.

Upon entering Aleisha noticed the two rows of six chairs on the right of the large room. She assumed this was where the jury would sit, if this had been a typical court session, but the space was reserved today for the offenders who were summoned to appear. A bailiff directed Aleisha to take a seat in the area, and soon there were eight other women sitting with her on the hard wooden chairs.

Most of the women were close to her age, and most of them had a skinny, unhealthy look to them, their skin drawn and pale. Only one wore makeup, with her hair styled as though she'd just left a salon. She wore a red dress that stood out in the crowd, with matching pumps and what looked to be a leather handbag. Probably a knock-off, Aleisha surmised.

The rest were, like Aleisha, dressed conservatively in well worn and comfortable clothing, as though hoping to blend in with their surroundings.

Aleisha didn't know any of the others, though two of them looked familiar to her. Perhaps she had passed them on the street before, on those nights she had wandered the city's sidewalks. They didn't seem to notice her, portraying no sign of recognition, caught up in their own issues and involved with their own concerns.

A few minutes after sitting down the girl behind her – a blue-eyed blonde with the fading vestige of a bruise on the side of her face – leaned over Aleisha's shoulder. Her voice was the husky intonation of the perpetual smoker.

"Your first time here, Sweety?"

"Yeah."

"You been stayin' away from the junk?"

Aleisha nodded in reply.

"Then you got nothin' to worry 'bout. Landers is pretty easy on first timers. Just don't step outta line and she won't fuck with ya."

"How often you been here?"

"Fuck, I lost count it's been so many times. Went through the whole routine couple years ago. Thought I'd actually beat it, you know? Then my friend Shelia shows up my place one night with some China White. Fuck, there I was, back at it again. Been straight the last four months, though. But it's hard. Know what I mean?"

"Yeah. Hits me mostly at night. I wake up shaking

sometimes."

"Been there. Me, I get the drive heaves. Feel like I'm about to puke my fucking brains out."

Anything further they might have said to one another was interrupted by a voice from the front of the courtroom. Aleisha focused her attention on the bailiff.

"Drug Court is now in session. The Honorable Carole Landers presiding. Please rise."

Judge Carole Landers was much younger than Aleisha expected, and her appearance a lot less threatening. She didn't look domineering or mean, or the type of person to order people around. She looked tiny, sitting behind her large bench, like a toddler playing a make believe game in a grownup's world. She had a pleasant smile, which she directed at the women gathered at the side of the room, and Aleisha found herself feeling more at ease.

"I want to thank you all for coming," Judge Landers began. "I appreciate the fact that this isn't easy for any of you. Nobody said it would be easy. But I want you to understand that you aren't alone. There are services available for the asking. If you run into hard times all you have to do is reach out to someone. Your case worker. Your therapist. Anyone here at the courts. There are a multitude of people ready and willing to help you achieve your goals.

"But it all begins with you, and the desire to turn your life around.

"I know many of you have heard this spiel before, but it bears repeating. I can sit up here and be your best friend. Or I can be your worst nightmare. The choice is up to you. Work with me and I'll do everything within my power to assist you. But go against me...."

She paused, allowing the lingering silence to answer for her.

"So let's get down to business."

The first girl was called, and she walked to the front of the courtroom to stand at the podium to the left of Judge Landers. Her name was Lisa – no last name was given, so there was at least a modicum of anonymity – and she stepped forward displaying an air of utter disregard. She appeared unfazed by her surroundings, like it was the most natural thing in the world to be standing in front of a group of strangers to discuss her drug problem.

"Good afternoon, Lisa."

"Hello, Judge Landers."

The Judge took a moment to review some information on a piece of paper in front of her. "This is your third appearance in my court, is that correct?"

"Yes it is."

"It says you've been living at your parent's house. How long have you been there?"

"Since I got out of rehab. Almost two months now."

"And things are going well?"

She shrugged.

"I'm afraid gestures don't appear too well in transcripts, Lisa. Would you say you've been doing well at your parent's house?"

"I guess so."

"You don't sound too sure of yourself."

"Everything's good there. They looking out for me okay."

"Good. I see too that all your tests have come back negative since you've been out."

"Yes ma'am."

"Splendid. I'm glad to see things are progressing the way they should be. Do you have any questions or concerns that need to be addressed?"

She considered a moment. "Can't think of none."

"Very well. You may have a seat."

And that was it. The entire exchange took less than five minutes, from the time Lisa's name was called until she was back in her seat with the other girls.

Aleisha was beginning to think Drug Court wasn't that bad of a thing after all. Sure, it was a pain in the ass to take time out of your day to head down here, and then to have to sit and listen to what the other girls had to say, but if it brought her closer to having this business over with then she figured it was worth while. It all seemed like so much busy work, rather than being productive in any way, but she supposed that was the way the system worked.

"Joannie. Please approach the bench."

Joannie, as it turned out, was the young woman in the red dress. She carried herself with a self-assurance that seemed out of place considering the surroundings. She sauntered to her position at the front of the courtroom, flashing a look toward the bench that bordered on contempt.

Whether it was due to the young woman's attitude, or caused more by the information she read in front of her, a marked change presented itself in the judge's demeanor. It may as well have been another person presiding over the court, so marked was the metamorphosis. A cold, precise tone set the mood as she distinctly voiced her opening statements. "I'm looking at your report, Joannie, and I'm not liking what I see."

Landers paused, giving the young woman the opportunity to reply, but when it became obvious there would be nothing forthcoming the judge continued. "You've missed three of your last four therapy sessions. Care to explain why?"

"I been busy. That's all. What difference does it make, anyway? All they do is talk about the same shit over and over again. It's just a waste of time."

"So you think your recovery is a waste of time?"

"Just busy work. That's all it is. Don't do me no good."

"And I suppose I'm wasting my time by seeing you here today as well?"

"Your choice. I just don't see why you got to make a big deal out of everything."

"Have you been staying clean?"

"Yes I have."

"For how long?"

"Three months now."

"That's not what it says here. According to this you tested positive on August 15th. And again on September 9th."

"That's bullshit. I don't know where they come up with that shit, but it's not right."

"How about last week? Looks like you had another positive when you dropped."

"That's 'cause of the meds they got me on. Ask my doctor. She'll tell ya."

"I find that highly unlikely."

She casually shrugged, as though the topic was of little interest to her.

Judge Landers leaned forward. "I think you need to work harder at recovery, Joannie. I detect a definite lack of effort on your part and I'm not pleased."

"I'm not doing nothing wrong. I'm staying clean and that's the truth. So there's nothing you can do about it."

"That's where *you're* wrong, Joannie. To begin with, I don't think you are staying clean. One time and I could consider giving you the benefit of the doubt. Three strikes is too many. These repeated infractions display an unwillingness on your part to put any effort into cleaning yourself up.

"I've also talked to your therapist. She doesn't feel you're progressing any. As a matter of fact, she thinks you're in worse shape now than you were two months ago."

"Well, I think you're both wrong, so what do you think of

that?"

"I'll tell you what I think of that, Joannie. One of the conditions for your release from lockup is that you abide by the rules and regulations as set forth by this court. That means staying clean, which you've clearly failed to do. That also means attending all your therapy sessions, which you've also neglected to follow through on.

"And on a personal note, it means showing some respect for this court, which you obviously have no intention of doing. You leave me no other choice but to remand you back to custody."

Until now Joannie had exhibited a total disregard for the proceedings, as though she considered any consequences that might occur to be not worth worrying about. The reality of the situation sank in when the import of the judge's words finally got through to her.

"That's not fair. You can't do that."

"I beg to differ. Since I'm sitting up here and you're down there I can do anything I please. And it would be wise of you to remember that the next time you appear before me."

Landers leaned back in her chair and, as if dispatching a bothersome bug, made a motion of dismissal with her hand. "Take her away."

A Police woman approached, removing the handcuffs from her belt and installing them on the young woman's wrists. Joannie was led away, a look of dismay on her perfectly made up face, while a stunned silence held the onlookers.

"Aleisha. You're up next."

The judge's words startled her, and Aleisha slowly rose to her feet. Great. Landers would be in a pissed-off mood now. Why couldn't somebody else have gone next?

Slow steps took Aleisha to the front of the room. She felt under a terrible scrutiny, with every eye turned in her direction and every ear attuned to what she was about to say.

"This is the first time I've seen you, isn't it Aleisha?"

"Yes, ma'am."

"Don't let that last episode worry you." She smiled, a faint expression of sympathy. "I have a responsibility to all of you and I take it very seriously. If it means I have to lay down the law at times then so be it. I'm not here to be your friend, but I don't have to be your enemy either. Understood?"

"Yes."

"Good. You've been out of Riverfront for three weeks now. Correct?"

"Yes, ma'am."

"And where are you currently residing?"

"At my sister's place. For now. It's a bit crowded but we making do."

"I'm sure you are. Looks like you're keeping all your appointments, which I'm glad to see. And you're staying clean. That's marvelous. I'm proud of you."

The words startled Aleisha. The judge's encouragement actually sounded sincere.

"Thank you."

"We'll be seeing each other a lot in the next few months. Keep up the good work and we won't have any problems."

"Yes, ma'am."

"You may return to your seat."

Chapter Thirty:

CURLED UP IN A CORNER OF THE COUCH, snuggled beneath her favorite blanket, Beverly awoke with a start. She didn't even recall having fallen asleep. The last she knew she had been reading a book, one of those romance novels she regarded as her secret vice, enticed by the all too familiar intrigue the story contained.

She blinked twice, wondering what had startled her, when she felt the vibration – and heard the muffled ring tone – of her cell phone, which had managed to slip beside her while she slept. The device lay nestled beneath the blanket.

Reaching down, feeling her way under the covers, Beverly managed to retrieve the phone. The display announced Jennifer as the caller.

"Hey, Mom. Are you busy?"

"No, Dear. Just relaxing."

"I wanted to remind you about tomorrow night. At Emily's school."

"You think I could forget about my oldest grandchild's Halloween play? I've been looking forward to it for weeks."

"I told you before, Mom. It's not a Halloween play. It's an Autumn Festival."

"Whatever. It's a Halloween play. I'm too old to worry about being Politically Correct at this point in my life."

"Well, whatever you want to call it, Mom, it's tomorrow night at 7:30 in the school auditorium."

"I know. And I'll be there."

"You sure you don't want Tom and me to pick you up? It's really no trouble at all."

"No, Dear. I'll be fine. You know how much I like my independence."

"Then I'll see you tomorrow night."

"Okay, Dear. See you then."

Beverly was about to push the red phone symbol to disconnect the call when she heard an exclamation from her daughter.

"One more thing, Mom. Did I tell you? Joey and Teri are coming as well. And they're bringing the kids."

Beverly beamed with the announcement. "Then I get to see my whole family tomorrow night. I wouldn't miss it for the world."

"See you then."

Chapter Thirty-One:

YOU SEEM MORE PENSIVE THAN normal this afternoon, Aleisha."

She made no reply, uncertain how he expected her to respond to his observation.

"Is there something you want to discuss?"

"Just had a busy week. That's all."

"Then let's start there."

Dr Bargalony leaned slightly forward, as though to reach out to her by bridging the gap between them, but it had the opposite affect, making her feel like withdrawing further. Aleisha still felt intimidated by the man. She had grown more accustomed to his ways. His overbearing manner was just part of his personality, and she realized that now. He had a self-assured attitude that he appeared unable to conceal, as though he knew the answer to everything and whatever he had to say mattered because it was the right way of dealing with things.

She shrugged, still reluctant to fully open up to him. "I guess I'm just gettin' tired of all the runnin' around. I don't see how they expect me ta get better when they keep me so busy all the time."

"So you're feeling an infringement into your life? Like the system is monopolizing your time?"

She had to consider a moment, to make sure she

understood what he was saying. "Yeah. Why don't they just leave me alone?"

"Supposing they did that. Supposing they just told you, okay Aleisha, everything's all right now. You can go home and forget all the obligations we've committed you to. What would you do then?"

"Maybe get some decent sleep for a change, 'stead of gettin' up every morning to catch a bus takin' me to some damn place I don't want ta go to."

He nodded, as though in sympathy with her feelings. "So you could maybe relax more, and alleviate some of the stress you're having to deal with?"

"Yeah. That's it."

"Fine. What else would you do?"

"I don't know." She considered for a moment. "Spend time with my kids, I guess."

"That's admirable. And it's important they have their mother available to them."

She smiled a weak smile, pleased with his acceptance.

He continued. "So coming to these sessions is infringing on your family time. Is that what you're saying?"

"Yeah. You got it."

"But your two older children are both in school now. Isn't that correct?"

"So?"

"So your activities – your counseling, and such – aren't really interfering with your time with them. Because if you were home right now two of your children wouldn't be there anyway."

She pondered a moment, feeling a bit confused with his logic. "I guess not." She was about to say more, to point out to the therapist that she could still be spending more time with Michael if she wasn't so busy, but before she could continue Bargalony was speaking once more.

"So let's presume you're home all day, relaxing by

yourself. The kids are at school. Your husband's at work. You've slept in, you wake up well-refreshed, and you're ready to face the day. What would you be doing?"

"I don't know." Aleisha was starting to feel annoyed. Dr. Bargalony was twisting her words and making something out of them that she hadn't intended. It was like he was trying to trap her into admitting things that weren't true. "What does it matter, anyway?"

He leaned back, crossing his legs as he settled into a more comfortable position. "Let's take a look at what you were doing a year ago, Aleisha. What did you do then to pass the time?"

She shrugged, saying nothing.

"Would you have gone out looking to score some heroin?"

She found herself turning away from him, reluctant to answer.

"I suspect you did that a lot a year ago, didn't you Aleisha?"

"I needed to," she slowly replied, the words barely above a whisper. "I couldn't help it. I needed to get away from things."

"What kinds of things?"

She shrugged. "I felt stuck in that damn house. Didn't have no job so I couldn't get out and do nothing. Two little kids underfoot and Michael on the way. I just felt trapped."

In spite of herself, and even though she fought to control the urge, Aleisha could feel tears beginning to form, the salty liquid welling up in the corners of her eyes before the liquid snaked its way down her cheeks.

For several long moments Bargalony said nothing, as Aleisha's body shook from a series of small convulsive sobs. When at last he spoke his tone was milder, like that of someone seeking to console a close friend.

"Have things changed at home since then, Aleisha?"

She shook her head slowly back and forth, still refusing to make eye contact.

"Then that's not a good environment for you, is it?"

She made no reply.

"Every one of us has stress in their lives. From family. Jobs. Just life in general. Stress is something we all have to deal with. Many choose the same route you took, seeking escape through drugs or alcohol. But that's not an escape, Aleisha. It's a temporary reprieve only, a few minutes or hours of solace that makes you think your life is better. But it's all artificial. It doesn't remove your stress, and it doesn't change your life.

"And it's not going to change until you make the conscious effort to rectify the situation."

The tears, which had continued in a slow but steady progression, were beginning to moderate now as Aleisha brought herself under control. When she spoke next she found the emotions distorting her voice, the tone a whine that seemed out of place with the persona she tried so hard to maintain.

"So what do I do?"

"You learn to cope."

Her face jerked upward, her gaze directed fully toward him. A smattering of the old defiance and anger showed on her face. "How? How do you learn to cope?"

"To begin with, you must start looking at the positive aspects of your life. Quit dwelling on the negative. What did you learn from our group sessions in rehab?"

"That life is a piece of shit. And not just for me. For everyone."

"That's a negative, Aleisha. Let's not dwell on that. What *positive* things did you learn in group?"

She considered for a moment, striving to understand what point he was trying to make but failing to grasp it. She struggled for an answer she thought would appease him. "I guess I saw that I'm not the only one who's got problems? That other people are messed up too?" She voiced the comments as questions, uncertain whether they were valid statements.

"And what makes that a positive point?" Bargalony asked.

She shrugged but failed to reply.

"If nothing else it should convince you that all of us have problems to contend with. Dealing with adversity, confronting situations that make us uncomfortable, is part of human nature. You can't hide away and lament the fact that things are happening to you. You can't expect your issues to resolve themselves and disappear on their own. It doesn't work that way. If it did then I guess I'd be out of a job, wouldn't I?

"Welcome to the human race. You're not alone, Aleisha. But you are unique, and how you handle your situations, how you approach your specific problems and what steps you take toward conflict resolutions, are things that only you can decide. I can't tell you what to do with your life."

He paused, apparently expecting a reply, and when none came he continued. "Consider Linda from our group. How do you think she's adjusting to coping with her issues?"

"She don't seem to be getting no better."

"I'd say that's a good assessment of her condition. And do you know why?"

Again she shrugged.

"Linda feels dejected by those she loves. She feels isolated and cut off from everyone else. And while there's a lot of truth to that, the sad reality is she is the cause of her own isolation. She has a martyr complex, where she wants people feeling sorry for herself. She thrives on the attention. But it does nothing to improve her situation.

"But look at Janelle. She has a support group, a mother and sister who are there to help her. But more than that – and I can't stress enough the importance of this – she embraces the strength and encouragement she receives from them. It helps her to grow, and cope, and adjust to the demands of getting herself better.

"You could learn from that, Aleisha. You have a husband.

And a sister. And three beautiful children. Use these people as a foundation to assist in your growth."

"I'm not sure they want ta help."

"That's a negative, Aleisha, and it doesn't help you to think in that manner. You've informed me how Mark is showing up for family visits with your children. That alone should tell you he hasn't given up on you. And your sister is allowing you to live with her. That wouldn't be happening if she didn't care about you."

"I suppose you're right," she grudgingly admitted.

"And look beyond your family," he continued. "You have a community of people working to assist in your recovery. A case worker looking out for the welfare of you and your family. People caring for your children until such time as you're able to resume your place as their mother.

"And while I know you haven't embraced the idea of attending Drug Court, that should be approached as a positive thing as well."

"How do ya figure that?"

"Because it's another avenue of support for you. It's an opportunity to feel less isolated and be part of a group. It can also be a valuable learning experience.

"Take a look at the other women in attendance. Which ones are succeeding and, perhaps even more important, which ones are failing? Ask yourself what the difference is between the two groups, and attempt to model your behavior on the individuals benefiting from the experience.

"This is your life, Aleisha. We can't live it for you. And we can't provide all the solutions. All of us – from your case worker to the people caring for your children – as well as the judges and magistrates in court – want to see you get better. I want to see you get better.

"But the important question here is, what does Aleisha Turner want? Do you want to get better? Do you want to live a rich and fulfilling life?

"Or are you content with your destructive behavior, serving no benefit to your children and family? Where the best you can hope for is to not end up at the hospital again – or the morgue – before it's all over."

He leaned forward, his penetrating stare making her feel weak and vulnerable.

"The choice is up to you."

Chapter Thirty-Two:

T HERE WERE ONLY A HANDFUL OF CARS in the parking lot when Beverly arrived for the Autumn Festival at Emily's school. She had expected to be early; she was habitually early for everything. But it still surprised her that the rest of her family hadn't shown up yet.

She considered going inside and finding a seat but decided to wait instead for the kids. The evening was a pleasant one. So she sat in her car with the windows open, leafing through a *Good Housekeeping* magazine she had picked up on a whim at the grocery store, and scrutinized every vehicle that arrived to see if she recognized it.

When the familiar blue mini-van pulled in, Joey driving with Teri in the front seat next to him, Beverly took it as a cue to get out of her car. She greeted them as the kids were just climbing out the back.

"Grandma!" Stephanie, still dressed in her soccer uniform, ran over to deliver a hug to Beverly. The third grader made no attempt to disguise her enthusiasm. "It's great to see you."

"It's great to see you too, Dear." She smiled, taking in her granddaughter's young face. She had Joey's eyes, that vibrant blue her son had inherited from his own father.

For a fleeting instant looking at Stephanie brought Russell's face back to her mind. It was a good feeling, knowing her husband lived on in his children and grandchildren, though it brought a pang of grief to her to consider he was gone to her now, and they could no longer enjoy these family activities together.

A few seconds later Andrew approached, arriving at a more sedate pace. "Hi, Grandma."

"I swear, you two look like you've grown since the last time I saw you."

"That was only a week ago," Andrew pointed out, his logical nature coming forth. "We couldn't have grown since then."

"Well, you look bigger to me," Beverly informed them.

"Hello, Mom. How you doing?"

Beverly turned toward her son. "I'm doing good, Joey. How about you?"

"Still running the rat race."

By now his wife had approached, pausing at Joey's side and squeezing his hand. "They've got him working a lot of extra hours right now," Teri announced.

"That's too bad," Beverly replied. "How about you, Dear? Everything going good at CONSOLIDATED?"

"Same as usual. The shop keeps turning out parts and I struggle to keep up with the paperwork." Teri smiled. Ever optimistic, Beverly's daughter-in-law seemed to always take things in stride. Nothing seemed to faze her. "But we get by somehow," she concluded, as the family began moving as a group toward the school entrance.

As they walked Joey looked around, giving the cars in the parking lot a quick perusal. "So where are Jennifer and Tom?"

Beverly shrugged. "Haven't seen them yet. I suppose we should go in and save them a seat."

"Probably a good idea," Teri agreed. "Knowing Jennifer, they'll be running late."

The family moved in to the rapidly filling auditorium. As

it turned out Jennifer and her husband arrived before the start of the show, but just barely. They had no sooner sat down when the lights began to dim and the curtain opened for the start of the performance.

If asked to describe what the production was about Beverly would have been hard-pressed to offer an explanation. There seemed to be no rhyme or reason to the activity on the stage. Rather than a single story-line it was a series of vignettes, with little connection between the parts. No doubt it was intended to showcase the talents of all the children, many of the acts featuring singing or dancing, with an attempt to allow each child their moment in the spotlight.

Emily's part was short, a humorous skit with three other students. It seemed to be well received by the audience. She performed her part with an enthusiasm Beverly could only assume she had inherited from her mother, beaming as she delivered her lines with evident gusto. Part way through she caught sight of the family sitting on the side of the auditorium and managed to flash a tiny wave, unobtrusively performing the motion as though it was part of the routine.

Jennifer leaned over to address her mother. "She's the star of the show, don't you think?"

Beverly naturally had to agree.

The closing scene brought all the sixth graders onto the stage together for a song. Their voices united in a wondrous medley of sound, their enthusiasm evident to the crowd.

Watching all those eager students, the glow in the young eyes and the smiles on the youthful faces, caused Beverly to reassess her daughter's words.

Emily wasn't the star of the show. They were all stars, each and every one of them, shining tokens of what the future held for them. So much potential appeared on that stage; so many possibilities of what lay ahead.

Beverly's mind wandered, considering those possibilities. Maybe some of these children would grow up to become doctors, holding future lives in their hands. Some might become the leaders of tomorrow, shaping the world and making decisions that could change things forever. So much potential.

Another image flashed through Beverly's mind. An image of Aleisha Turner, a strung out addict sitting in a hospital recovery room after a heroin overdose. It was the portrait of a life wasted and ruined because of a horrible drug.

Aleisha had been like these children on the stage, and not very long ago, a young girl with a lifetime of possibilities ahead of her. Maybe her parents had sat in a school auditorium just like this one and watched their daughter perform.

She had been the star of her own world, but somewhere along the line that star had fallen.

Or, what might be equally true, maybe the opportunity to shine had never arrived for Aleisha. Maybe her home life had been so bleak and miserable that her only escape had been the path she had eventually chosen, precipitating a fall into a life of street walking and drugs and bad decisions that had come close to ruining her life.

Beverly couldn't help wondering if it was too late to catch her before she fell any further.

Chapter Thirty-Three:

Laying on the couch, staring up at the ceiling, Aleisha's eyes adjusted to the early morning sun as it penetrated into the tiny apartment. She struggled for a few minutes to stay alert, alternating between sleep and wakefulness, her mind wandering between awareness and slumber. Something had disturbed her rest, but it took a few moments to pinpoint the cause.

Then she heard it again. Voices emanated from the back room, muffled noises that barely made it through the bedroom door, informing Aleisha that Kareen and her boyfriend were awake.

Leroy seldom stayed overnight. Aleisha didn't know where he stayed most of the time. She didn't really know a lot about him; whether he was employed somewhere or merely a drifter, moving from place to place. Sometimes he'd be gone for days at a time. At those times she could see a concern on her sister's face, an unvoiced apprehension that gripped her with a nervousness that increased with each day Leroy was absent. Then he would show up and crash at the place, like it was the most natural thing in the world.

Kareen seemed to accept his comings and goings as a part of their relationship, one she obviously didn't care for but had grown to accept. He would often show up in the middle of the night, like he had last night, and Kareen would welcome him back – at least as far as Aleisha was aware – without a word of explanation passing between them. He would disturb both women as they slept with his pounding on the door until one of them – usually Aleisha – let him in. Then, without a word, he would head back to the bedroom, followed by Kareen, looking for all the world like a lost puppy following a friendly child home.

Aleisha wondered why her sister put up with it. She'd always been so strong-spirited; the independent one of the family. It had taken strength for Kareen to leave home when she did. Even though Aleisha had felt betrayed with the departure, which left her to fend for herself in a house that was anything but nurturing, a part of her had always admired the way Kareen behaved.

When had the change come over her sister?

But, since it was really none of her business, she didn't say anything. No reason to stir up trouble where it didn't belong. She was a guest in the apartment and felt no need to upset the arrangement by bringing up topics better left alone.

She heard footsteps heading into the bathroom. From the light tread she suspected it was Kareen. This was followed by the sound of the shower, a rhythmic cadence that nearly put Aleisha back to sleep, like a soothing reminder of a gentle spring rainfall.

She was still struggling with wakefulness when her sister – fully dressed now and ready to face the day – walked past the couch and into the kitchen, fumbling for a cup from the cupboards with what seemed an unnecessary amount of clutter, and then prepared herself some instant coffee.

"I see you're awake." Kareen spoke the words as she sat down across from Aleisha, perched on the edge of her chair, sipping at the hot beverage.

"Getting there. Where you off ta this early?"

"They got some sorta special going on at the store today." Kareen worked at Devon Mall, in one of those specialty clothing stores with the type of over-priced items Aleisha couldn't imagine people actually purchasing. Even with her employee discount Kareen couldn't afford to shop there. "We need to do a inventory this morning. Before we open. So I got me an early day. How 'bout you? What you got going on?"

"Another therapy session at Riverfront. This afternoon. I just wish this would all end. I'm getting so tired a doing everything some joker down at Children's Services says I gotta do."

"Guess you had your fun. Now you got to pay for it." There was no trace of sympathy in the words as Kareen took another sip of coffee. She glanced at her watch and abruptly stood up. "Gotta go. See you later."

It seemed no sooner had the door closed when a shadow crossed over Aleisha. She hadn't heard Leroy entering the room, his footfalls quiet as he padded across the carpeting. Something in the back of her mind questioned whether this had been intentional on his part. He stood at the end of the couch, blocking the light from the kitchen, looking down at her. He was bare-chested and wore an old pair of gray sweatpants that drooped further below his stomach than they should have. He was a towering figure, particularly from her vantage point reclining on the sofa.

He smiled as he drew nearer.

Aleisha felt instantly aware of their closeness. It wasn't a pleasant feeling, the two of them alone in the cramped space. She pulled her blanket against her chest, feeling no warmth from the action.

"What you up ta, Leroy?"

He continued to grin at her. "You don't remember me, do you?"

The question puzzled her. "What do you mean?"

"I remember you," he continued, as though she hadn't said a word. "Was 'bout a year ago. I was drivin' around, no particular place to go. Feelin' a bit horny." He smiled at the recollection. "I remember seein' you at the side a the road. Thinkin' that there's a fine lookin' woman."

As he spoke he moved closer until he reached her side. He sat down on the edge of the couch, his body forcing her further into the cushions. He leaned up against her, and ran his hand out to feel her leg under the covers, the touch of his fingers cold and harsh against her skin.

"You is one fine lookin' woman, Aleisha. Yes you is."

"What are you doin'?"

"Now don't be gettin' shy on me, girl. I just thought it about time we got together agin'. You can't tell me you forgot how good I was. Last time we was together you was moanin' and groanin' and sayin' I was the best thing you ever had."

"I'm not interested in that no more, Leroy. I don't want none a your money."

He laughed, as though she had made an absurd suggestion. "I ain't 'bout to give you none a it. I figure we practically family now. Don't see no reason I should be payin' for it. It should be comin' to me for free."

She tried to move, to raise herself up from the couch, but his position against her prevented it. She was finding it harder to breath now, his bulk pushing against her.

"This ain't right, Leroy."

"Sure it is. Can't think a nothin' that would be more right. Just you and me. Alone like this. I got me a nice black dick that's just achein' for some a that sweet pussy of yours. You can't tell me you ain't int'rested."

She reached down with her arms and attempted to push off from the couch, striving with all her might to extricate herself from the vulnerable position. She managed to raise herself up, but in doing so only drew closer to Leroy. In his cravings of the moment he took it as a sign of acceptance. With a swift motion he pulled the blanket aside and lifted the flimsy t-shirt she wore, forcing the fabric up and above her head. The collar slipped behind her neck but, with her arms still in the sleeves, it left her more helpless than before.

He pushed her back against the cushions, actually throwing himself on top of her.

She was about to scream when another voice interrupted.

"What the hell's going on here!"

Leroy stepped away from the couch as though propelled. "Hey, babe. It's not what you thinkin'."

Kareen stormed into the room, leaving the front door open in her haste. "Is this what's been going on when I'm not here to watch you two?"

"It's not like that." Leroy's demeanor had changed on the moment, his inflection one of stunned dismay. "Your sister started comin' on ta me. Hell, you know I'm only human. What was I supposed to do?"

"Comin' on to you, my ass," Kareen exclaimed. "You think I ain't been seein' the way you been lookin' at her ever since she moved in?"

"It's not like that. Honest."

Kareen stormed around him, grabbing the jacket he had left on the chair the night before. She threw the garment at him. "Get the hell outa here."

"Now Kareen...."

She lurched toward him. Before he was even aware what was about to happen she delivered a resounding slap across his cheek.

"Just get out. Just get the fuck out. Now!"

He hesitated, as though about to say something, then apparently thought better of it. Without a word he walked out of the apartment.

By now Aleisha had extricated herself from the t-shirt and had her chest covered. As she stood the blanket slipped to the floor at her ankles, exposing her to the cool air blowing in from the still open front door, but she noticed none of it.

"Kareen, I'm sorry. I...."

Her sister held her hands over her ears a moment in a bid for silence. "I don't want to hear about it."

"But Kareen...."

"I just come back for my cellphone. Didn't expect to see my sister and my boyfriend going at it on the couch."

"It wasn't like that."

"I already told you once," she snapped. "I don't want to hear nothin' from you."

Kareen disappeared to the bedroom, her footfalls heavy with anger.

Aleisha fell back onto the couch, still stunned from what had just happened. Looking down at her hands she detected a slight tremor in her fingers. Trying to ignore it only made things worse, and soon she was shaking even more.

Kareen didn't bother to look her way as she arrowed for the front door. Pausing with her hand on the knob she turned toward Aleisha.

"I thought you was trying to change. I thought maybe this time you'd make somethin' of yourself. But you always was a fucking whore. You ain't never gonna change."

She turned to leave.

"I want you outta here. Today. I don't want to see your sorry ass here when I get home from work. Understand?"

She left without waiting for an answer.

Chapter Thirty-Four:

IT WAS CROWDED ON THE CITY BUS, which under normal circumstances would have been bad enough, but hefting a garbage bag of belongings with you didn't make things any easier. Aleisha managed to maneuver down the center aisle – past an elderly gentleman with his cane precariously blocking the aisle, then between two teenage boys, one on each side of the bus, trading occasional jabs at one another as they laughed over some private joke – until she found an empty seat near the rear. She plopped down exhausted on the worn plastic cushion, but whether from physical exertion or mental stress she couldn't have said.

When she reached her stop twenty minutes later it was another hassle to exit the bus, retracing her journey through the gauntlet of crowded seats, and finally she reached the secure footing of the city sidewalks. She held the bag clutched against her chest, clinging to the belongings within. It wasn't much, barely more than she had left Riverfront with such a short time ago, but it was everything she had from Kareen's place. Everything she owned in the world.

At least the bag wasn't too heavy, a fact she was glad of as she walked down the street with the burden, ignoring the occasional glances from the people she passed.

She reached the psychiatric clinic with time to spare. She had, after all, left the apartment much sooner than she had intended.

It had all happened so suddenly, she reflected. The entire episode with Leroy was still a blur to her, a scene that had unfolded too quickly for her to comprehend and was over before she even realized the consequences. Kareen's reaction, following her boyfriend's advances, had made a bad situation even worse, the unexpectedness of her sister's declaration forming an unbelievable accent to the event.

She wondered again if she had done the right thing in leaving without an argument. Maybe she should just go back and talk things over with her sister. Maybe, having had time to cool down, Kareen would be more understanding about the incident, recognizing that it was through no fault of Aleisha's that Leroy had behaved the way he had.

Aleisha realized, however, that she couldn't go back there. In some respects it had been a mistake to even move in with her sister in the first place.

Kareen had been cool, even distant, when Aleisha had first broached the subject of moving in with her. Her time at rehab had been nearing an end, and she needed somewhere to stay, but as she sat in her room and considered the possibilities she came to realize there was no one to turn to.

Going back to Mark was out of the question. Aleisha hoped, someday, to pursue that route, to see if they could recover some of the feelings they had shared at the beginning of their relationship. But for the time being Mark was just another complication in her life. She needed time to sort out what it meant to be on her own; to discover who she really was. She owed it to herself to do that much. Going back to Mark would be returning to a routine that had been detrimental to her from the start.

Some habits just weren't worth repeating.

She considered her friends, the people she associated with

on a regular basis, though when she stopped to consider there was only a handful of possibilities. There were the girls she knew in the neighborhood, and a few she had gone to school with that she still occasionally saw. But Aleisha realized that none of them could provide the kind of stability she needed to get through recovery. They all had issues of their own, lives of drama Aleisha wasn't prepared to adapt to, and she didn't want to be drawn in to their complications.

Other than Kareen she had no family to speak of. She had lost touch with her mother long ago, with an ambivalence regarding her parent's present whereabouts. Whether the woman was even alive or not no longer concerned her. Aleisha had lost any regard for her mother long ago.

Her brother Willy – whom she had always been closest to – had moved to Detroit several years ago, with the notion that he could buy a house for next to nothing, fix it up, then return with some extra money to show for his labors. At least he was trying to make something of himself, and was willing to put some effort into his life.

She hadn't heard anything from him since he left town.

Of her two remaining brothers Aleisha knew nothing; they were no better than strangers to her. Like Aleisha they had left home with no interest in ever returning to the abusive household they had been raised in. They had no desire to retain contact with a family that had never been a unit and consequently had severed all connections with one another.

That left Kareen as her only alternative.

Her sister had initially balked at the suggestion.

"My place is pretty small." Her tone had betrayed an obvious reluctance to warm to the subject. "You wouldn't even have your own room."

"That's okay. I don't take up much space." Aleisha had smiled then, attempting to lighten the moment. "I am a *little* sister, after all."

"And I'm not very close to the bus line," Kareen had pointed out, ignoring Aleisha's attempted humor. "I can drive you once in a while, but with my schedule you won't be able to depend on me. I can't be haulin' your ass all over town for one thing or another."

Aleisha felt a returning anger, a frustration that made her feel like saying the hell with the whole thing. But she realized her options were limited and she needed to swallow her injured pride. She had to fight the urge to lash out against what her sister was saying.

"I don't expect you ta be playin' taxicab for me. And I don't need no baby sitter. I just need me a place ta stay for a while. 'Till I get things sorted."

In the end Aleisha had resorted to the only thing she could think of.

"Please don't ask me ta beg, Kareen. I have no place else ta go."

Kareen had capitulated, agreeing to help out. But looking back at it now Aleisha suspected that her sister had been just waiting for something to happen to use as an excuse to send Aleisha on her way.

Which left her back where she had been after leaving Riverfront; on her own, with nowhere to go and no one to turn to.

"So what are you going to do?"

Aleisha considered Dr. Bargalony's question, though not for the first time. It was all that had been on her mind the entire day.

"I just don't know. I'm tired of not feeling like I belong anywheres. I just want ta get away from it. Escape for a while."

"Are you talking heroin, Aleisha?"

She considered her feelings, and how much she wanted to reveal to him, then slowly nodded her head. "Maybe. I guess. I don't know. It always made things seem so much easier. So I didn't have ta think about things as much."

"But addiction isn't a solution, is it? When you wake up your problems will still be there."

"I know." She buried her face in her hands, rocking back and forth.

"You do realize there are places you can go, don't you? There are a number of homeless shelters available in the city. I could make a few phone calls...."

"No."

The simple exclamation surprised the therapist, causing him to pause in mid-sentence. In truth it startled Aleisha as well, the word coming forth as though of its own initiative, like she had found a hidden reservoir of strength she had known nothing about.

"I'm tired of my life," she exclaimed, realizing as she said it that the words were true. "I want ta change. And I know it's somethin' I got ta do on my own."

"But you're wrong, Aleisha. You don't have to do this yourself. That's what I'm here for. That's what your case worker is here for. There are a lot of understanding people willing to assist you."

"I know." She sniffed back the beginning of a tear. "I guess I just need ta know I can do this. On my own. If not, I may as well go back ta how I was living before.

"And that's not fair. Not for me. Not for my kids. They need their Mama."

"That's the kind of determination a therapist longs to hear. I do believe you can succeed, Aleisha. In the time since we met I've seen you at your worse, but I've also seen how you've grown, overcoming some tremendous difficulties. I have all the confidence in the world in you."

She felt some response was necessary, but could think of nothing but a meek "Thank you."

Chapter Thirty-Five:

J ANELLE BAILEY WAS FINALLY BEGINNING to feel like she had her life back on track.

It hadn't been easy.

The accident that had taken her boyfriend had been devastating to her, disrupting her life in a manner she could have never imagined before the event. She had come to rely on David for so many things; he was her strength, the one she depended upon when things got too difficult. He was her reason for living.

The fire had taken everything from her – clothing, personal items, mementos she had accumulated over the years – but those were just things. Their worth paled in comparison to the true loss she had suffered, a loss that had driven her to the point of desperation and nearly over the edge of a precipice from which there was no returning. She still missed him constantly, and spent the majority of each day thinking of him, but she had finally grown to accept the fact that life would go on without him.

But it would never be the same.

She didn't go out much anymore. Since being released from Riverfront Rehab she had kept to herself. The friends she used to have, in the days when she was obsessed with heroin and it motivated everything in her life, were no longer important to her. She had left them behind with her recovery. Part of her still missed them, and longed for the companionship she had felt in the past, but she knew that was a portion of her life she would never return to. She realized she was still weak and needed to avoid temptation. That's all her former friends represented to her anymore. Temptation.

It was peaceful staying with her mother and teenage sister, though sometimes it was too quiet in the big old house. The family home she was raised in had become as melancholy as she had with the passage of time. Her old room still felt familiar, still brought to mind the dreams and aspirations she had entertained within its walls, but it was no longer the comfortable haven it had been during her younger years.

It was like visiting a family member you hadn't seen for years. You wanted things to remain the way they were, reliving the pleasant memories of the past, but time had marched on, changing everything around you.

Or maybe it was only Janelle who had changed. She certainly had gone through enough in the past few years to warrant a transformation. Perhaps she was merely looking at things from a different perspective, the tribulations of her life having readjusted for her the concept of what that life encompassed.

She pushed the matter aside. She knew she dwelt in the past too much. It was unhealthy, a nonproductive state of mind she worked at intentionally to avoid. And the best way to do so, she had found, was to interact with others.

Edna Mae Bailey was sitting at her computer, puzzling over the crossword puzzle on the monitor, when her daughter entered the room.

"You at it again, Mom?"

"Can't help it. Guess I'm addicted to these things."

"I wish you wouldn't use that word."

Edna Mae turned, the smile leaving her face. "I'm sorry,

Janelle. I didn't mean nothing by it. I spoke out of turn."

"It's my fault, Mom." Janelle was at her mother's side by now, giving her a quick hug. "I shouldn't be so sensitive. But you know addiction is a real thing to me. What I went through...."

"Hush, child. That's all behind you now. We're a family again, and that's what counts. I can't tell you how much it pleases me to see you and your sister spending time together. She needs you in her life right now."

"I don't know about that." Janelle sat down in a flowered-print chair, sinking into the comfort of the plush cushions, facing her mother. "I'm not exactly the best role model for a teenage girl. Considering what I've gone through...."

Edna Mae cut her off, reaching over to grasp her daughter's hands in a tender embrace, her wrinkled fingers stroking her daughter's smooth brown skin. "But that's just it, child. You been through some tough things, so you know what's out there. Theresa don't know nothing about them things yet. She's at that age where she thinks she knows it all. And she thinks nothing ain't ever gonna happen to her. Like she's invincible or something. And even though she seen everything you been through, even though she know how much bad there is out there, she still think nothing like that gonna ever happen to her. She don't know what a cruel place this world of ours can be."

Janelle managed a weak smile. "Oh, to be seventeen again. To have your whole life ahead of you. What I wouldn't give to go back to them years."

"That's foolish talk, child," her mother advised, an edge of harshness in the words. "It's the bad times we face in our lives what make us the people we are. The adversity we rise up to that defines us. If my grandpap had stayed in Alabama all them years ago just think how different things would be now. For all of us. You think it were easy for him, picking up his family like that and heading north when he don't have no idea what's up here and don't know nobody what lives up here?"

It was a story Janelle had heard many times growing up; about the horrible working conditions for her great-grandfather in the cotton fields, and how he finally decided for the sake of his family there was no alternative but to leave the South. It was a part of their family history her mother was proud of and referred to often whenever the opportunity arose.

Edna Mae continued. "So don't be putting yourself down none, Janelle. We all got things in our lives we ain't proud of. What's important is to get past them things and make the most of what's left of your life."

"I know that, Mama. And I try." She offered a returning squeeze to her mother's hands. "And I am glad I got you and Theresa to look after me the way you do."

She intended to say more but the conversation was interrupted by the ringing of the front doorbell. Edna Mae glanced at the clock on the wall. "Landsakes. Who do you suppose that could be?"

Janelle shrugged. "Don't know. I'll go check."

Before she could follow through on her comment another voice chimed in, accompanied by the sound of footsteps in the front hall as Theresa sprinted for the door.

"I got it."

Standing on the front stoop, shivering from the cold night air, a young woman stood, a black garbage bag slumped beside her. She carried a worn, world-weary look to her.

"I'm looking for Janelle Bailey," the stranger announced. "Is she here?"

"What you want her for?" Theresa's words carried a tone of suspicion.

"I...." She stumbled with the words, weary with fatigue. "Can you tell her Aleisha Turner here to see her? She knows who I am."

Before Theresa could respond Janelle approached from behind. "Aleisha? Is that you?" She squeezed past her sister to grab Aleisha by the hand, startled by the frigid feel of the new arrival's fingers. "It's too cold to be standing out there. Come on in."

Janelle escorted Aleisha into the house, practically pulling her through the doorway, while Theresa grabbed the bag the young woman had neglected to carry in. They entered the parlor, a room with a warmth that seemed to embrace Aleisha, bringing instant comfort. By the time she was seated in a plush rocking chair Edna Mae had joined them, pulling herself away from her puzzles for this latest distraction.

"You look so tired," Janelle observed. "Is everything okay?"

Aleisha had struggled all day to be strong. Even while talking to Dr. Bargalony, with whom she now felt comfortable enough to express her feelings, her emotions had been kept in check. She was upset with Kareen for assuming the worst, and not even allowing her the opportunity to explain things, but had managed to control the outrage and anger she felt following the morning's events.

Now, having spent the day aimlessly searching through the city in an attempt to find somewhere to stay, and having finally found a warm place to just sit down for a minute, the full import of her situation overwhelmed her. How unfair everything was. Not just with Kareen, but with her entire life, which had been a struggle for her since before she could remember.

The tears came quickly, as between sobs she recited a brief description of the encounter with Leroy. It never occurred to Aleisha that she was revealing an intimate part of herself in front of a group of total strangers. The desire to unburden was overwhelming to her. She let the words flow.

She felt better having completed the recitation, like just

talking about things had eased the pain.

In silence the three spectators listened, a silence that continued until Aleisha found the strength to stifle her crying at the story's end.

Janelle spoke first. "You don't have to face things alone, Aleisha. We have plenty of room. You're welcome to stay here as long as you need to."

"Are you sure?"

Edna Mae took a cue from her daughter. "Of course, child. Wouldn't be Christian of us to turn you out, now would it? Theresa, take Miss Aleisha up to the spare room. See if she don't need anything."

Aleisha stood. Her legs felt wobbly, like all the strength had departed her. She could think of nothing better than to lay down and rest, drifting off to sleep and forgetting all about her day. A warm bath sounded enticing, but like too much of an effort. Tomorrow was another day.

She followed Theresa out of the room.

Footsteps sounded on the stairs. Once they reached the back of the house Edna Mae faced Janelle. "You sure this is okay?"

"What do you mean?"

"I ain't never heard of this girl before. How do you know her?"

"We met at rehab."

"So she's trouble."

"Mom!" She shot the elder woman a scornful look. "I was in rehab. Does that mean I'm trouble?"

"That's different. I know where you been. What you gone through. Just how much do you know about this girl, anyway?"

"I know she needs our help. Isn't that enough?"

"Lot a people out there need help, child. We can't be there

for all of them."

Janelle gave her mother a hug. "It will be okay. I promise. Aleisha's a good girl. She won't be no trouble at all."

"I hope you're right."

Chapter Thirty-Six:

"SO HOW ARE THE CHILDREN DOING IN school?"

Peggy Kale seemed to hesitate before answering Beverly's question. "They're doing okay. Neither one is a straight A student, of course. But how many kids are?"

Beverly felt a note of concern with the announcement. "Are their grades getting worse?"

"No. I don't think so, anyway. They're both intelligent children. I just don't think they try hard enough. Especially Nataya. She's so quiet all the time."

"I'm sure they're having a hard time dealing with everything. With their mother's problems and all. It can't be easy for them."

"They do seem better after they've seen her," Peggy agreed. "They always come home from visitation in better spirits. I actually think it would do them good to see more of her."

"The second hearing is next week," Beverly remarked. "Things have been looking good. Aleisha's been following her case plan, been attending her therapy and making a good showing in Drug Court. I don't see any reason why she wouldn't be permitted longer visitations."

"Some overnights would be good. It would give me a break from things over here."

"I'm sure the magistrate wouldn't be against that. I just don't know how it would work out, with Aleisha staying at her sister's and all. The place is pretty small."

"I figured she'd be moving back in with her husband by now."

"She hasn't said much about it. Neither has he. I don't think they want to rush into things and make the same mistakes they did before."

"Who's rushing? It's been over five months now. How long's it take them to get their act together?"

Beverly detected a trace of irritation in the woman's voice. "Are there problems with having the children stay here?"

"Of course not. It's just that it's a full time job that adds a strain to my own family. We've been through it before, with other children. I'm sure things will be okay. From the sounds of it the family will be back together in no time."

Beverly left the Kale house and drove over to visit with Michael. Things had pretty much become routine in the case, a circumstance she had noticed during previous CASA assignments as well. The hustle of initial activities – the preliminary investigation, the written court reports, and everything involved with immersing herself into the troubled lives of a shattered family – had slackened by now. Her role as a watchdog had become a wait-and-see one.

There wasn't much more she could do for now.

It was times like this that made Beverly question her role as a CASA volunteer. She felt like she just wasn't doing enough. She wanted to be more involved with the children on a day to day basis. Take them places. Enrich their lives. Be there for them in ways their mother no longer could be.

But these activities were denied her, and for a number of significant reasons.

She couldn't help but become attached to the children she

worked with. This was a fear she had considered when first joining the program. All children were wonderful, in Beverly's eyes, each and every one of them a special joy. How can you work with children, removed from their parents and often living with strangers, without becoming emotionally involved in what they were experiencing?

But she realized the importance of keeping her distance. She knew she couldn't let the children see her as more than an authority figure. The children she worked with had already suffered a lot, through neglect or abuse. Their lives had been torn apart; disrupted by a well-meaning court with only the children's best interests at heart, but torn apart regardless. Family allegiances had been shattered through separation or, as in Aleisha's case, the family members had suffered a long duration apart from one another.

When the case was over Beverly would never see Willard and Nataya and Michael again. Her role in their lives would be complete. It was necessary for her departure to be painless to them, so they wouldn't be losing someone else from their lives. Thus the need to stay detached, even distant, from the children. As hard as that was for Beverly, she knew it was important for the children's sakes.

She pushed the thoughts to the back of her mind as she drove to Mary Bradley's apartment. Arriving there, Beverly was struck again by how difficult it was to remain detached. Over a year old now, Michael had picked up walking easily, though he still relied on help for most of his steps by clinging onto an end table or a chair or whatever was available. As Beverly sat down the toddler made a beeline in her direction, taking two tentative steps on his own before latching on to her leg, tiny fists clutching to the hem of her skirt as he smiled up at her in obvious satisfaction with his accomplishment.

"I can't get over how well he gets around now."

Mary nodded in agreement. "Tell me about it. I don't get any work done around here anymore. Just spend the day chasing after him."

Beverly lifted Michael onto her lap. He seemed heavier than she remember – more plump – which meant he was doing well in his environment. He seemed content to sit on her knee, playing with the scarf she wore around her neck, feeling the texture of the material with his hands. He was still an innocent, Beverly reflected, untainted by the hardships his mother was dealing with.

"And his visits are going well?"

"Yes they are. Aleisha sees all three children at the same time. At Children's Services. Aleisha's always on time and seems to be responding well with all of them. No complications as far as I can see."

"And Mark?"

"Michael's been seeing a lot of his father lately, both here and downtown. Mark seems to be more accepting of his role as a parent. I honestly think Mark wasn't ready for fatherhood when he met Aleisha."

"He is several years younger than her," Beverly observed, referring to the information she had absorbed at the beginning of the case.

"That's right. And, not to put it too bluntly, a lot less experienced. But he seems to be growing into it."

Michael began to squirm, apparently having tired of the scarf, and Beverly sat him down on the floor. He instantly crawled to a box of toys in the corner, rummaging through the contents.

Beverly resumed the conversation. "You realize there's another hearing next week, don't you?"

"Of course."

"I'm sure things will change some after that. Aleisha's been doing great with her case plan. She hasn't had any positive drops, which shows she's staying clean. I expect her to be able to see a lot more of the children."

"That will be great. For all of them." As she spoke Mary moved over to where Michael sat on the floor, helping him retrieve one of his toys that stubbornly refused to be pulled from the box.

"Though I don't know how Aleisha will be able to handle three kids in her sister's apartment," Beverly observed. "Have you seen the place?"

Mary, still occupied with the toddler, answered. "Aleisha's not living at her sister's anymore."

"What?"

Mary turned at the surprised sound of Beverly's voice. "Didn't you know?"

"No. When did this happen?"

"It was just a couple days ago. She probably didn't have a chance to tell you about it yet."

"What happened? Why'd she leave?"

"I don't know. I think Mark knows. He's the one that told me. But he didn't say much. Some kind of trouble between Aleisha and her sister."

"So where's Aleisha staying now?"

"Some friend's house. I don't know the name."

By now Michael was happily banging on a toy xylophone, managing to make a great deal of noise even though he failed to strike any of the keys on the instrument.

Mary stood to face Beverly. "I'm sorry I can't tell you more, but that's all I know."

"That's okay. I'll talk to her at the hearing and find out what's going on."

Chapter Thirty-Seven:

BEVERLY KEPT A CONSTANT WATCH ON the elevator doors, waiting for a glimpse of Aleisha, anxious to find out how the young woman was doing. It concerned her that Aleisha had moved so abruptly from her sister's apartment, especially considering she had failed to provide any prior notice of the change. It made Beverly feel a problem had occurred between the two siblings – some unforeseen issue – one she couldn't help but think could affect the outcome of future proceedings.

The idea had occupied her mind for nearly a week now. She had repeatedly attempted to reach Aleisha but her calls had been sent to a voice mail account that apparently was full. She wasn't even able to leave a message.

Which left her still perplexed concerning what had happened between Aleisha and her sister, and no closer to an explanation.

It wasn't idle curiosity alone that motivated her desire to resolve the issue. If something was going on in Aleisha's life that might ultimately affect the children it was Beverly's responsibility to know about it. The longer a problem festered the more difficult it became to correct.

For a change Beverly wasn't the first person to arrive at a hearing. The participants from Children's Services were already at the Juvenile Center when Beverly reached the scene. She approached Patrick Zimmerly to speak with him concerning Aleisha's living arrangements, assuming he would know the particulars of the situation.

The case worker appeared unfazed when Beverly questioned him. "I know Aleisha isn't staying at Kareen's any more. I have a new address for her," he offered, giving Beverly the information. "She contacted me last week about it."

"Did she tell you why she isn't staying at her sister's?"

"She told me some of it, though I'm guessing not the whole story. Seems there was an incident at Kareen's place."

"Incident?" Beverly's expression betrayed her confusion. "What's that mean?"

Patrick paused to glance around, ascertaining no one was within earshot before continuing. As though they were co-conspirators in a plot Beverly found herself drawing closer.

"Her sister's boyfriend – Leroy Jackson – attacked Aleisha. Apparently she was fighting him off when Kareen walked in the door."

"Is Aleisha okay?"

"A bit shook up. And pretty angry over the whole thing, especially after Kareen kicked her out."

"That doesn't make sense. Why would Aleisha's sister kick her out? From the sounds of it, she didn't do anything wrong."

Patrick offered a noncommittal shrug. "I don't think Kareen was too crazy about having Aleisha move in to begin with. This just gave her an excuse to tell Aleisha she had to leave."

"So what happens now?"

"Aleisha's found someplace to stay, with one of the women she met at rehab, so I guess everything's okay. As long as she continues her therapy, continues to drop negative, and stays out of trouble, she can live wherever she wants."

"But doesn't it concern you? Shouldn't something be done?"

"What can we do? Aleisha doesn't want to press charges. She can't see any sense in stirring things up further."

"But it isn't fair. Aleisha's working so hard to get through this. And then to have something like this happen to her...."

"Hold on, Beverly. I realize how involved you are with this case. I applaud your work and compassion. But you have to understand something. I have a dozen other cases, just like Aleisha's, sitting on my desk. Plus child abuse cases. Juvenile Delinquent cases. You name it, I got it. I can't afford to become emotionally attached to each and every one of them."

"How can you say that? Don't you care?"

"Of course I care. But it's a job. If I didn't look at it that way I'd go crazy. I always try to consider what's in the best interests of my clients, but I can't be a full-time nursemaid to them. Good or bad, they're going to live their own lives. And there's not a whole lot I can do to change that.

"You have to remember as well that transience is often a part of the lifestyle for the people we deal with. There are dozens of reasons why they don't stay in one place for long. Aleisha's experience isn't as unique as you might think. Many of them don't even know what it means to have a permanent residence. They drift from place to place, living wherever is convenient, then move on to somewhere else."

"You can't be all right with that."

"As a permanent solution, no, I'm not all right. If Aleisha expects to have her children returned to her she needs a more stable home life. But for now she's dealing with other issues and still finding her way through things.

"I already have an appointment to visit Aleisha's new residence next Tuesday afternoon. To verify that it's a safe environment for the children. You're welcome to come join me and see for yourself. I've run background checks on everyone living there and everything looks okay, so I'm sure things will work out fine."

The conversation apparently having ended, Patrick walked away to speak to someone else, leaving Beverly more informed but less at ease concerning the situation.

When at last Aleisha appeared Beverly made it a point to intercept her while they were out of hearing distance of the others.

"Good morning, Aleisha."

"Morning, Miss Beverly." The reply was soft-spoken; nearly meek.

"Is everything okay, Aleisha?"

She merely nodded.

"I heard you moved out of Kareen's apartment."

She appeared to nearly blurt something out, then thought better of it. "It just weren't working out. That's all."

"Is it something you want to talk about?"

"No. It's okay. Really. I'm better off outta there."

"I understand your reluctance to talk about things," Beverly continued. "I can't imagine it's easy, having everyone pry into your business. But we are here to help you."

Aleisha flashed a hesitant look. "I thought you was here because of my children? I thought they was your concern?"

"That's true, Aleisha. But you're such an important part of their life. I can't help them if I'm ignoring you. Your recovery is the most important thing in their life right now."

"This ain't got nothing ta do with my recovery," Aleisha responded, the trace of insistence in her tone reminding Beverly of the angry young woman she had first met in rehab. "It's something between me and Kareen."

She walked away without another word, and Beverly silently followed her into the courtroom

*****

"Aleisha Turner." Magistrate Peterson paused after announcing the name. "I've been hearing good reports about you," she finally said.

Aleisha managed a quiet reply. "Thank you, Your Honor."

Her attorney, Lucy Lemly, spoke up. "My client has been compliant on all issues, Your Honor, showing what I feel is exemplary behavior regarding her recovery."

The magistrate reviewed her paperwork a moment longer before replying. "From what I see here that does appear to be the case. Mr. Zimmerly, do you have anything to add regarding Miss Turner's performance?"

"Our only concern now is with the mother's living arrangements. She recently changed where she was staying and has yet to establish a permanent residence."

"Miss Turner? Do you care to comment on this?"

The young woman's attorney provided the reply. "A temporary setback. Miss Turner is still working on procuring permanent residency, but otherwise has followed through on all the particulars of her case plan."

"And you see nothing to be concerned with regarding this issue, Counselor?"

"I do not, Your Honor."

"Very well. But until this matter gets settled all parties need to be aware that the court can go no further regarding reunification."

"Understood."

"Mark Bradley," Magistrate Peterson continued. "I see you have completed your training as set forth in your case plan. Do you have anything to add to this?"

"No, Ma'am."

"Then I would just like to say I commend both of the participants regarding the work they have accomplished so far. It pleases the court to see parents who are so willing to put forth the effort required in these matters.

"However, at this point, I see no reason to change custody regarding any of the children. Willard and Nataya shall remain with the Foster Parents. And while I'm pleased with your progress, Mr Bradley, considering that your wife is still working on her residency issues I see no reason to disrupt things further by relinquishing care of Michael from his present situation. Are there any objections to this?"

Each party present agreed to the decision.

"Is there anything else?"

Lucy Lemly stood. "Your honor. My client would like to increase visitation time with her children. In light of her performance I think this is a reasonable request."

"Agreed. Mr Zimmerly. Any objections?"

"None, your honor."

"Miss Johnson. As CASA for these children do you have any objection to increased visitation?"

Though still concerned regrading Aleisha's move from her sister's apartment, Beverly could in truth voice no reason for denying more family time. Under the circumstances it was the best for everyone. The children were obviously missing their mother, and for Aleisha it meant a return to more normalcy and an opportunity to grow with her children.

"No objections, Your Honor."

"Very well. Visitation will be increased to what is agreeable for all parties."

Beverly left the Juvenile Center pleased with the events of the day, satisfied that the end was drawing near for the case involving Aleisha Turner and her family.

Chapter Thirty-Eight:

"HAPPY TURKEY DAY, MOM!"

Aleisha had no sooner walked in the house than Willard was all over his mother, throwing himself against her in obvious excitement.

He continued, his enthusiasm unabated. "You should see the turkey Aunt Mary brought over. It's as big as Michael."

"It can't be that big."

"It is. Go see."

Aleisha hung her coat on the rack by the door and entered the living room. Mark sat on the couch, watching the football game, Michael sleeping propped up against him. He made no acknowledgment of her arrival, his attention apparently captivated by what was on the television.

Nataya sat on the floor in a corner of the room playing with Miss Jasmine. A stable's worth of plastic horses surrounded her, a menagerie of mismatched sizes and outlandish colors. Nataya took turns with the steeds, giving her doll a ride on each while attempting to make horse sounds to accompany the action. The best she could manage was a garbled gibberish.

Miss Jasmine didn't seem to mind in the least.

"Where's your sister?" Aleisha asked Mark.

"She's in the kitchen."

Aleisha followed the aroma of basting turkey into the

soothing warmth of the kitchen. The tiny room was filled with the moist emanations from the bird in the oven. A large pot of peeled potatoes boiled on the stove, the water so high it threatened to overflow the container. Next to it sat a small pan of simmering okra.

Mary was rummaging through the cupboards when Aleisha entered the room. She paused in the doorway, taking in the scene. "I can't believe you went ta all this trouble."

"No trouble," Mary replied. "Just a little dinner."

"Looks more like a feast. You should a waited for me. I could have helped out."

"I figured you'd want to spend time with the kids." Mary turned from the cupboard with a distracted look. "Don't you guys have a gravy boat?"

"Gravy boat? What the hell you think this is? Some kind a fancy restaurant? We don't got no gravy boat."

Mary returned to the cupboard. "Then I guess a bowl will have to do." She retrieved the article, placing it on the table next to an assortment of serving utensils, and continued with her preparations.

"At least let me help with somethin'," Aleisha pleaded.

"I got it. Really."

Aleisha hesitated, then walked toward Mary, who by this time was poking at the potatoes to check whether they were done or not. Wrapping her arms around Mary, Aleisha delivered a hug.

"What was that for?" Mary asked.

"Ta thank you."

"For what?"

"For everything. For all this. For taking care a Michael when I weren't able ta." She shot a glance into the adjoining room, smiling at the sight of the toddler resting on the couch beside his father, then faced Mary again. "For everything."

"That's what family is for." Mary cleared a space on the

counter as she talked. "So why don't you go in there and spend some time with yours?"

The meal was done, the dirty dishes stacked in the kitchen waiting to be attended to. Mary had slipped away upstairs to take a nap, worn out from all the food preparation. Mark sat once again on the couch, watching yet another football game, but he found his mind wandering.

Today had been something he had never expected. He and Aleisha had lived together for over two years before her overdose disrupted the household. In all that time, with the five of them living under the same roof, it had never felt like a family. The kids were Aleisha's kids, not his. Mark had at times done things with Willard and Nataya, sharing activities with them, but it had always been prompted of necessity, when he grudgingly had to assist them with something. They were strangers to him. Someone else's children. He felt no bond with them, and certainly little responsibility for the two children.

Today had been different. Sitting at the table together, sharing their holiday meal as a family, there had been a closeness between all of them that he had never detected before. It was a sense of belonging he had never anticipated.

He glanced now at Aleisha, sitting on the floor beside Nataya, the two playing together like friends. He had never noticed the similarity between them. Nataya was a miniature replica of her mother. The same curly black hair. The same deep brown eyes. The same enchanting looks that had attracted Mark to Aleisha in the first place.

He found himself staring at them, amazed that he was seeing the similarity for the first time.

Looking up, Aleisha caught sight of his attention toward them. "What you looking at?"

"Nothing."

"You looking at something, all right. Don't tell me you

not looking at anything when you looking at something." Her voice contained a mocking accusatory tone, further accented by the smile on her face.

Mark felt suddenly embarrassed; as though he'd been caught at something he shouldn't have been doing. "I was just thinking how much she looks like you."

Aleisha glanced at her daughter. "She does a bit, don't she?"

Mark nodded.

Aleisha stood and walked over to the couch, sitting down beside him. Her hand reached out to rest on his leg, rubbing up and down against the material of the jeans he wore. A smile graced her face. "Today was nice, wasn't it?" she finally admitted.

"Yes it was."

As they talked Willard approached. He tapped his mother on the knee to catch her attention.

"What you want, Willy?"

"Why do they call this Thanksgiving?"

"Because that's what we're supposed ta do today. Give thanks for what we got."

"What we got to be thankful for?"

"Oh, lots a things. I thankful I got you, and your sister, and your brother. Them's good things, ain't they?"

He nodded. "I just wish we could be together again. All the time. Like before."

"We will be, Willy. Soon." She turned toward Mark. "Won't we, Mark?"

Mark hesitated.

As good as today had been, he didn't know if he was ready for it on a regular basis. He was still young. This family thing made him feel like an old man.

When he had first met Aleisha he was captivated with the excitement of it all; the attractive young woman he had found, filled with a spark that brought a certain zest to his life. They had known each other for months before he even realized she had two children, though at that point they had become so attached to one another that he felt like it didn't matter.

He hadn't realized until recently how much his life had changed by having Aleisha and her children around. Raising children was a full time occupation. He saw that now. It wouldn't be as bad if he was assured of Aleisha's cooperation. Together the two of them could get by.

He wasn't sure if he could handle things if Aleisha turned back to her old ways.

She did seem better, but he couldn't help wondering if she had really changed. She had always been wild. Impulsive. Would the old Aleisha return in the months ahead?

He felt her staring at him, waiting for an answer. "Well, Mark? Won't we be tagether soon?"

He faced Willard, not wanting to look Aleisha in the eye. "There's still things to be worked out. Between me and your mother."

She stood, feeling the approaching anger. "What things?"

"I just don't want to see the same things happening to us that did before. I want to be sure we're both ready for this and that you don't....."

He stopped abruptly, realizing that he had said too much.

"That I don't what?" Aleisha asked, hands placed defiantly on her hips.

"I need to be sure you don't...." He paused again, aware that Willard, and now even Nataya, were watching him, hanging on every word he said. "I don't want to see you get sick again. Like before. When you ended up in the hospital."

"What the hell you mean by that? Ain't you seen how hard I been working? I been going to their damn classes. Listening to that asshole of a doctor. Hell, I been having ta drop my pants and pee in a fucking cup in front of somebody just ta show I ain't been using no more. Don't any of that mean nothing to you?"

Mark was speechless. He had ruined the perfect day. But he had only said what was on his mind. At least he was being honest with her.

Willard broke the silence before his step-father could respond. "Mommy? Are you gonna get sick again?"

She glared at Mark while answering her son. "Hell no I ain't getting sick no more."

She stormed to the front of the house, grabbing her coat from the rack as she opened the door. "I tell you another thing I ain't doing. I ain't staying in this fucking house another minute longer than I have ta."

A moment latter she was gone, the slamming of the door behind her accenting the departure.

Mark was immediately off the couch and heading for the front entrance. Willard started to follow but stopped at sight of the stern look Mark delivered.

"Stay here," he commanded, then followed Aleisha out the door.

She stood on the sidewalk at the edge of the porch, as though uncertain which direction to go. Mark's footsteps sounded across the porch and she whirled to face him.

"'Leisha...." he began.

The rest was interrupted by her reply.

"I don't want to talk to you. Just get back in the damn house and leave me alone!"

He stepped closer, reaching out to her, and received a slap on the wrist for the attempt.

"Don't you touch me. I don't want nothin' ta do with you!"

"I'm sorry. Really. Can't we talk this over?"

"Sounds like you already said ev'rything you wanted to say. That I'm no good and you don't want nothin' ta do with me."

"That's not what I said."

"But that's what you meant. Weren't it?" She approached him, thrusting her face close enough to him that he could feel the exhalations of her breathing against his cheeks.

"I just think you still have some issues to work through, that's all."

"What sorta issues you talkin' about?"

Exasperation showed on his face. "Your anger, for one thing. There's no need to explode over this."

"So what should I do? Thank you for pointing out what an awful mother I am in front a my kids?"

"That's not what I was trying to say."

"It sure as hell sounded like it ta me."

"Don't be that way, 'Leisha."

He reached once again for her, and once again she slapped his hand away, before turning her back on him and walking away.

He nearly said something. He came close to following her down the street.

Instead he turned, shaking his head, and retraced his footsteps across the porch and to the house. Willard stood in the opened doorway, watching his mother as she walked away. Mark stepped around the youngster, refusing to make eye contact.

Mary stood at the top of the inside stairway, looking down at her brother. "Is everything okay, Mark?"

"Yeah."

He plopped down on the couch beside Michael, who was fussing and waving his arms in the air. Nataya looked at him from her corner of the room, eyes wet with tears, then turned around to face the wall.

"Yeah," Mark repeated. "Everything's just great."

Chapter Thirty-Nine:

ALEISHA WANDERED THE STREETS, HER anger keeping her warm. She failed to notice the temperature hovered below freezing as she plodded through the snow. She nearly returned to the house but she wasn't certain what she would say.

Mark had it so easy. His life had barely changed with everything that had gone on. He still lived at the house, residing in familiar surroundings, following the same routines he had before the children had been taken from them. Even that was probably no more than an inconvenience for him. He had always complained he needed time away from the kids and now he had all he could ever want.

Aleisha was the one whose life had been disrupted by everything. On top of all the bullshit she now had to put up with she still had the cravings, the urgings, to escape it all again.

The physical withdrawal seemed to be over now, which was at least one positive in her life. She had suffered through intense pain the first few days in rehab; the muscle aches and shakes and the seemingly constant vomiting that left her weak and tired and barely able to drag herself out of bed each day. To complicate matters, she had even reacted adversely to some of the medication they were treating her with, which made her even more sick.

At least that was all over with, left behind months ago.

But the mental craving was something Aleisha fought each day; the desire to escape from it all. There seemed no end in sight to her frustrations. It would be so easy to turn a trick, pick up a few bucks, and stop in at Pete's for a fix. Then this would be all behind her.

After all, it was her life. Why did it matter to the county and the court and every one else what she did? Why couldn't they just leave her alone?

The buses were running on a reduced schedule, due to the holidays, and she found herself waiting longer than normal at the stop. As she stood waiting she watched the tiny flakes of snow filtering down from the gray sky above. The precipitation seemed minimal, next to nothing really, but with time the snow managed to cover her boots in a mantle of white. When the bus approached she stamped her feet to dislodge the accumulation of snow, then stepped inside to join the handful of riders already within.

She found a seat in back, by herself, and stared unseeing out the window as the snowfall increased in intensity during the long ride.

By the time Aleisha arrived at Janelle's house in the early evening her anger had abated some, though she still felt pretty upset with Mark. Things had been going so well, and then for him to be so completely noncommittal regarding their relationship had really disturbed her. She knew she was working hard to get her life back on track. It bothered her that he didn't appreciate the effort she was putting into things.

Janelle and her family had just finished cleaning up after their dinner and were relaxing in the living room when Aleisha walked in the door. She would have liked nothing better than to be left alone; to just go to her room and lay on the bed and, if necessary, have a good cry over the whole thing. But Edna Mae had insisted she join them.

She could hardly refuse, considering how generous they had been to her the last few weeks.

All three of them were dressed for the holidays. Edna Mae wore a pearl necklace that would have looked ostentatious on anyone else, but somehow it seemed to fit her.

"It belonged to my Grand Mama Angelique," she explained, as her fingers played with the little white beads. "God rest her soul. Poor woman didn't have much in the world but she did manage to leave me this. It was a present from her first husband."

"First husband?" The revelation seemed to surprise Theresa, who managed to look up from her cellphone. "I didn't know Angelique was married more than once."

Theresa, who normally dressed in the type of scruffy attire she seemed to think befitted a teenage girl, had bothered to wear a dress for the Thanksgiving holiday, a simple garment of light tan with short sleeves. She had done something with her hair as well, a braiding technique Aleisha hadn't seen her wearing before, which highlighted her face in a pleasing manner and made her look more mature than usual.

"Angelique didn't talk much 'bout her first marriage," Edna Mae admitted, returning to her story. "After they married Joseph was enlisted. Sent over to Germany. That was in 1944."

The old woman paused, recalling to mind what little she had heard regarding the incident. Silence held the room while the others waited for her to continue.

"Joseph never did make it back. Never found out what happened to him, either. Like so many others, he turned up missing and they figured he were dead."

"That's too bad," Janelle offered in a subdued tone, her mother's words recalling to mind her own lost. David's image flashed for a moment in her mind. It was bad enough to have someone close to you taken from you, but to not even be certain what happened to them must have made the lost even more devastating.

"It's God's will," Edna Mae countered. "Besides, if she hadn't done got married to your Grand Pap none of us would be here now."

The conversation continued between Edna Mae and her daughters while Aleisha looked on in silence, listening to the litany of unfamiliar names and unknown incidents. From time to time they would say something to her, in an attempt to include Aleisha in the conversation. But the vague replies she offered contributed little. Moments later they would resume where they left off, discussing Aunt Margaret or Uncle Tanner or cousin Bethany. The names became a blur after a while, to the point where Aleisha gave up all pretense of trying to follow what they were talking about.

At last Edna Mae pushed her chair back from the table and rose to her feet.

"I think that does me for tonight. I'm feeling plumb tuckered out."

"No wonder," Janelle said. "After all the work you did preparing Thanksgiving dinner."

"It's no work, Child. It's always a pleasure to do things for my daughters. And Miss Aleisha. I'm sorry you couldn't join us. But there's plenty leftovers in the kitchen, so don't be shy 'bout helping yourself if you get hungry."

"Thank you, Ma'am."

Her mother's departure seemed to be what Theresa was waiting for. As soon as Edna Mae left the room the teenager was out of her chair as well. She, too, left the room, saying nothing as she exited.

Janelle turned toward Aleisha. "You were back earlier than I expected today."

"Was earlier than I expected, too."

Janelle detected the trace of irritation in her friend's voice.

"I guess things didn't go too well at dinner, then?"

"Oh, dinner was fine," Aleisha admitted. "It were afterwards when that husband of mine...."

She stopped, wondering if she really wanted to rehash the day's events.

"It might help to talk about it," Janelle prompted.

So before she even knew what was happening Aleisha told everything. By the time she was done she had broken down in tears, her frustration obvious.

Janelle gave her time to get the tears out before saying anything.

"You know, I think all people are selfish," Janelle began. "But I think drug users are the most selfish of all."

"What's that supposed ta mean?"

"Everyone looks out for themselves. It's only natural. We look at life as how it affects us. How we can do the things we want to do. And avoid the things we don't want to do.

"Only drug addicts take it to the extreme. All they can think of is themselves. I know. I've been there. Sure, the heroin gets a hold of you, and after a while you need it. Really need it. But what attracted us in the first place? The selfishness. The desire to escape from whatever problem we have. Or think we have. The need to feel better. The selfish urge to look out for ourselves."

"What's any of this got ta do with me and Mark?"

"I've given this a lot of thought. I know what you're going through, Aleisha. I went through it myself. I had the same self-pitying thoughts you do. Why me? Why do I have to put up with this? Can't everybody see that I'm going through hell here?

"But they don't see it, Aleisha. They're caught up in their own lives. Their own selfish needs. They may feel sorry for you, and try to help, but so much of it you have to do on your own."

She paused, thinking once again of her boyfriend. "I was

lucky. I had David. And he was simply wonderful to me. I couldn't have done it without him. He saw me through my recovery."

"Why can't Mark do that? Why can't he be here for me?"

"Because we're all different. We all handle stress in different ways. I've never met Mark, but from what you've told me I think he does care for you Aleisha. And I'm sure he wants to help.

"Give him time. Don't give up on him, and he won't give up on you. You owe it to yourself to hang in there."

They talked a bit longer, senseless prattle as far as Aleisha was concerned that did nothing to alleviate her problems, and at last Janelle decided to call it a night. She left Aleisha alone in the by now darkened room and headed upstairs.

For several minutes Aleisha sat, thinking of nothing, her mind an empty slate of ideas. She was too tired to think. Too tired to plan ahead. Too tired to even be mad at Mark anymore. All she wanted was to get away from everything.

Detecting a creaking sound, she turned to discover someone standing in the doorway, staring at her.

Theresa walked into the room. "Didn't want to startle you," she explained. "You looked like you was thinking about something."

"Actually," Aleisha corrected, "I'm tryin' *not* ta think of something."

"So did Janelle give you her spiel about how everything's gonna work out great and there ain't nothing to worry about?" Theresa didn't wait for a reply. "I get so tired of her bullshit all the time."

"I think she means well."

"Well, just because my sister screwed up her life don't think I'm gonna let her mess mine up. I got one more year of school then I'm outta here."

Aleisha nearly replied, then paused for a moment. The

words Theresa had used, even the intonation, sounded so familiar to her. They might have been thoughts she herself had voiced not too long ago.

"It don't seem too bad here, Theresa."

"Are you kidding? This place sucks. My mother with her holier-than-thou attitude. Spouting out like she's some kind of Christian and she better than everybody else. Who's she to tell me how to run my life?"

"I'm sure they just looking out for you."

"Well, I'm sick of it. I turn seventeen next month. That means I got one more year to put up with them. Then I'm outta here."

She turned and left the room, heading for the kitchen, and moments later Aleisha could hear the clatter of articles being moved around in the refrigerator as Theresa apparently searched for something to eat.

Aleisha found herself sympathizing with the girl. She could understand Theresa's frustration, and the urge to be out on her own. But she couldn't help but wonder if Theresa had any idea of what the world was really like outside her mother's home.

Chapter Forty:

T HINGS RETURNED MORE TO NORMAL after the Thanksgiving holiday.

Aleisha felt herself growing stronger, more independent all the time. She had finally come to the realization that she was going to make it. The yearnings were still there, the cravings to slide back to the old routines and escape from it all, but as each day passed the urgency of the need decreased. It seemed less important to her now than it had in a long time. Even the thought of her former routines – the bad habits she had adopted to satisfy her need to escape – left her feeling ashamed of herself.

That was another person, she told herself. The old Aleisha Turner. Those things, the mistakes she had made in the past, were all behind her now. They no longer mattered.

The important thing now was to get her children back and return to a life with her husband.

She had thought long and hard about the scene at the house on Thanksgiving. Yes, she had been angry, upset that Mark wouldn't acknowledge the hard work she had done so far. But there was more to it than that. There was also the dread that she and Mark might never get back together again.

She hadn't realized how important he was to her. Through rehab, and the beginning of her recovery, Aleisha's mind had been focused on her own problems. What she was going through. She hadn't considered the children – or her husband – until recently.

Maybe Janelle had been right. Maybe all along she had been just too selfish. There was more to life than being self-centered. There were the people that mattered to you as well.

She would just need to prove to Mark – and to herself – how much she had changed.

The weather moderated, with unseasonably warm weather for the beginning of December. Aleisha had another appointment at Drug Court, but she was no longer bothered with the routine. It still seemed a waste of time to have to sit there and listen to all the other girls and what was happening in their lives, most of them bitching about how hard things were, and that what was expected of them was too much.

But with time Aleisha had grown to see it as a kind of therapy, similar to the group sessions in rehab. It made her aware that she wasn't the only one dealing with the issues she had. Sure, there were some girls that had it easy, the ones that weren't that far into their addictions and seemed to have an easy time pulling away from it.

But there were just as many who, you could tell just by looking at them, would never recover. The ones like Joannie, from her first session at Drug Court, that wound up being taken away because they either wouldn't, or couldn't, change their lives.

Aleisha was determined not to be one of those girls.

It was a relief to leave the Juvenile Center and have that ordeal behind her. Aleisha was done for the day, as regarded her scheduled routine, with no more appointments with doctors or visits to the clinic or any of the other countless activities that seemed to be occupying her days lately.

Normally she would have returned to Janelle's house, but the family had planned an outing for the afternoon, shopping and lunch and just spending time together. They had invited Aleisha to join them but she just wasn't up to it. Plus her afternoon schedule would have forced them to change their plans to accommodate her.

She could have gone to the house anyway. She had a key to the place now, Janelle having finally convinced her mother it would make things easier for Aleisha if she could come and go without disturbing the family. But she didn't really want to sit in the place all by herself.

Her thoughts drifted to Mark.

Aleisha pulled her Obama cellphone from her purse, taking a quick look at the display, and realized her minutes were up for the month. She was hoping to call Mark, but it looked like that was out of the question. She had no idea what time he was working today – his hours varied at the auto parts store – but she decided to take a chance and see if he was home.

The bus arrived as she reached the corner, so at least she didn't have to wait for it, and ten minutes later her trip was over and she was walking the remaining two blocks.

The neighborhood was a mishmash of decorations. Many of the places had Christmas lights on display, with an occasional plastic tree or reindeer standing in the front yard, though a few houses still sported garish ornaments – ghosts and skeletons and spiders and bats – left over from Halloween weekend, their normal rundown appearance seemingly just another part of the decorations.

Turning the corner she approached the house.

Her house.

The house she and Mark and the kids had shared for a year and a half. She hadn't been back since Thanksgiving. She had left angry and she still felt hurt over it. But she wanted to mend things. She needed to move on with her life.

She couldn't help wondering if Mark felt the same way.

Mark's Impala was in the driveway. Parked out front of

the house – looking strangely conspicuous considering the neighborhood – was a blue Corvette, a bright ornament in an otherwise drab street setting. It didn't belong there, she thought, and wondered why anyone would chance bringing it to this neighborhood.

Walking closer, Aleisha saw Mark sitting on the front porch talking to someone she had never met before. Both men wore light jackets, like it was the middle of fall instead of the beginning of December. They didn't notice her until she was almost to the porch, and even then it wasn't Mark but, rather, the other man that saw her first.

He had a cold look to him, with gray eyes that managed to look her over minutely in a moment's glance but, at the same time, betrayed the fact that he considered her an insignificant thing in his world. There was no warmth to him, no sign of a friendly greeting.

"What have we here?" His tone was self-assured, the words delivered with an easy carelessness.

Aleisha was glad when Mark turned and noticed her. "Leisha. I didn't know you were stopping by today."

"It was sort of a whim. Just ta say hi. But if you're busy...."

"No." He stood, started toward her, then seemed suddenly aware that they weren't alone. "This here's Brad. He was just helping me with my car. You know, that trouble I was having with the tie-rod."

"Hi." It was all she could think to say.

Brad stood, appraising her once more, standing in a ramrod straight military posture as though he considered it the proper way to address someone. She almost expected him to bow to her, though if he had it would have been a mock gesture. "So this is Aleisha. I've heard about you."

She scowled in Mark's direction.

"Nothing bad," he assured her. "Really."

"Sure." She gestured toward the Corvette. "Yours?"

"You bet. She's a beauty, don't you think?" Admiration filled his voice. "Done a lot of work on her myself."

"Ain't you afraid to leave your car out here?" She took a look around. "In this neighborhood?"

"Never leave her out of my sight. That's why we're out here, and not in the house."

She was on the porch by now, standing between the two men. A cool breeze blew in from the street, and she shivered slightly as the wind crept against the exposed skin of her face. She turned toward Mark. "Can we go inside? To talk?"

Before he could reply Brad spoke up. "You two go ahead. About time for me to get my ass out of here anyway."

Mark reached behind him, opening the front door, and beckoned Aleisha to enter. "Go on. I'll be right in."

As she walked through the archway into the house Brad called out. "It was nice meeting you, Aleisha."

She made no reply.

Brad watched her until she disappeared in the shadows of the darkened house before turning toward Mark. "That's a nice piece of ass you got there, my friend. I wouldn't mind a taste of that myself."

Mark wasn't sure how to react. He assumed this was Brad's way of giving a compliment, but part of him couldn't help wondering if there was a hidden meaning behind the words. It was as though Brad was insinuating something concerning Aleisha, something Mark didn't want to even consider.

When it came right down to it the two men didn't know each other very well. They had met at the auto parts store, and from their initial meeting there was no denying Brad was knowledgeable about cars. When he offered to help with the Impala Mark had accepted, but once he found himself spending time with Brad he was anxious to get it over with. Something about the guy just rubbed Mark the wrong way. He was so sure

246

of himself and quick to criticize others.

Feeling some reply was necessary Mark searched in his head for something to say. "I thought you had yourself a girlfriend already?"

"Who, Jackie? Nothing serious there. She's good to come home to once in a while but she's a bit too quiet for my taste."

Glancing toward the front door, his mind obviously still focused on Aleisha, Brad continued. "It would be great to have something wild to come home to once in a while."

Then he turned away, headed toward his Corvette.

Mark called out from his position on the porch. "Thanks again for your help."

A feeling of relief struck him as the blue car drove away.

Aleisha was standing in the front room, nervously worrying her lower lip, when Mark finally entered. No lights were on in the house, the only illumination in the room the afternoon sunlight sneaking in through the windows, and Aleisha appeared as an indistinct figure for the few moments it took his eyes to adjust to the dim surroundings. As she came into focus Mark marveled at how attractive she actually was.

Months ago, before everything had fallen apart between them, he had been aware of a change in her, though he hadn't suspected the reason. Or, to be honest, he had refused to admit to himself what the reason could be. She had lost weight, particularly in her face. Her eyes sagged, giving her a doleful, dog-eyed look that wasn't attractive in the least. She cared less and less about her appearance, over time disregarding how her clothes hung on her, or how disheveled they were.

He had ignored the alterations, telling himself that he was making something out of nothing. Even when he did begin to suspect the worse – the nights she was out too late, the days she refused to get out of bed – he ignored the obvious implications of what was going on around him. Instead he had adjusted to the situation, learning to live with the woman Aleisha was turning into.

She looked different now, more like the woman he had first been attracted too, and it pleased him to see her returning to her former self. She had put on some weight, enough to give her a filled-in look, and the color had returned to her skin. She had done up her hair recently. Probably not at a salon, because he doubted she could afford such a treatment, but it was obvious she had prepped herself for the day, braiding her long black hair into a style that made her look younger, more vibrant, than she had for a long time.

"You're looking good, 'Leisha."

Never one to be shy about her attractiveness, she nonetheless turned her head, stifling a blush. "Thanks. I feel good."

"How's everything going? With therapy, and all?"

"Okay. It gets old after a while, but what the hell. It's something I gotta do. But it has made me see things...." She paused, searching for the right words. "I don't know. Different than I done before, I suppose."

"In what way?"

"For starters, I was being unfair ta my kids. They deserved better than they got from their Momma. I see that now."

"They learned to adjust. Guess they had no choice. Just like me."

"I know I wasn't fair ta you, Mark. And I'm sorry."

"No. I should be telling you that. I wasn't very nice to you on Thanksgiving."

"That's okay. Maybe I deserved it. I know I done some bad in my life. I'd say I'd make it up ta you but I'm not sure I can."

"You're not doing drugs again, are you?"

"No. Course not. That's behind me now. I promise."

"I'm glad to hear it."

"It's been over half a year now since I OD'd." As they spoke she had been moving closer to him, bridging the distance between them. By now she was directly in front of him.

"There's something else I ain't done in over half a year."

She was against him now. His arms encircled her, reflexively. Their lips connected as he pulled her closer.

Chapter Forty-One:

ALEISHA HADN'T INTENDED TO SPEND the night with Mark. She really hadn't planned anything when she showed up at his doorstep, other than to keep the lines of communication open between them, in the hopes that they could find a way to work things out.

Apparently the way had been found.

The night had been unlike anything Aleisha had ever experienced before. It recalled to her mind the first time she and Mark had ever made love. He had told her afterwords that it had been the greatest sex he ever had. That she had been so attuned to his needs, and so adept at conforming to his urgings, that he could never imagine a more satisfying experience.

Aleisha remembered none of it.

She had been high on heroin that first night, and while it had apparently heightened her senses, bringing her to new depths of arousal, it had also left her mind a blank when the occasion was completed. All she could do was smile at him, envying him his satisfaction, knowing it was lost to her through a drug induced stupor.

She wasn't always high when they had sex. But on countless occasions she was coming down from the last hit, or anticipating the next fix, to the point where sex was just a series of moves to her, something to occupy her until she found the glorious release she desired through heroin. Mark was like the strangers who paid to enjoy her body for a few minutes. It was something she did – consider it an obligation – and not something she derived pleasure from.

Until last night.

Something had changed last night.

They had somehow anticipated each other, moving together perfectly, with a freedom of feeling that was completely new to Aleisha. It was the first time in her life she had enjoyed the experience of being intimate with a man.

And it made her realize more than ever how important it was to get her life back together.

The morning came too soon, reminding them of obligations they each had. They had showered together, then dressed in silence, each of them absorbed in their own thoughts. When it was time to leave – Mark for his job at the auto parts store, Aleisha planning on heading back to Janelle's – neither wanted the moment to end.

Chapter Forty-Two:

$\mathbb{J}$ANELLE GRABBED ALEISHA BY THE ARM the moment she walked into the house, herding her into the parlor. She kept her voice low, barely a whisper.

"Tell me you didn't do it, Aleisha."

"Do what?"

"My mother's fit to be tied and I don't blame her. My father's wedding band. Her grandma's necklace. I just don't understand why you would do that to us."

"Janelle, I don't know what you're talking about."

"They're gone, Aleisha. Someone took them."

"And you think...." Aleisha paused, realizing the significance of what her friend was saying, stunned with the accusation. "But I didn't...."

"You!"

Edna Mae's voice thundered across the room as she stormed toward Aleisha. "What did you do with my jewelry? Where are my things?"

"I don't know nothing about no jewelry. Honest, Edna Mae. Believe me."

"So you saying my things just got up and walked out of my house on their own? What kind a fool do you take me for."

"I didn't do nothing. I swear I didn't."

Too enraged to even hear the young woman's pleas, Edna

Mae continued. "After all we done for you. We welcomed you into our house. We sheltered you. And this is the thanks we get."

Janelle appealed to her friend. "Please, Aleisha. Just give the things back and nothing else will be said about it. My mother just wants her jewelry returned."

"I don't have it. I didn't take it. You got ta believe me."

Aleisha looked from one to the other of the two women, pleading with them, but no speck of sympathy was displayed on their faces. Her guilt was not even questioned. Her innocence never considered. They had trusted a stranger, reached out to help someone in need, and had been betrayed. Hurt enveloped them.

"Maybe it was somebody else," Aleisha suggested, grasping for some sort of straw to relieve her of the predicament she found herself in. "Maybe somebody broke in while you was gone."

"Don't make things worse, Child," Edna Mae scolded. "I've had Mama's ring in my jewelry box for over twenty years. Harold's wedding band been in there eight years now, ever since I had to say my goodbyes. And I'm supposed to believe someone just happen to break in here right after you move in with us? Right after we give you a key so you can come and go anytime you want? I'm not a dummy, you know."

"But I didn't...."

"Aleisha." Janelle grabbed Aleisha's hand. "If you're having problems we can help. We want to help. But don't be doing this to us. It ain't fair to us."

Another thought occurred to Janelle then, and any trace of sympathy in her voice was replaced with coldness. "Did you sell the stuff for money? For heroin? Is that what you did?"

"No. I been clean. I been staying away from the junk. I wouldn't do that. And I wouldn't take your things. Please Janelle. Edna Mae. You got ta believe me."

Long seconds dragged by, until at last Edna Mae broke the silence.

"You pack your things. Right now. I want you outta here. Understand? And don't you come back."

With that she stormed out of the room.

Aleisha appealed again to Janelle. For a moment she thought a glimmer of sympathy could be detected on the young woman's face. But then Aleisha recognized the look for what it was. She had seen that look before. At Drug Court. At the Free Clinic. In the faces of strangers staring at her.

The look of pity, directed toward someone they felt so far gone that redemption was no longer an option.

Aleisha could do nothing but walk away in silence, head bowed low in defeat. She held no anger; no outrage over the events. All that remained was the accusation from Janelle and her mother and the feeling that somehow she had let them down.

A sick feeling gripped her stomach, along with the realization that no matter how hard she tried she could never get her life back on track.

Chapter Forty-Three:

Once AGAIN ALESHA FOUND HERSELF wandering the streets, aimlessly meandering through familiar neighborhoods in an attempt to make sense of it all.

She barely noticed the buildings she passed. Mickey's Pawn Shop. The First National Bank. Subway. Ernie's 24-Hr Grill. She had seen them all so many times before that Aleisha didn't need to look at them to know they were there. They didn't interest her anyway.

Her mind was somewhere else, lost in private thoughts that, no matter how hard she tried, she failed to be able to make sense of.

She didn't notice the car pulling to the side of the road, nor did she notice as the window slithered down on the passenger's side and a head leaned out the window. A woman's voice called out in her direction.

"Aleisha! Hey Aleisha."

Lifting her head, Aleisha detected a barely recognizable face, a young woman with short black hair and a world weary look to her. The woman in the car beckoned Aleisha to approach with a casual wave of her hand.

"It's me. Veronica."

"Okay." Recognition came slowly. They had seen each other a few months ago, on the first of many days Aleisha had made a drop at the Free Clinic.

The heater must have been blasting in the car. The warmth assaulted Aleisha through the window as Veronica continued. "What you doin' walkin' the streets on a day like this? You gonna freeze your ass off, girl."

"Does it matter?"

Veronica ignored the comment. "Climb in back, girl. Get yourself outta the cold."

Aleisha hesitated, considering her alternatives. She felt tired and listless, uncertain of her actions, aware of nothing but the overpowering desire to be anywhere but where she was. She felt detached, barely aware of her actions, as she opened the back door and climbed in.

It was hot inside the car. The sudden change in temperature from the frigid city streets outside made her suddenly aware of how cold she had been. She shivered and pulled her coat closer.

"You want us to drop you off somewheres?" Veronica asked, once the car was in motion.

"Got nowhere ta go."

"Well that's a bitch, ain't it?" Veronica gestured to the man driving the car. Aleisha had seem him around a few times but didn't know his name. "Me and Eddie are headin' over to Pete's. Want to join us?"

This time she didn't hesitate at all.

"Sure. Sounds like a good idea."

Aleisha lay back, to rest her eyes for a moment. It felt good to be out of the cold and off her feet. The steady hum of the car's engine, combined with the soothing movement of the vehicle, brought a degree of comfort to her. She sighed and rested her head against the car door.

Aleisha felt a hand shaking her shoulder.

"Wake up, sleepy head," Veronica's voice announced. "We're here."

Aleisha shook off her lethargy and stepped out of the car, glancing over the familiar surroundings she had once frequented. It seemed like a lifetime ago since she'd been here, but seeing the place again brought a degree of comfort to her. As though happiness beckoned within.

Pete's place looked much the same as it had the last time she was here. It looked more miserable than she remembered, in worse repair than she recalled, but at least the covering of snow that had fallen recently covered up a multitude of sins. It almost looked peaceful with the blanket of white in the front yard.

Veronica and Eddie, who had as yet not bothered to say a word, stepped onto the porch and to the front door. Aleisha followed, then hesitated at the foot of the steps.

"Ain't you comin' in?" Veronica asked.

"I don't know." Aleisha felt suddenly nervous, recalling what it was like on the other side of the door; remembering the last time she had been here and the consequences following the event.

"Maybe this ain't such a good idea."

Veronica shrugged, dismissing Aleisha's hesitation. "Suit yourself. If you want to sit out here and freeze that pretty little ass of yours off then go ahead. Me, I'm headin' in where it's warm."

The two of them disappeared into the house, leaving the door open behind them.

A moment later Aleisha followed them inside.

Chapter Forty-Four:

PATRICK ZIMMERLY SPENT THE MAJORITY
of each day out of the office. It was an occupational hazard for
him. After visiting client sites, appearing at court dates or
meetings, or any one of a number of activities that needed the
attention of a busy case worker, he had little time remaining for
office work. He had just completed a court appearance and had
stopped in to check if he had missed any messages. As he was
reaching for the phone it buzzed, announcing an incoming call.

"Patrick Zimmerly here."

"Hello. This is Mark Bradley."

"Hello Mark. Everything okay?"

Patrick detected a slight pause before the voice continued.
"I don't know." The words came slow, the trace of concern
obvious. "Have you been in touch with 'Leisha?"

"Not for a few days. What's going on?"

"She was here yesterday. Everything was looking good.
Real good. We spent some time together. When I left for work
she took off as well. Guess she had an appointment or
something. But since she left...."

He paused in mid-sentence, as though to collect his
thoughts. "I haven't heard from her since."

"And this was yesterday?"

"Yeah. In the morning. That's when I saw her last. I was

expecting to hear from her last night, but nothing. So I waited until this morning, figuring she'd get hold of me. But I haven't heard anything."

"I know she's been staying with some friends. Janelle Bailey. Do you have the number?"

"I tried there a couple times but couldn't get hold of anyone."

"Did you call Kareen's?"

"No. I'm sure she wouldn't be there. Not after...." There was another pause while Patrick waited for Mark to continue. "She's not there. Believe me."

"Don't get yourself worked up, Mark. I'll check around. Make a few calls. I'll get back to you later this afternoon."

There was no answer on Aleisha's cellphone, which hardly surprised Patrick. She had one of those pay-as-you-go phones and generally could be counted on to run out of minutes long before she had the necessary funds to replenish the allotted time.

This was another of the many frustrations of the job, Patrick mused. Transient people were difficult to get hold of. Even when they did have a moderately permanent place to live they often couldn't afford the price of a telephone. There were agencies that offered assistance, and many people relied on the help. But just as many more simply did without what a lot of suburban families would consider the basic necessities of life.

Regardless of what Mark had said Patrick decided to call Aleisha's sister. It seemed the logical place to start.

Kareen answered her phone on the first ring.

"Hello."

"Am I speaking to Kareen Turner?"

She paused, a note of suspicion entering her voice. "Who is this?"

"This is Patrick Zimmerly from Children's Services. I'm Aleisha's case worker."

"I know who you are." Her tone had become cold once he identified who he was. "I just don't know why you're bothering me."

"I'm just trying to determine Aleisha's whereabouts."

"She ain't here. I ain't seen Aleisha since I threw her sorry ass out of here."

"Then you don't know where I could get hold of her?"

"Don't know and don't care. I'm tired of pickin' up after Aleisha. It's about time she took care of herself ."

Patrick went over his case notes, finding the information regarding the home review for Edna Mae Bailey. Everything had come through okay on the background checks. The only item of concern was regarding Janelle Bailey, who, like Aleisha Turner, had been investigated by Lucas County because of heroin addiction. There had been no children involved, but Social Services had been called in when Janelle wound up at Toledo Hospital from an overdose.

Not having been involved with the case, Patrick was ignorant concerning the particulars. He had delved deeper into it, contacting the case worker who had worked with Janelle. There didn't seem to be cause for alarm regarding the young woman, who seemed to have made a positive adjustment in her life. Consequently Patrick had approved the locale for a safe place for Aleisha to meet with her children.

The phone was answered on the second ring.

"Hello."

"Hello. This is Patrick Zimmerly. From Lucas County Children's Services. Who am I speaking with?"

"This is Janelle Bailey."

"Hello, Janelle. I'm calling about Aleisha Turner. I don't know if you remember me, but I was out a few weeks ago for a home check...."

"I remember you, Mr. Zimmerly."

"Good. I'm trying to get hold of Aleisha. Is she there?"

"No she isn't."

"Do you know when she'll be back? I need to get hold of her."

"Aleisha doesn't live here anymore, Mr. Zimmerly."

"I see. Do you know where she's staying now?"

"No I don't."

"Well, if you should hear from her, please tell her to get hold of me."

"I'll do that."

"Thank you Janelle."

He had nearly hung up when he heard the voice on the other end resume. Until then the voice had been distant and uncaring, conducted in a businesslike tone. For the first time he noted an expression denoting concern.

"Is everything okay?"

"Excuse me, Janelle. I didn't quite catch that."

"With Aleisha. Is everything okay? Is she all right?"

"Everything's fine," he lied, wondering just what was going on with his client. "Thank you for your time."

Chapter Forty-Five:

$\mathbb{T}$HE TINY BELL ABOVE THE DOOR OF Mickey's Pawn Shop made a delicate tinkling sound as the young woman walked in the store. With her came a blast of cold air from outside. The man at the counter shivered, wrapping his sweater tighter, as she approached where he stood.

"May I help you?"

"I have some jewelry that was handed down to me. From my Aunt. I was wondering if it's worth anything."

She placed the items on the counter. A man's gold wedding band. A pearl necklace. Several opal rings. An assortment of gold and silver earrings.

He took a quick look, pushing his glasses back on to the bridge of his nose, before replying. "We're not here to do appraisals, Miss. Maybe you should take these to a jewelry store."

He pushed the items back to her side of the counter but she made no attempt to pick them up.

"How much...?" She coughed, to clear her throat. "How much are they worth to you?"

"Are you interested in a loan, ma'am? Using this as collateral?"

She nodded, not saying a word.

He took a minute to look her over before replying. A young, attractive, black girl walks in with a handful of jewelry, it has to make you wonder. He knew there was a story behind all this. He suspected there was no Aunt that had handed these down to the girl.

But he also knew he wasn't paid enough by the store he worked at to worry about such incidentals as proper ownership of the items people walked in with. That was the boss's problem, not his.

"Let me check."

He turned behind him and began punching numbers into a computer, searching online for similar items. As he did so he noted the young woman's reflection in the screen. Fidgeting, casting occasional glances about, she seemed uncomfortable in her surroundings. He could only imagine why.

"Will this take long?" she asked, her anxiety obvious.

"You want to get your money's worth, don't you?"

"Sure."

So she waited, pacing the small space at the front of the store and glancing casually at the merchandise on display, as he delved deeper into the research.

At last he found what he was searching for, and he began jotting numbers down on a piece of paper. He returned to the counter, adding the figures together, then announced his decision.

"I can give you $35.00 for the lot."

She looked heartbroken. "I was hoping for more."

He suspected she wasn't in any kind of position to argue with him. "Take it or leave it. $35.00. That's the offer."

She considered a moment, then pushed the articles further to his side of the counter. "I'll take it. Can I get cash for that?"

He smiled. "We always deal in cash."

It didn't take long to finish the transaction. She had to provide a name and address, but he opted to save her further humiliation by not asking for identification. He barely looked at the name she entered in the ledger, assuming it was a false one. Unlocking a glass display case he placed the jewelry within, being certain to lock the case behind him. His fingers flashed on the cash register, the drawer slid open, and he removed the money.

Saying nothing, she thanked him with a nod. He watched as she left the Pawn Shop and walked away down the sidewalk out front.

She felt guilty about the whole thing. There was no denying it. It didn't seem right taking the stuff from the old lady. But it wasn't like she was going to do anything with it, other than have it take up space in her jewelry box. Why not make some money on it and put it to good use?

Besides, the timing was right. If she had waited much longer the opportunity to sneak into her room and grab the stuff might have been gone.

It hadn't been easy. Her stomach had reacted like it was trying to turn itself inside out while she waited for her chance. Many nights she had laid in bed, listening to the sounds of the voices downstairs, wondering if now was the time to make her move. And many nights she had resisted the urge, fearful of being caught, aware of the change that would come over the house if they knew what she was planning.

When she had finally crept into the room, conscious of every sound she made, she feared any moment someone would walk in on her and catch her in the act.

Even after it was done she had waited a couple of days to visit the pawn shop, afraid to be seen with what she had taken.

She finally decided she had waited long enough. She needed the money. Or, rather, she needed the fix the money would bring her. And she knew just where to get it.

Moving down the empty sidewalk, a few flakes of snow swirling from the pavement as she walked past, she paused outside a convenience store, peeking in through the metal-slatted windows. The few people within making late night purchases never noticed the young black girl staring in the window. Why should they? Like her, they were involved with their own lives.

Withdrawing the cash from her pocket she counted it once again, just to be sure. Thirty-five dollars. It was enough. She would have liked more, but it was enough.

Theresa Bailey crammed the money back into her pocket, satisfied that everything had worked out fine. She never bothered to think of Aleisha Turner, or the fact that Aleisha had taken the blame for her actions.

The only thing on her mind now was where to score her next hit.

Chapter Forty-Six:

HE FAMILY WAS GATHERED AROUND the Christmas tree, the presents spread out beneath the bottom branches, the display twinkling from the white lights adorning the holiday totem. Music played softly in the background, the Christmas songs Russell had always enjoyed so much and subjected the family to each year. It still seemed wrong that he wasn't with them to share in the happiness.

But he was with them, Beverly reminded herself. He was with them always. In every one of her thoughts. In every place she traveled. Russell was there.

"Merry Christmas, Grandma."

Beverly turned as Stephanie approached, opening her arms wide to accept her granddaughter's hug. "Merry Christmas to you, Dear."

Andrew, always the logical one, spoke up from the doorway. "It's not Christmas yet. We still have another week to go."

His mother shot him one of those looks parents seem to be born with, the kind that broaches no argument. "Andrew. We already discussed this," Teri pointed out. "Uncle Tom and Aunt Jennifer will be out of town next weekend, that's why we're all getting together a week early. Right?"

"Yes, Mom."

"Now go give your grandmother a hug."

The duty performed, the family gathered together. Beverly took the seat in the corner of the couch, from force of habit, while Teri sat beside her. Joey joined his kids on the floor.

"We can pull some chairs in from the kitchen," Beverly pointed out.

"I'm okay, Mom. Really. This kind of reminds me of Christmas time when I was little, all of us sitting on the floor together, watching Dad put together some monstrosity you guys decided we needed to have. One that always came with those three little words on the side of the box."

Beverly and Teri joined him as all three recited the words. "Some Assembly Required."

"Every year it was the same thing," Joey continued. "Dad would spend all day putting something together for us. Some Lego spaceship with a gazillion parts. Or a dinosaur that transformed into a spaceship or something equally ridiculous."

"And by the end of the day," his mother put in, continuing with the story, "it was in so many pieces that there was no way it could ever be salvaged."

"I don't know what you and Dad were thinking of."

"We never did learn, did we?"

"The Legos must have been for Joe," Teri observed. "I imagine Jennifer's gifts weren't as hard to handle."

"Are you kidding?" her husband remarked. "You should have seen all the Barbies that girl had. And the accessories. She could never get enough of them."

A voice called out from the front of the house. "I still can't get enough accessories." Jennifer entered, followed by Emily, who immediately sat down by her cousins.

"Where's Tom?" Beverly asked.

"He'll be right in. Just getting some things from the car."

As if to prove the point her husband walked in with an armful of presents. "HO-HO-HO!"

"Oh, Dad!" Emily looked away, embarrassed by her father's behavior.

"It's Christmas," he pointed out. "We're supposed to be jolly. There's nothing to be unhappy about, is there?"

"I guess," Emily grudgingly acknowledged.

Beverly, glancing over at Teri, noticed an abrupt expression of grief cross her daughter-in-law's face. She held out her hand, touching Teri lightly on the arm. "Are you okay, Dear?"

"Yeah. I suppose."

Her husband spoke up in her defense. "She's just had a hard time. With the accident last week and all."

Jennifer grasped for this latest morsel of gossip. "What accident?"

"At the shop where I work," Teri explained. "There was a mishap in the foundry. Sent two people to the Emergency Room."

"That's awful," Jennifer put in. "Are they okay?"

"One of them is. The other one...." She paused, the others hanging on to what she had to say. "He's still alive, that's the main thing. I guess we can be grateful for that."

Again silence prevailed, even the children aware of the import of Teri's words. And, even more disturbing, what she hadn't said.

Beverly, still rubbing her daughter-in-law's arm, was first to recover. "Don't go there, Teri. Don't dwell on the bad things that happen. If you saw some of the things I've seen, some of the children I've had to represent, you'd wonder how any of them get by. But it's incredible how resilient people can be. How they can recover and turn their lives around. I've seen some wonderful success stories working for CASA. It's what gets me through the hard times, knowing there are better times ahead."

"I still don't know how you do it, Mom," Jennifer observed.

"Because I believe every child out there deserves to have the type of Christmas you and your brother had growing up, with happy family gatherings like this. And if I can help to make that happen then I've done a good job."

"Good for you, Beverly," Tom put in. "But isn't it about time we started doing some celebrating here instead of just talking?"

Beverly smiled. "Of course. So are you kids ready to start opening some presents?"

The answer was a resounding affirmative.

Eventually all the presents were opened, and while the kids enjoyed their gifts the adults visited and snacked on the homemade cookies Beverly still insisted on making each year. While stepping into the kitchen for another tray of goodies Beverly heard the buzzing of her cellphone. She nearly ignored it. All her family was here, so who could possibly be calling at this time of night?

Still, it could be important. It would only take a moment to answer.

Patrick Zimmerly's name came up on the caller ID.

"This is Beverly."

"I hate to bother you, Beverly. I hope I'm not disturbing anything."

Beverly glanced at the family in the other room, the kids visible through the doorway as they played on the floor, the sounds of the adults talking wafting out to her. "No problem. What is it?"

"Have you spoken to Aleisha Turner lately?"

"No." Her senses were immediately on the alert. "Is there a problem?"

"Could be. Her husband called earlier. Hasn't heard from her for a few days."

"Should I be concerned?"

"Not yet. Just let me know if you hear anything about her. Okay?"

"Sure. I'll do that."

Preoccupied with this latest morsel of information, Beverly nearly forgot her reason for going to the kitchen. As her mind wandered she prepared a tray of cookies – peanut butters, gingerbread, and the Russian tea cakes Russell had never cared for and affectionately termed saw-dust cookies – and took them back in to her family.

Teri was the first to notice the distracted look on Beverly's face.

"Everything okay, Mom?"

"Yes. Everything's fine."

"Were you talking to someone on the phone just now?"

"Some CASA business. Nothing important."

She set the cookies down and resumed her position on the couch. And though she tried to enjoy the rest of the evening with her family she found her mind wandering, drifting to thoughts of another family.

What would Christmas be like for Willard and Nataya and Michael? What gifts would Santa be bringing them? Certainly not the abundance her grandchildren were enjoying.

But her greatest concern, rising above all others, had been sparked by the phone call a few minutes ago.

Where was Aleisha?

Chapter Forty-Seven:

IT WAS QUIET IN THE HOUSE, FILLING THE rooms with an oppressive stillness. Somewhere a clock ticked, a rhythmic pattern that under normal circumstances would have gone unnoticed. But not tonight. Tonight it was an ominous chiming that intruded on the silence.

Janelle tried to ignore the sound, attempting to block it from her thoughts, but found herself struggling with the deed. Like the anonymous narrator from the Edgar Allan Poe story, the more she fought to ignore the ticking of the clock the more intrusive it became, until – like the beating organ in "The Tell-Tale Heart" – the sound overpowered everything else.

Poe's storyteller had been guilty of murder. Janelle – though her crime was considerably less – was guilty as well. Guilty of betraying her family. Her misguided sense of compassion and decency had allowed someone to enter their midst, an unknown entity she knew nothing about, who had deceived them all by taking advantage of the family's goodness.

Janelle was no stranger to the actions of a drug addict in need. She too had betrayed the people she knew and loved while under the thrall of heroin. She had felt its influence, its power to convert an otherwise normal person into a lying, cheating wretch of a being, where rules of decency were abandoned in the quest for fulfillment of their longing. Family ties meant nothing, friendships were forgotten, to the junkie determined to obtain that next hit.

Yes, Janelle knew only too well the characteristics of the addict, having lived with them herself.

But she hadn't detected them in Aleisha Turner. The young woman seemed so sincere in her attempt to leave that life behind her. When Aleisha spoke of her family, as she did often when the two women were together, Janelle had marveled at the intensity of the young mother's feelings. Determination seemed to motivate her actions; the determination to redeem herself and restore her marriage, reuniting the family that had been torn apart through her recklessness.

Obviously Aleisha had fooled Janelle.

Maybe Aleisha had even fooled herself into believing that she could change.

Janelle sighed in exasperation. Once an addict, she pondered, always an addict. She knew that to be true from personal experience. She knew the longing would be with her always, the desire to escape to the false sense of contentment that beckoned from heroin's embrace. It took all her strength, all her fortitude, and all her family's support and caring, to stay clean.

Apparently Aleisha hadn't been strong enough.

The front door opened, worn hinges squealing slightly in protest. Footsteps sounded from behind her. Turning, Janelle watched Theresa crossing the hallway.

Sniffing loudly as she entered, as though battling a monster head cold, her sister's stride was unsteady, her movements sluggish. Janelle attributed it to the lateness of the night. Theresa approached the steps leading upstairs, unaware of her sister's presence.

Janelle forced aside her concerns for Aleisha, attempting a light-hearted tone with her words. "Where you been, Theresa?"

Theresa paused a moment. She said nothing, as though uncertain of what was expected, or even aware that a response was necessary, sniffling once again as she proceeded to move forward. Lifting her foot to mount the stairway she apparently misjudged the location of the step. Losing her balance, she nearly stumbled, managing to prevent falling only when she grabbed the banister. The motion seemed exhausting to her. She took a deep breath, as though gasping for air, the act followed by repeated sniffling.

Janelle, suddenly alarmed, rose from her seat.

"Theresa! Are you okay?"

By the time Janelle reached her sister's side Theresa had slumped to the floor. Light bathed the scene as Janelle threw the switch on the wall. Bending down, she cupped Theresa's chin in her hand, forcing her head back to more clearly examine the face.

Theresa's nose was red and raw. Moisture dribbled from her nostrils. Her eyes held a glazed look of confusion, a lack of understanding Janelle had seen in the past. Countless times the expression had stared back at her from the mirror after snorting the white powder that had ruled her world several years ago.

"What did you do?" Janelle's tone betrayed her anger at the situation, while masking her sorrow at finding her sister in this condition. There was no denying what was going on.

Then another thought occurred to her, a revelation that explained so many things. Janelle's hand flew to her face, covering for a moment the exclamation that sought to escape her lips.

"It was you! You stole Mom's jewelry." She voiced it, not as a question, but rather as a statement of fact, her dawning awareness attesting to the reality of the situation. "You sold Mom's stuff to get money. So you could buy drugs. How could you do such a stupid thing?"

Theresa made no reply, her face a mask of blurred thoughts and incomprehension.

Another voice intruded, calling from an upstairs room.

"Is everything okay down there?"

"Yes, Mom," Janelle lied, not wanting to involve her mother in what was happening. "Everything's fine."

Janelle slumped to the floor beside her sister, throwing an arm around Theresa and drawing her closer. For a moment she felt better, offering what little comfort she could to the young woman.

Then a picture flashed through her mind, the image of another young woman walking away from their house, the sorrow and dejection on her body all too obvious now that Janelle knew the truth.

"What have I done?" The whispered words barely disturbed the scene. It was doubtful Janelle even realized she had spoken out loud.

She started to cry, hanging her head.

"Aleisha, can you ever forgive me?"

With the awareness of Theresa's guilt came the determination to set things right. Janelle started to stand up, intending to get her cellphone and try calling Aleisha. As she rose Theresa slumped forward, as though her body had lost control of itself. Her breathing was shallow, a slow rhythm that barely seemed sufficient to draw air into the lungs.

Janelle realized her sister was in a vulnerable position. She couldn't leave her side. Not now. Theresa needed her, like she had needed David during her bad times. She would worry about Aleisha another time. There would be plenty of opportunity to take care of that problem later.

Chapter Forty-Eight:

HE INSTANT THE HEROIN HIT HER bloodstream the drug's potency overwhelmed her. Aleisha felt the warmth enveloping her arms and legs and shoulders, her breasts and genitals, the sublime sensation delivering the euphoric high her body had been denied for so long. At that moment she felt impervious to all outer stimuli, her inner being providing everything she could ever require. Everything she had ever needed. There was no warmth and no coldness. No light and no dark. Time and distance and space were meaningless entities, obliterated along with everything else.

All pain was forgotten, all stress erased, as the drug performed its potent magic on her, releasing her full potential and delivering her to a place of pure tranquility.

She was no longer Aleisha Turner, troubled girl of the cruel city streets. Instead she was the radiant queen of all earthly paradise.

She no longer sat in a squalid rat-infested house, where Veronica and Eddie grappled naked in the corner in the throes of their togetherness and Pete slumped in a chair, his corpulent body glistening with sweat and smelling of raw animal musk. She was a goddess in a castle of light and wonder.

No longer was she encumbered with the base demands of mere mortals. She could go anywhere. She could do anything.

She was unstoppable.

Nothing could contain her. She was meant to be free, to revel in the glory that was her being.

With no awareness of her actions she rose to her feet, her limbs apparently moving of their own accord as her mind concentrated on the mysteries of the universe and ignored everything else, her body leaving the others behind in the ramshackle house.

The winter air rippled over the ebony surface of her skin as she walked outside, her body feeling no sensation of coldness, no awareness of the dark. Yet, conversely, she was cognizant of each soft petal of snow as it touched her, marveling with every sensation the exposed beauty of the flakes. As she wandered down the street her bare feet left delicate tracks in the freshly fallen snow, like the passage of a mythical fairy from some long forgotten universe. Crystals of ice formed between her toes and against her bare fingers but she continued forward, blissfully unaware of the sensation.

She was free now. Free of stress. Free of heartache. Free from pain and humiliation and the depressing realities of life. Free to explore the night in her euphoric high.

Minutes only had passed since her blood had accepted the heroin, but already the incredible high was waning, the heightened sensations nearly forgotten. She felt a lethargy overtake her, a peaceful feeling of bliss. She wanted nothing more than to lay down and enjoy this newest pleasure.

Armand Stravichio had driven a taxi for years. The hours were often long, with the pay barely adequate, but at least it was an honest way to make a living. Many were the times he worked late into the night, trolling the streets as he observed the pedestrians making their way down the sidewalks. Armand kept a vigilant eye open for customers, hoping for that final fare before returning home to his wife and children and a few hours sleep before he woke up to begin the cycle once more.

As his gaze drifted from side to side, ignoring the harsh glare from the streetlights he passed under, he failed to detect the shapeless form slumped in the middle of the street ahead. Even as he pulled closer, and his headlights illuminated the delicate arm reaching for the heavens, he didn't realize what was in front of him.

His first inclination of something amiss was the jolt as his tires drove over the body laying on the cold pavement.

At 11:43 PM Edgar Newton, Lucas County Coroner, stepped out of his car and walked over to a still form laying on the street. Snow had drifted already against the body. The white flakes stood out in harsh contrast to the woman's skin, though the temperature of the flesh matched the snow for coldness. A handful of uniformed policemen and plain-clothed detectives surrounded the figure.

The onlookers parted at Newton's approach, allowing him access to the body. A cursory glance told him more than enough.

Black female.

Mid-twenties.

Dead at the scene.

There was nothing left to do but shove the remains in a black bag and haul it back to the morgue.

Chapter Forty-Nine:

NATAYA WAS NO LONGER AFRAID OF stepping through the metal detector at the entrance to the Juvenile Center. Weeks of visits had helped her to overcome her initial fears of the contraption. The excitement of knowing her mother waited upstairs for them also assisted in the process, a cause and effect pattern the little girl had been quick to perceive. Enthusiasm showed on her face at the thought of the encounter awaiting them.

The mood of her brother was different. Willard felt apprehensive. It was a word he wouldn't have understood the meaning of, but it was a sensation that had gripped him just the same ever since leaving the foster home. The feeling had started the moment the case worker arrived that afternoon to pick them up.

With a subdued voice Mrs Kale had instructed the children to wait in their room while she talked with Patrick. The two adults had kept their voices low, speaking in hushed tones so the children wouldn't overhear. By the time Willard and Nataya were summoned to the front of the house a change had come over Mrs. Kale. She seemed more quiet than normal, saying nothing as she helped Nataya with her coat and watched as the children slipped their boots on. Perhaps what was even more surprising was the hug she gave each child before they left the house, a show of affection contrary to her normal behavior.

Patrick was quiet on the drive to the Juvenile Center, not even asking them how things were going at home or if anything new was happening at school. Even the questions Nataya asked, the nonsensical queries she normally came up with concerning doll clothes or cartoons or other things she considered important, were answered with curt replies, as though the man's thoughts were somewhere other than with them.

His sister didn't seem to notice, but to Willard all the signs indicated this wasn't going to be a normal day for the children.

Approaching the glassed-in visiting room on the third-floor Willard spotted Mark pacing the floor, his step-father's face expressionless, his head hung low. Willard turned toward Patrick Zimmerly as his sister ran eagerly toward the visiting room.

"What's going on?" he asked the case worker, his voice quivering with nervousness.

"I think you need to talk to Mark about that."

Willard still hesitated. Inside Mark was already hugging Nataya, enveloping the girl in his arms and holding her close. As Willard walked in Mark lifted his face. Moisture was evident in his eyes.

"Where's Mom?" Willard asked.

The answer was slow in coming, the words delivered in a hesitating manner. "I need to talk to you guys about that. About your mother." He stumbled over the words, uncertain what to say next.

Willard remained standing in the doorway, afraid to enter. Nataya stepped away from Mark.

"Is Mommy sick?" The little girl's words expressed no concern other than a casual wonder.

Mark nodded his head.

"Is she in the hospital again?"

Mark fought back the tears. "Not this time."

"Then where is she?" Nataya held up her doll. "Miss Jasmine has a new dress. I want to show it to Mommy."

Mark bent at the knees, stooping down to the little girl's level. His hands caressed her shoulders as he stared into her eyes. "I'm sorry, Nataya. You won't be seeing Mommy anymore."

"I don't understand." She was beginning to shake, a tremor of nervousness that she couldn't control. "Where's Mommy?"

She withdrew from Mark, pulling away from his reach.

"I want my Mommy."

Willard, still standing in the doorway, became suddenly aware of the reality of the situation. When he spoke the tone was without inflection. "She's dead."

Mark turned away, then slowly nodded his head, acknowledging the truth of what had been said.

"No." Nataya's lips quivered as her eyes glazed over with tears. "Mommy can't be dead."

No one spoke to calm her fears. There was nothing to be said. There was no way to explain away the senselessness of what had happened. For several long seconds silence lingered.

With a high-pitched wail the little girl ran out of the room. Willard turned to watch her passing, then without a word followed his sister down the corridor.

Patrick Zimmerly paused a moment, his indecision obvious. "I'm sorry, Mark."

It was all he managed before leaving, following the siblings down the hallway and joining them at the elevator. No words were spoken as they waited for the cage, and in silence they entered the tiny cubicle.

Mark watched the doors close on the children, neither one of them turning to look his direction as they disappeared from sight. With a sigh of frustration he slumped onto a chair, his head hung low in despair. He had anticipated telling the children would be a difficult thing, but it had been far worse than he had imagined.

He had managed to shatter their world with a few simple sentences. Things would never be the same again.

For any of them.

Stranding at last, he took a final look around the room before leaving. Something caught his eye, a crumpled form just inside the doorway.

He picked up Miss Jasmine, holding the doll in his arms as he left the room.

Chapter Fifty:

MARK SAT IN THE DARKENED ROOM, THE
house quiet around him, staring ahead but seeing nothing. The
day's activities were a blur to him. He barely remembered the
whirlwind tour of events, a grueling schedule of tasks that had
left him confused and bewildered. He hadn't bothered to shave
that morning, or even put on clean clothes, but had spent the
afternoon wandering aimlessly around the house, looking for
someone he knew he would never see again.

The reality of the situation had fully hit him – especially
after seeing the still form laying cold and empty of life on a slab
at the City Morgue – but he still found himself disbelieving the
events of the last few days. It was all so unreal. It was like
something that you read about happening to other people, or
watched on a television show, but certainly not something you
ever expected to encounter yourself.

A knock came at the door but he made no response. In
truth he failed to even register the interruption.

The visitor tried the knob, found it to be unlocked, and
walked in.

Mary paused at sight of her brother, wondering if she had
done the right thing by coming over. She didn't want Mark to be
alone, but she had no idea what to say to him. She had never

prepared words for such an occasion. Who does?

So she said nothing. With quiet footfalls she approached her brother, then sat down on the couch beside him. Her hand found his arm, in an attempt to offer comfort, but he made no response.

So they sat there in silence and she waited.

"I suppose this shouldn't be a surprise to any of us," he said at last, not looking at his sister. "Aleisha was courting danger for a long time and it finally caught up to her."

"I just don't understand what happened," Mary said. "What was she doing in the middle of the road?"

"She was...."

He stopped abruptly, not certain how to continue, then forced himself on.

"The police traced her footsteps to a nearby house. The three people inside were all strung out on heroin. There was drugs. Needles. Everything. Must have been having a regular party."

Mary, shocked, remained speechless, realizing her brother had more to say.

"They found Aleisha's purse in the house," he continued. "With her identification. So they figured she had been there as well."

Mary's hand covered the exclamation that sought to escape from her mouth. "I don't believe it. Are they sure....?"

"The autopsy verified it. The heroin was still in her system."

Mary searched her mind for the right words to say – for a way to relieve the anguish Mark was obviously facing – but managed little more than a meek attempt at consolation. "Maybe it was at least peaceful for her," she offered. "Maybe she didn't suffer any."

"No. Aleisha suffered for a long time. That's why she resorted to drugs. As an escape.

"But what I don't understand is, why now? Things were going so good for her. She'd been clean for months. We were actually starting to become a family. I know she felt that. I know she wanted that.

"So why now?"

There was no answer to the question, because there was no one alive to ask it of. They would just have to accept what had happened and move on.

Chapter Fifty-One:

BEVERLY WALKED UP THE STAIRS TO THE third floor, her movements slowed with hesitancy, rather than taking the elevator. The cramped little space seemed somehow frightening to her. Reminding her of a coffin.

She didn't know what to do next. Nothing in her training had prepared her for Aleisha's death. There were hundreds of success stories in the CASA office. Countless families reunited and thriving, their children at last safe in a nurturing environment.

Beverly realized as well that there were bound to be failures along the way. But she had never envisioned anything as shattering as this.

She felt lost, and needed someone to talk to.

Pausing at the landing on the third floor she looked down into the front atrium of the building. A Christmas tree, colorfully decorated and bright with lights, stood in the front lobby, greeting visitors as they entered. It was no doubt intended to bring good cheer but it only made Beverly feel more depressed.

Susan Grant stood when Beverly entered the CASA office, her typical enthusiastic greeting stifled. "Are you all right, Beverly?"

"I don't know."

"Do you need to talk to someone?"

She nodded, holding back the tears, and sat in one of the

chairs in the reception area while the secretary disappeared in back. A few moments later Susan returned.

"Malcolm would like to talk to you, Beverly."

She led the way down a hallway, and from there into a suite of rooms Beverly had never seen before. The CASA Director's office was smaller than Beverly had expected. It was crammed with books; in cases along the wall, on the corner of the desk, it seemed every available space was taken up with the printed word. Susan led her into the room then left without a word.

Malcolm McDougal got up from his desk, closed the door for privacy, then pulled his chair away from the wall, choosing a position across from Beverly.

"It's truly tragic what we have to deal with sometimes," he began. "The many success stories that come out of this office are easily forgotten when something like this happens. But it's a part of life that we have to deal with. Sometimes there are no happy endings."

"It just doesn't make sense to me," Beverly began, her attention focused on her hands, clasped together in her lap. "It all seems so unfair."

For a moment Beverly recalled the training she had taken months ago, remembering the statistics Alexis Rawlings had presented. Every five hours someone in Ohio dies of a heroin overdose. It had seemed an appalling figure, but that's all it had seemed at the time. A number. A statistic on a piece of paper concerning the faceless multitude of drug abusers.

But now it seemed so real. Aleisha Turner had become one of those statistics. Only now the statistic was no longer faceless.

"It all seems so unfair," Beverly repeated.

"It's not fair, Beverly. It's life."

"But everything was going so well. Aleisha was doing fabulous. She was starting to see her kids more often. Her whole life was ahead of her."

She looked up now, confronting the Director. "I failed her."

"Why do you say that?"

"Because I should have been there for her. I should have offered more assistance. I should have...."

She paused, running out of words.

"There was nothing you could have done for her." The words sounded cold, startling Beverly. She was surprised to hear Malcolm speaking in such terms.

"Aleisha's fate was decided long before you met her. I'm not talking anything metaphysical or religious here, Beverly. What I'm saying is she started down a road a long time ago that was a tough one to navigate. Aleisha Turner's life was filled with bad decisions. It's regrettable that she didn't have the opportunities many of us have. Maybe she would have made better life choices otherwise. But you could have done everything for her – and I'm sure you *did* do everything you could – and the results would have been the same."

"Then what's the point? Why do we even attempt to make a change when it ends up like this anyway? When the people we're trying to help are beyond help?"

"You're upset, Beverly. I understand that. And your obvious compassion regarding the events does you credit. But I think you're forgetting some important things.

"This city – this state – this country – is filled with people like Aleisha. Many of them are a lost cause. We do what we can for them, but when it comes right down to it their lives are in their own hands. We can't live it for them. We can't make them get better. We can offer guidance and assistance, but the rest is up to them."

Beverly sat in silence a moment, reflecting on his words, until at last he resumed.

"But you shouldn't let that discourage you. There is still a tremendous amount of good that comes from the CASA office, in no small part thanks to dedicated volunteers like yourself. For every one we lose, every case that doesn't end the way we want it to end, there are dozens and dozens of successful outcomes. You've seen them yourself."

She nodded silently, reluctantly agreeing to what he had to say.

"We can't give up because of one setback. If anything this should encourage us to be more diligent in the future."

"So you're saying I should have seen this coming? That maybe I could have prevented it?"

"No. That's not at all what I'm trying to say. I think this was a good learning experience. For all of us. And maybe it will help us to be on the lookout for problems in the next case that comes our way."

He stood, towering over her.

"But more than anything else, Beverly, there's something that you cannot forget."

"What's that?"

"You were not brought into this case for Aleisha Turner. Your purpose was to look after her children, and see that their needs were met, and their well-being provided for. That need still remains, Beverly. Now, more than ever, the kids need you."

Beverly forced a smile, considering his words. What Malcolm said made perfect sense. Beverly had entered the office feeling depressed, and upset, and thinking the case had ended with Aleisha's death.

But that wasn't true. Willard and Nataya were orphans now, having never known their father and now truly without a mother. The rest of their lives was anything but certain.

And while Michael still had a father, it was unclear what future the toddler had to look forward to.

Obviously there was more work yet to be done.

Chapter Fifty-Two:

THE SLEEPING FIGURE SPRAWLED ON the recliner was snoring loudly, the rough sounds emanating from the open mouth competing with the television in the corner of the room for dominance in the otherwise silent room. A football game played on the tube, the action contributing the only light to the otherwise darkened space. Several empty cans of beer rested on the worn carpeting beside the chair. One can had fallen over, leaving a soggy stain on the floor, the moisture leaving its pungent odor as the liquid evaporated.

Sylvia Bradley stood in the doorway leading from the hall, watching her husband as he slept. Her coat was on, purse slung over her shoulder, as though she intended to go somewhere, but indecision held her back. Her emotions overwhelmed her, the urge to do what she felt was right competing with the fear of reprisal should she follow through on her decision.

Determination decided the issue. She took a deep breath and stepped silently forward.

A gruff voice called out before she had made it halfway across the living room.

"Where are you going?"

She paused, saying nothing. She made no attempt to face him, preferring not to acknowledge his presence.

"I asked you a question," he persisted, the tone one she was accustomed to living with.

She could have lied. It would have been easy to make up some excuse about running to the store or something equally lame. That would be the intelligent thing to do.

The safe thing to do.

Instead a streak of defiance rose up in her. "I'm going to see our son, Frank."

"Like hell you are." She heard his footsteps then, a shuffling gait that matched the slurring of his words, as he approached from across the room. A moment later his hand gripped her arm with a tightness she was all too familiar with. He spun her around.

"I told you I don't want you going anywhere."

"Mark needs his mother. He's in pain...."

"He's a goddamn worthless piece of shit," Frank interrupted. "And he has been ever since he hooked up with that tramp. He's better off without her."

"That's a horrible thing to say. No matter what she was, how can you possibly be so cruel?"

"She had it coming to her. Damn whore only got what she deserves. What kind of an asshole gets hooked on drugs anyway?"

He paused a second, as though expecting an answer, but before Sylvia could respond her husband continued.

"A loser. That's all she was. Her bad habits caught up with her and she got exactly what she deserved."

Without even thinking she glanced at the debris on the floor beside the recliner, the empty beer cans a testimony to how Frank had spent the evening. "There are other habits that are just as bad."

Perhaps, had she been facing her husband, she would have seen the blow coming. Maybe she could have braced herself, or moved in time to avoid the brunt of the attack. As it was the open palm striking savagely against her cheek caught her totally unprepared. She nearly fell down, the only thing restraining the motion her husband's other hand as it continued to grip her arm.

The next blow, though she was prepared for it, was every bit as painful as the first one had been.

Chapter Fifty-Three:

KAREEN TURNER, PULLING THE cellphone from her purse, saw her friend Rosalie's name on the display. The cell chimed a third time as she answered.

"What's up, girl?"

"I just wanted to...." The voice on the other end of the line paused, stumbling for the words. "I heard about Aleisha."

"What about her?"

A heavy intake of breath followed as Rosalie continued. "I just wanted to say I'm sorry, Kareen. About what happened. I thought she was gonna beat it this time. It's too bad the way things happen sometimes, ain't it?"

Kareen paused, not certain how to respond. She wasn't following what her friend was saying. Something seemed wrong. That was obvious. But Kareen felt like she had entered a movie theater halfway through the film. She had missed something important but failed to grasp what.

Rosalie continued. "So when's the funeral?"

"Funeral?"

The word, together with what had been said previously, finally registered with Kareen. She felt her body grow weak. She slumped onto one of the folding chairs, like she had lost control of her body.

"I just wanted to pay my respects. You know?"

"Yeah. Yeah." Kareen answered instinctively, barely hearing what her friend had to say. "I appreciate that. But, you know, things haven't really been decided."

She stopped, at a lost for words, while her friend continued.

"I understand. Listen, you need anything just give me a ring. You got it?"

Kareen said nothing in reply, but a moment later it didn't matter. The call was over, disconnected on the other end, and without even realizing what she was doing Kareen let the cellphone slip from her hand. It landed with a dull clunking sound on the table in front of her, totally forgotten by this point.

For a moment she sat there, dazed, uncertain how to respond, until she felt a touch from someone behind her. The hand rubbed against her shoulder, jerking her back to reality.

"You okay, Babe?"

She turned slowly, just barely managing to respond with a nod of her head.

"So what's going on? Something happening?"

"No." She considered a moment. "Nothing important."

"I don't know. You look like you could use some cheering up. And I know just how to do it."

He reached for her hand as he backed away, pulling her off the chair and toward him in a single motion. Releasing his grip he smiled, then turned to walk down the hallway.

Without giving it another thought Kareen followed Leroy into the bedroom.

Chapter Fifty-Four:

THE CHILDREN WERE SITTING IN AN outer room at Children's Services, with Mary Bradley in attendance, when Beverly arrived on the scene. They were quiet. Subdued. They failed to greet Beverly with their usual gusto. They said their hellos but made no attempt to interact with her. Willard's face remained buried in a book he held, while Nataya stroked her doll's hair in what seemed to be a purely reflexive action. Michael lay stretched out on the floor, sound asleep on a blue blanket.

"They're both still pretty shaken over the whole thing," Mary explained, keeping her voice to a whisper as she indicated the two older children. "And no wonder."

"What do you mean?"

"They never even got to say goodbye to their mother. There was no closure for them."

"Surely at the funeral...."

Mary, shaking her head back and forth, interrupted the next words. "There was no funeral. No showing. Nothing. Aleisha had no insurance. There was no family to help out. Mark was on his own.

"He wanted to do right by her. He doesn't have much, but he was willing to try. But I talked him out of it."

The words startled Beverly. "I don't understand. Why

would you do that?"

"What good would it do Aleisha now to have a funeral? Or a fancy casket? Or a big procession with a big black limousine? She's dead, and none of those things is going to bring her back. What little money Mark has will be better off spent on the living."

She made a motion with her head toward the three children.

"On them. They need to be his priority now."

Beverly, feeling suddenly morbid about the whole thing, nevertheless found herself voicing the question that came instantly to mind. "So if there was no funeral, what happened to...." She stopped abruptly, not wanting to be callous.

"Lucas County took care of things. A simple burial in Westwood Cemetery. An unmarked grave." Her words trailed off to nothing as she turned away.

Beverly barely caught the last thing she said. "Such a horrible waste."

The conference room seemed crowded with people. Patrick Zimmerly was of course there from Children's Services, along with Judy Dencher. Mark, sitting quietly, his fingers playing with a pencil in a gesture Beverly was quite certain he was totally unaware of, was present with his attorney. Lucy Lemly, Aleisha's attorney, was also present. It seemed sort of odd to Beverly, considering the circumstances, that the woman had even shown up.

Once everyone was seated Mark's attorney, Carl Hemmings, stood up to address the group.

"I know we are all overwhelmed by the sad turn this case has taken. To think a young woman, who fought so hard through rehab and afterward to restore her family, is now gone, is surely a tragic reminder to us all of how fleeting life can be.

"But life goes on, as it must, and now more than ever the

future of the children Aleisha Turner left behind is in doubt."

The attorney paused, glancing over at Mark Bradley. Mark sat motionless at the table, staring into space, as though barely aware of the people around him. Beverly could see him shaking slightly, the show of emotion somehow incongruous in light of his strapping physique, but understandable considering the circumstances.

"Mark has followed through on his case plan," Hemmings continued, "proving his desire to follow the rulings set down by the court. The only thing preventing him from reuniting with his son was the uncertainty of Aleisha's future, a condition that – tragically – is no longer an issue. At this point in time I see no reason to delay the reunification of Mark and his son, Michael, and submit that we should speed things up to achieve this goal. They both need order restored to their lives, so the sooner we proceed the sooner the healing process can begin."

The attorney sat down, and for several seconds no one spoke. Judy Dencher, the coordinator from Children's Services, took up the conversation.

"I agree, Carl. I'm certain that, considering the unusual circumstances, we can get the date pushed ahead for the next hearing. I see no problem with Michael returning to his father's custody."

Mark, his eyes still downcast, his demeanor quiet, muttered a meek reply. "Thank you."

"What about Willard and Nataya?" Beverly asked.

Judy motioned toward Patrick Zimmerly. "We've talked about this at length, to determine the best solution to their status."

"We've looked once again into Aleisha's relations," Patrick began. "Other than her sister Kareen, who shows no interest in becoming involved, Aleisha had no close ties to family members. As such, there is no suitable candidate to raise the kids. With this in mind, we feel Lucas County should be granted permanent custody of the two children until such time as placement, in the form of permanent adoption, can be obtained."

"I don't understand." Beverly's gaze swept the faces of the people gathered around the table, looking for a show of sympathy, and found none. "Those two children have been through so much already. There must be something we can do for them. Instead of...." She paused, struggling for the right words. "Instead of just abandoning them."

"No one is being abandoned," Patrick was quick to point out. "The children will be well-cared for. They will most likely need to be placed with a different foster family, but Children's Services will maintain contact and assure everything is going smoothly with their new living arrangements."

"Why do they have to move? Everything seems fine where they're at now."

The case worker shook his head as he replied. "The family they are currently with accepted the children with the understanding that it was only until reunification or, barring that, until other arrangements were decided upon. They never intended to have the children long term."

"So besides just losing their mother, Willard and Nataya have to start all over again?"

"It will be best for them in the long run, Beverly."

She turned toward Mark Bradley, who still sat dejected and detached across the table from her, as though separated from the proceedings. "Do you have anything to say to this, Mark?"

He shook his head, a slow back and forth motion, a listless effort that reflected his present state of mind. His voice, when he finally managed to speak, was a low tone of acceptance. "Whatever's best for the kids. I guess that's the way it has to be."

Mark rose then, refusing to make eye contact with anyone, and silently left the room.

Chapter Fifty-Five:

IT ALL SEEMED SO UNFAIR.

Beverly reflected on this as she sat in her kitchen, staring at the case reports and documents haphazardly spread out on the table before her, neglecting the cup of tea she had poured for herself earlier but that now sat cold and forgotten off to the side. She had cried earlier, as evidenced by the redness that colored her eyes, and though there was a certain amount of cathartic release with the action it hadn't changed the situation any. Things still remained the same.

It all seemed so unfair.

It was so frustrating to think Aleisha Turner had worked so hard to recover only to succumb at last to the deadly drug she'd been trying to distance herself from. The sad reality of the situation – a fact Beverly had come across repeatedly during her online research – was that many heroin addicts overdosed shortly after leaving a detox program. Time away from heroin often lessened the addict's resistance. A dose that would have been normal six or nine or twelve months earlier could easily be lethal once the victim had been away from the drug for a while. Ironically, the time in rehab could have been the reason Aleisha hadn't survived her final fling with heroin.

Beverly forced herself away from such thoughts. There was nothing she could do for Aleisha anymore.

But that didn't mean she couldn't do something for the young woman's children.

Willard and Nataya had been through enough already. It was time to resolve their future, not to extend the uncertainty that surrounded them. There had to be a better solution than the scenario presented at Children's Services, a plan that would do little more than to leave them lingering in the system. Though she was certain the agency had their best interest at heart, she was equally convinced that there was a better alternative.

"Mom?"

The gently delivered word, accompanied with a light touch on her shoulder, drew Beverly from her thoughts. Turning in her seat, she smiled up at her daughter.

"Jennifer? I'm sorry, Dear. I didn't hear you come in."

"You seemed preoccupied with something. Is everything okay?"

Beverly sighed. "I guess so."

She considered a moment longer. "Oh, I don't know. I just don't know what to do."

Jennifer sat down in the chair beside her mother, taking the older woman's hand, caressing it lightly. "About what?"

"This CASA case has me so frustrated. It's not like reading a book, or watching a show on television. These are real people I'm dealing with. You can't just turn off your emotions and forget about what they're going through."

Jennifer recalled the last time they had spoken about it, remembering the warning she had delivered. What was it she had told her mother? *You may as well cut your losses and move on to the next case.* It seemed so prophetic now, like she had foreseen the dire circumstances to come. But she hadn't realized how involved her mother would become in the lives of the people she was dealing with.

"I'm sorry, Mom. About what happened. I really am. I

guess it makes you realize how good your life is when you see the bad things that happen to other people. I feel awful for what that woman must have gone through."

"She must have led a very unhappy life," Beverly agreed. "To be driven to do the things she did. But that's really not what's bothering me. I have other concerns on my mind."

Jennifer pulled away in uncertainty. "What is it, then?"

"It's the children."

Beverly stood from her chair, walked over to the kitchen counter, and for a few seconds fiddled with the sugar bowl resting on the counter, before turning around to address her daughter. "I can't do anything for Aleisha. It's too late for that. But now I feel like I've let the children down as well."

"In what way?"

"I keep thinking about what they're going through. It's bad enough they lost their mother. Now they"re stuck in the system for who knows how long. They may end up moving between foster homes, being shuffled from one family to another, while they wait for someone to adopt them. If that ever happens at all."

"What can you do about it? After all, they don't have many choices, do they?"

"It's just not what I would have decided for them. That's all."

"Okay. Then what's your solution?"

"I would have kept them with the step-father. That way the three kids would still be together. And, instead of living with a bunch of strangers, they'd all be in a familiar place. The place they lived in with their mother. At least then something in their life could return to normal."

"Then why don't they do that?"

"Children's Services thinks it's better this way."

"But you don't?"

Beverly shook her head.

"Has everything been decided, then?"

"Well, the court hasn't issued a verdict yet. But it's pretty much a done deal."

Jennifer stood up, taking two steps toward her mother's side.

"Why did you become a CASA volunteer, Mom?"

"What do you mean?"

"The CASA program. Why did you join?"

Beverly turned away, reliving the memories in her mind, recalling how difficult it had been following her husband's death. She had felt lost. And, even with her children's support, alone. There had been an emptiness that needed filling, a desire to do something, that had been fulfilled with her commitment to CASA.

"You know the reasons. How hard it was after your father passed away. How empty it was in my life."

"That's not what I'm talking about."

Beverly looked up. "What do you mean?"

"You told me once you did it for the children. That there were kids out there that needed someone looking out for them."

"That's true. If I can make a difference in a child's life...."

Jennifer stepped closer, interrupting her mother's next words. "Then make a difference. If you feel this isn't in the best interest of the children then you should say something. Or, better yet, do something. Before it's too late. Isn't that what a guardian is for?"

Chapter Fifty-Six:

THE IMPALA STILL SAT IN THE DRIVEWAY; the front porch was still piled high with boxes. Outwardly, things had remained unchanged at the Bradley house.

With mixed emotions Beverly approached the front door. Her first impression of the way the family lived hadn't been a favorable one. She recalled vividly the clutter within the house, especially the messy appearance of the kitchen. She rang the doorbell, hoping as she did so that, for the kids' sake, things had changed some inside.

Mary Bradley opened the door. "Beverly? I'm sorry, but we weren't expecting you."

"I know. I just decided to stop by. May I come in?"

Mary hesitated a moment, as though this was an unwelcome intrusion into their privacy, but then stepped back, holding the door open in invitation. "Certainly."

Beverly entered, walking into the front room. Like before the room was cluttered, a disarray of crumpled clothes and dirty glasses and wrinkled papers, but as Beverly examined the room closer she detected a change from her last visit.

Or maybe things hadn't really changed, after all. Maybe Beverly was just viewing things from a different perspective. Previously she had been judgmental; looking for fault, and finding it everywhere she turned.

Now she was seeing things from a family point of view. Recalling in her mind the disruptive nature of her own kids when they were small, and her never ending battle to restore sense to the seemingly endless chaos around her, she couldn't help but to smile inwardly at the memory. The majority of the clutter in the room was from playthings, children's toys scattered about the house, as though waiting for Willard and Nataya's return. She could picture in her mind the two of them playing together, racing with the plastic cars, or assembling the various puzzles in the room, pieces of which appeared to be distributed everywhere. She could almost hear their tiny voices echoing off the walls.

Maybe the house wasn't as messy as she had originally surmised.

A look into the kitchen satisfied her that it, too, had changed in character. It had received a cleaning recently. Some dishes rested on the counter, a couple of cereal boxes took up space on the kitchen table, but for the most part it looked neat and, though not necessarily organized, at least livable. It looked like the kitchen of a family.

Mark, reclining on the couch, failed to acknowledge Beverly's arrival as Mary took up the conversation. "Michael's upstairs. Taking a nap. Do you need to see him?"

"Actually, I came to talk to Mark."

He turned to face her, slowly, but said nothing.

Beverly entered and took a seat across from him. "I know you have a lot on your mind, Mark. I know how hard this is for you. Believe me. I realize how devastating it can be to lose a loved one." For a moment an image flashed in her mind, of the last time she had spoken to Russell; the last time she had seen his face, and looked into his eyes.

"But it gets better, Mark. Believe me. You'll get through this."

"Is that why you stopped by, Beverly? To give me a pep talk?" The tone of voice failed to match the anger inherent in the words. Rather, it betrayed the weariness, the loneliness, that enveloped Mark. "Are you here to tell me how I should forget about Aleisha and get on with my life?"

"Of course not," Beverly replied. "If you loved Aleisha then you'll never forget about her. And you shouldn't. Memories, even painful ones, are often all that remains after we lose someone. Cherish the memories as you loved Aleisha."

Mark, obviously confused with her words, stumbled with how to respond. "Then why are you here? I'm sure you mean well. But I can't imagine what you could say to change the way I feel right now."

"It's not you I'm worried about, Mark. There's somebody else – actually, two very special people – that I'm thinking about."

Mary had followed Beverly into the room, remaining standing as the CASA volunteer talked with her brother. But with Beverly's last words came understanding. "You're talking about Willard and Nataya?"

Beverly nodded, her attention still focused on Mark. "Of course. Look at what you've gone through, Mark. How hard it's been for you. Now imagine what it must be like for those children. Aleisha's children. You've lost a wife. But they've lost not only their mother, but one of the few people in their lives they've ever been close to."

"I can't change that. And there's no way I can make it up to them."

"That's where I think you're wrong."

"What do you mean?"

"You're a part of their life too, Mark. Someone they should be able to depend on to be there for them. Someone to help them get through this."

"How?"

"By truly being there for them. By taking them into your life. By not abandoning them."

Mark said nothing, taking in the import of the words, while his sister drew closer. "You want my brother to raise the kids himself?"

"I only think it would be in the best interest, of all three of the children, if they weren't separated."

"That's ridiculous. Mark already has Michael to take care of. On his own. How's he supposed to raise all three of them?"

"With love. And understanding. And compassion."

"Those are just words, Beverly. They don't pay the bills. They don't put food on the table. I think you're expecting a lot."

"So you're okay with having Willard and Nataya left in the system? Moving from one foster family to another?"

"Of course not. I feel awful for what those kids are going through. But don't forget. They're Aleisha's kids. Mark wasn't even part of the picture when they came along. I'm sorry, but they aren't his problem. Hasn't he been through enough already without expecting even more from him now?"

Before Beverly could respond Mark stood. Silently he walked across the room, pausing for a moment as though to collect his thoughts, then turned to face the two women.

"When I married Aleisha a year ago," he began, "I made the decision to be the father to her children. I'm the first to admit I had no idea what I was getting into. How demanding of a responsibility it would become, especially after..." He coughed to clear his throat, wiping at the corner of his eye as he did so. "After Aleisha's death.

"I don't want to see this family torn apart. I don't want to separate Michael from his brother and sister, and I don't want any of them to forget their mother. Aleisha had her problems. I know that better than anyone else. But she was a good person, who deserved more from life than she got.

"If keeping Aleisha's memory alive, and keeping her children together, means I have to raise all three of them, then that's what I should do."

"Are you sure that's what you want?" Mary asked.

He turned to face Beverly. "Would I be able to do that? Receive custody of Willard and Nataya?"

Beverly's smiled betrayed her joy regarding his decision. "I don't see why not. You are their legal step-father. Who has a better right than you to decide what's to become of them? But I can't lie to you. It won't be easy. Being a single father and raising three children will be a handful."

"I know."

Just then a sound intruded, the beginning of a cry from the toddler upstairs. Mark looked toward the ceiling and managed a weak smile. It was as though he was seeing through the wood above him, admiring the youngster on the other side. He turned back to face Beverly.

"But it will be worth it. I'm sure of it."

Chapter Fifty-Seven:

 HERE WERE OF COURSE ISSUES TO BE resolved before everything could be finalized. Mark, though never wavering in his desire to keep the children together, found it difficult to stay on task when it came to arranging things. So Beverly stepped in, spending time with Patrick Zimmerly, and others from Children's Services, to ensure that everything would follow according to the young man's wishes.

By the day of the final court session all the particulars had been agreed upon. Mark's petition had been granted by the courts for him to raise all three of the children, with no disagreement from any of the parties involved.

Beverly felt a sense of satisfaction with the turn of events, pleased to know she had been a part of keeping the family together. But, in spite of that, she found no joy the day of the hearing.

Beverly had attended reunification cases before, so she knew what to expect. But the mood today was markedly different from her past experiences. The specter of Aleisha Turner's passing haunted the proceedings. Beverly's joy at seeing the three children reunited paled from the memory of what they had lost.

Once things came to their logical conclusion Beverly was the last to leave the room. As she walked into the hallway she watched Mark approach the elevator. He held Michael, carrying the toddler in his left arm, while Nataya held hold of his right and took small hesitant steps beside her father.

Willard was several steps ahead, ready to push the button to make the elevator doors open. Once the cage arrived the family stepped in.

Beverly reflected on the word. Family. The group was a family again. They had suffered a terrible hardship and weathered the strain. They would no doubt have other struggles ahead. All families do. It wouldn't be easy for Mark, being a single father and raising three kids. But they had each other.

Beverly took her last look at the children she had grown to know over the past eight months. The doors closed on them, closing a chapter of Beverly's life as well, and she made her way out of the building and out of their lives.

THE END

Afterword:

THE COURT APPOINTED SPECIAL Advocates Program – CASA – began in 1977 in Seattle Washington. In the forty years of its existence it has grown tremendously into a truly national organization, with all 50 states now enlisting the aid of volunteers to help children in need. Nationwide, approximately 70,000 volunteers in over 1,000 CASA programs speak up on behalf of the nearly 280,000 abused and neglected children they worked with last year alone.

CASA volunteers deal with issues of domestic violence and child neglect. They work with families whose parents suffer from a dependence on alcohol, or struggling with mental illness. They see daily children living below the poverty level. Children who go to bed each day hungry. Or cold. Or alone. And, at an increasingly alarming rate, more and more of the cases dealt with by CASA volunteers involve a problem that is currently plaguing our country.

Heroin Addiction.

Aleisha Turner's story is a work of fiction, a drama concocted from the author's imagination. But the dangers of heroin addiction – and the life altering affects that are the consequences of its use – are all too real.

The statistics presented in this story are accurate, but they only paint part of the picture.

In 2012, 697 people in Ohio died from a heroin overdose.

In 2013 that number jumped to 983 people. In 2014 it increased once more, to 1,177 deaths. These are alarming statistics that are played out with similar increases on a national level.

Or consider the case of Lucas County, the site of this story. The Lucas County Coroner's office oversees 21 Counties in Northwest Ohio and Southeast Michigan. Those 21 Counties witnessed 215 heroin related deaths in 2015. For the first two months of 2016 that number stands at 38, for a projected estimate of 228 deaths for the year. And those in the know expect that number to only increase.

It's obvious to all that this is a problem that will not go away soon.

To counteract this epidemic the Lucas County Sheriff's Office – under the leadership of Sheriff John Tharp and with support from the Attorney General of Ohio and many local area businesses – is involved in an ambitious program known as D.A.R.T., or the Drug Awareness Response Team. Their mission: "To stop the profound number of deaths of loved ones caused by opiate overdoses while helping victims to overcome their addictions."

And while there are many Aleisha Turner's out there – young women drawn to prostitution to support their drug habit, abandoning their children for the insatiable desire toward that next high – the reality of the situation would surprise many people.

Dr. Robert B. Forney, Chief Toxicologist with the Lucas County Coroner Office, reports that 89% of the heroin deaths they investigate are white. 84% of the victims are male, with 37.7 the average age. They could be your neighbor. Your child's teacher. Or the handyman that comes to work on your house.

In the words of Sheriff Tharp: "Heroin addiction does not discriminate."

As tragic as it is to consider the lives lost through this

epidemic, this is only one part of the story. There are always family members involved, like the children in Aleisha's story. There are parents, and siblings, and friends, who can do little but stand by and watch as loved ones waste their lives away.

SOLACE of NW Ohio – an acronym that stands for Surviving Our Loss and Continuing Everyday – is a wonderful support group for families. Belinda Brooks of Solace offers advice for family members. "We have to educate ourselves on addiction and disease and try to keep ourselves mutually healthy so we do not end up destroying our lives as well. It is a roller coaster journey that does not end and parents have to pace themselves so they do not burn out emotionally."

It is obvious the war against drugs is being waged on many fronts. Whether it's the medical and emergency personnel that treat the drug abuser, the law enforcement officers that fight to keep our streets safe, or the rehabilitation centers that work to cure the sickness that grips the addict in its deadly embrace, countless people around the country are doing their part in the battle.

It's not an easy task.

But it has to start somewhere. And one person can make a difference.

If you have a drug problem seek help. There are facilities across the country that can offer assistance.

If you have a family member that is struggling with addiction do something about it. Educate yourself about the problem. Speak out about the issue. And – perhaps what is toughest of all – take the hard steps necessary for your loved one's survival. Don't feed their habit by enabling them. Be firm in offering your love, but be just as firm in denying them any assistance that can prolong their behavior. You're not doing them – or yourself – any favors by contributing to their condition.

Author Bio

Originally from Erie Pennsylvania, Keith has lived in the Toledo Ohio area since 1982, where he and his wife raised their two boys. The children live now in Missouri and Kansas while Keith and Colleen reside just north of Toledo, across the border in Southern Michigan.

www.KeithJulius.com

Also available from Keith Julius:

Daniel Jameson was living the American Dream. With a secure job, a house in the suburbs, and a wife and two children, he seemed to have everything he ever desired out of life.

His storybook existence is thrown into turmoil when he witnesses a tragic accident at his workplace. Following the event Daniel begins to question aspects of his life he had long taken for granted. He manages to become separated from his wife Becky and on his own, aimlessly adrift and uncertain of his future.

A chance meeting at a restaurant introduces Daniel to Jackie Somerset, a younger woman to whom he is immediately attracted. His infatuation runs counter to the wishes of Jackie's boyfriend, Brad Wilkens, who unleashes a torrent of violence - beginning with a brutal attack against Daniel - that soon escalates to much more.

Daniel finds himself involved in situations and events he could have never imagined, fighting not only for his peace of mind but for the life of his family as well.

34693113R00176

Made in the USA
San Bernardino, CA
04 June 2016